MZUNGU'S WIF

That night, when Patrick came home from the factory, she challenged him. 'Is it true?'

'Of course it's true.'

'Why didn't you tell me? Why didn't you tell me what happened?'

He yawned. 'What good would it have done you to know?'

'You brought me to this place, Patrick. I had a right to know.'

He spoke as if he was tired, yawning again. Julia wondered what emotion the tiredness concealed.

'It was a long time ago, Julia. Things like that don't happen anymore.'

'But didn't it make you hate them, didn't it make you afraid?'

'Of kaffs?' He laughed. 'You can't be afraid of a kaff, my love.'

'But you must have hated them.' He shook his head. 'You wouldn't hate a dog.'

Mzungu's Wife

Philippa Blake

CORONET BOOKS
Hodder and Stoughton

First published in Great Britain in 1988 by The Bodley Head

Coronet edition 1989

British Library C.I.P.

Blake, Philippa
  Mzungu's wife
  I. Title
  823'.914 [F]

  ISBN 0 340 50825 6

Printed and bound in Great Britain for Hodder and Stoughton Paperbacks, a division of Hodder and Stoughton Ltd., Mill Road, Dunton Green, Sevenoaks, Kent TN13 2YA.
(Editorial Office: 47 Bedford Square, London WC1B 3DP) by Cox & Wyman Ltd., Reading.

For my parents,
Phil and Helen Blake

GLOSSARY

asante sana	thank you
ayah	nanny
bahati njema	good luck
bibi	peasant woman
dawa	medicine
dhobi	laundry
hapana	no
huko	there
jambo	hello
kikapu	basket
kusema	speak
kwaheri	goodbye
mbaya	bad
mfua	rain
mtoto	child
mwivi	thief
mzungu	white man
ndiyo	yes
panga	long blade
sasa	now
shamba	smallholding
tafadhali	please
tatu	three

1

A crowd had gathered; pickers in brightly coloured aprons collected near the Beechcraft, excited faces lit by mirror-bright sun on the fuselage. The loading bay gaped open, ready for the coffin.

Not a real coffin, rough planks hastily nailed together in the factory. Kangeni had arranged it, settling easily behind Patrick's desk to give instructions to the foreman; smooth black forearms resting on the blotter as he wrote the slip to draw the wood from the store.

Harry had borrowed Kangeni's sunglasses. The plastic frames were too wide for his face, but he wore them gratefully, holding his head at an angle to keep the lenses between his eyes and the sun.

All the whites were there, clusters of women standing a little apart from their men, pools of truncated shadow at the edge of the strip. They nodded to Harry as he approached.

There was nothing to say. The women looked at him, and away. Vera clutched a posy of flowers. Her pinched, narrow face stared into the distance.

'We might have done something,' she said.

The other women turned to her.

'We tried,' said Madeleine Waugh.

'God knows we warned her,' said another, whose name Harry couldn't remember.

Vera shook her head. 'We didn't do enough.'

Hearing the conversation, some of the men began to drift across.

1

'Don't you fret, Vera,' said Jack Bowen. 'She brought it entirely on herself.'

Harry moved away from them. Weariness clung like weights to his limbs. He had not slept. There had been no time for rest, no night. Only the plunging darkness of the township, running back to see the faces in the doorway – five pairs of eyes flickering in the lamplight. Harry had poured change into an outstretched palm.

'Fetch the police. Tell them there's been an accident.'

The faces had remained, figures squatting on the step, a silent wake until, after an hour, a policeman had come. A single man in khaki shorts and maroon stockings. The watchers melted away. He scraped the mud from his boots on to the step. They were loud on the concrete floor. Harry pointed to the corner and the policeman crossed the room. His face bore no expression as he squatted down to pull a shotgun from the lifeless hands.

'This is confiscated,' he said. 'No private guns are permitted on these estates.' He took a rag from his pocket and began to clean the gun.

Harry backed away. 'Shouldn't you unload it first?'

The policeman paused. The rag was patched with blood. He raised the gun to eye level and took aim at a large spider high up on the wall. Harry covered his ears and the policeman smiled, repeating the action, grinning with pleasure as he swung the gun up to his shoulder and squinted down the barrel. 'This is confiscated,' he said again.

He put the gun against the wall and took out a notebook. It was attached to his belt by a thin chain but the socket for a pen was empty. He turned to a clean page and patted his pockets. Automatically Harry reached for his own pen but the officer was bending down, extracting a silver ballpoint from the body on the ground.

With a flourish he looked at his watch. It was the gesture of a schoolboy. I have a watch and I am looking

2

at it. Laboriously he wrote the time at the top of the page: one fifteen a.m., and the date: 21st March 1979.

'Your name?' The policeman clicked the ballpoint impatiently.

'Thomas, Harry Thomas.'

'You are employed by Chaachi?'

'Yes.'

'You are working here, on the estate?'

'No. At the Coast.'

'What are you doing here?'

'In Ledorot? – I'm staying with friends.'

'No. I am asking what are you doing here – in this place?'

'We – we came to find someone.'

The sergeant looked up, meeting Harry's eyes for the first time. He tapped the pen speculatively against his teeth; a small clicking noise in the silent hut.

'The name of this man?' Pointing with the pen.

'Patrick Whitman. He's a manager for Chaachi.'

Harry spelt out the names and the sergeant wrote slowly in his notebook. 'Patrick Whitman, Chaachi Tea Company Limited, Ledorot.'

'Next of kin?'

Harry hesitated.

'Next of kin?' repeated the sergeant.

'His wife, Julia.'

2

Over the intercom Mrs Holu's voice sounded sharp and brittle.

'I have a message for you, Mr Thomas.'

Harry put down his briefcase.

'What is it?'

'Mr Whitman telephoned while you were out. He has come down from Ledorot.'

'Patrick's in town!' Harry exclaimed. 'Will he be coming in to the office?'

'No. He said he is catching a plane at two o'clock.'

Harry opened the door that linked his secretary's office with his own. There was a strong smell of acetone.

'Where is he going?' asked Harry, ignoring the brush loaded with pink varnish, poised above her thumbnail.

'To London. He said he would phone you from the airport.'

'Is anything wrong?'

Mrs Holu shrugged. 'He sounded all right to me.'

Harry returned to his own room, wondering why Patrick should suddenly decide to go to England. He had no family there, no family at all except the women of Ledorot, who mothered him.

Perhaps he's just going for a holiday, thought Harry, God knows I'd want one after a few years up there. He sat behind his desk and thought of the tea estates; Ledorot, Kibwezi, Nalali. The tea plantations covered an area the size of an English county; remote hilltops where fifteen years of Independence had scarcely penetrated; a place where even in 1978 Africans leapt off their bicycles to make way for a white man's car. Where the whites still called the Africans 'kaffs', 'nigs', 'bushheads', answering Harry's astonished face with the assurance, 'It's all right, we can speak freely up here.'

Things were different at the Coast. The process of Africanisation had left Harry, out from England on a short-term renewable contract, the only white in the Chaachi office.

'And so it should be,' he said, speaking aloud to the empty office.

He took a pile of papers from his briefcase and was hard at work when the telephone rang.

'Mr Whitman, for you,' Mrs Holu announced.

'Can you hear me, Harry?' Patrick's voice boomed in his ear. In the background Harry could hear the airport public address system.

'Very well.'

'I'm going to England. It's time I was married.'

Harry laughed. 'Who are you going to marry?'

'I don't know yet, I'm going to find a nice English girl.'

'Just like that? How long is your leave?'

'Two months.'

'You'd better work fast then!'

'I shall.' Patrick was shouting to hear himself over the airport announcements, but his tone was perfectly serious.

'The wedding should be in about eight weeks.'

'You're kidding me, Patrick, you don't even have a girl in mind.'

'I'll find one. Maybe you should come with me and we could find one for you too.'

Harry laughed. 'Why not? We could have a double wedding, take two sisters as a job lot.'

'I'm serious, my friend, there are lots of nice girls in England.'

'You don't go and get a wife like a tin of peas!'

His remark went unheard. 'Can you fix a trip to look

6

at those new packing machines? Then Chaachi will pay your fare.'

'Why do you want me there?'

'To be best man, of course.'

'But . . .'

Patrick interrupted. 'That's the final call for my flight. I'll have to go. Take care, my friend.'

'You take care of yourself,' Harry called. Patrick had gone.

Smiling, he put down the phone. Mrs Holu came through almost immediately.

'Lunchtime, Mr Thomas.'

'All right then.'

He waited for her to go and then cleared his own desk and took the back stairs down to the street. The Chaachi liftboy was squatting by the main door, a frayed janitor's hat pulled down over his eyes. The boy had been issued with shoes too, but complained that they gave him blisters. Harry thought it unlikely that anything so timid as a blister could flourish on the liftboy's leathery soles. No doubt the shoes had fetched a good price – paid off a debt or provided a few meals. He waved in response to a cheeky salute and turned into Government Road.

Outside the supermarket a hoard of ragged boys surrounded his car and blocked his path. Punnets of strawberries, damsons, tomatoes – even small shells – were thrust towards him.

'Is the best!'

'Is the cheapest!'

'I give you a good price!'

He pushed through them all and mounted the steps to the store. Above the door was a sign in English, repeated in Swahili and Arabic: 'No spitting on these premises.'

The checkouts were busy. A woman had dropped a carton of milk; Harry stepped aside to avoid a thin stream that gathered pace as it ran through the door and down the steps outside.

That the hawking boys ignored the milk no longer surprised Harry. When he had first come to Africa the plight of the street boys had torn at his heart. Not wanting their wares he had offered gifts of food and money and been surprised by the offence it gave. 'I'm not begging from you, white man!'

He found the real beggars soon enough; the cripples near the Cathedral, the dark bundles on the pavement at night. This was Independence: breath-taking architecture and children dying for want of clean water.

'They were better off under the British,' Patrick would claim, pointing to Ledorot for his example. 'No emancipation nonsense up there, and look how happy they are.'

Would he make such a remark in England, Harry wondered? Or would he behave differently there? Would an English girl see only the man out of Africa: the strong, tanned tea planter; be taken in by the rough charm and miss the real Patrick altogether? One of a dying breed; bred in Africa with a white skin, a child of the colonies, staying on after Independence because nowhere else would feel like home.

It was the bride herself who would need to be strong. Strong enough to stand up to Ledorot, to the closed society of tea planters and their narrow-minded wives. She would have to agree with Patrick or hold her tongue. Better still, be brainless, ready for the boredom, the weeks and years of unchanging routine.

Harry doubted Patrick would find such a woman. Or even that his friend would know what kind of woman to look for.

3

The hospital was a maze of prefabs, hasty grey blocks that clung like a sow's litter to the red brick of the original building. There was a pond at the side of the steps, ornamental concrete, a mossy sculpture thrusting out of the slime.

PADDLING IS STRICTLY FORBIDDEN

Paddling. The word brought a flurry of memories. An only child with her mother. Summers in guest houses. Bare feet, goose-stepping over pebbles; the joyous splash and suck of the sea. Crazy golf. The sign at the end of the pier: 'Dancing Nightly'.

Mother's memories.

'Your father was such a fine dancer, so handsome. I was the happiest girl in the world.'

TV in the lounge after evening meal. A whiff of vinegar from the chip shop. 'No, darling, we're not that sort.'

Candy-floss was permitted; and pink, tooth-shattering rock in the afternoon, strolling along the promenade, past the pastel-painted beach houses, peering in at kettles on primus stoves, fat women with cardigans over their bikinis.

The consultant was dapper. Wavy grey hair and a pale grey suit.

'Your mother has had a stroke,' he said, beginning

before she had even sat down. 'I am afraid the damage is extensive.'

I know that, thought Julia. I haven't waited two weeks to be told she has had a stroke.

A group of students passed by the window, white coats unbuttoned, laughing loudly.

The consultant paused to watch them, turning his back on Julia.

'Will she get better?'

'It is not impossible.' Reluctantly, it seemed, he turned back to the room. 'It is remarkable that she has not lost the power of speech, but we must not hope for too much.'

'Will she be paralysed?'

He gave a little shrug. 'With physiotherapy she might regain the use of her legs. But there will always be disablement and, possibly, incontinence.'

'Incontinence?' Julia's voice rose and for the first time the consultant looked directly into her eyes.

His expression softened. 'I am afraid so, my dear.'

'I couldn't bear it,' cried Julia, 'I couldn't nurse her like that.'

'Arrangements can be made.'

He had tried to sound sympathetic but Julia realised that for him this was routine. His hands strayed to the pager attached to his breast pocket. He clicked the little red button. On, off. On, off.

'First we must see if she survives. Then we can think of the future.'

'You mean she might not?' The interview was over. He held out his hand, not to shake but to guide her to the door. 'We'll just have to keep our fingers crossed, my dear. A great deal depends on the patient's will.'

He opened the door. 'Don't hope for too much.'

The corridor was noisy, trolleys rattled over the shiny linoleum; the same group of students were laughing on the landing. She followed the signs to the ward, familiar now. She had come every day, since the telephone call from Mrs Pritchard, her mother's friend and neighbour for thirty years.

'She was lying on the path, my dear. She must have just left the house. It can't have been long – I'd have seen her, I was waiting for the milk . . .'

Julia shuddered at the memory; the hours of waiting; Mrs Pritchard clucking beside her.

'She'll need a lot of nursing, you know. You won't be able to go gadding about.'

'I don't go gadding about, Mrs Pritchard.'

'Well, you weren't at home last night. I don't know why your mother puts up with it. It's the strain on her heart that's done it, I expect.'

'I went to a party, Mrs Pritchard. There's nothing wrong with that.'

Julia turned away and stared out of the window. The hospital faced south, looking down over London. Below in the street the rush hour was beginning, a long snake of traffic creeping through the dusk.

'She'll need someone all the time.' Mrs Pritchard dragged her back into the present. 'You can't leave an invalid alone.'

'Shall we wait and see what the doctor says?'

'You don't need a doctor to see how bad she is. Don't forget it was me that found her. Lying on the garden path she was, with her lips going blue.'

'Blue?'

'Yes, my dear, blue. She would have been dead if it weren't for me. That's why I keep telling you. You can't think of yourself from now on. You'll be nursing her night and day – that's if she lives.'

Eventually Julia wept, leaning on Mrs Pritchard's shoulder.

'I don't want her to die. I want her to be well. I can't think of that house without her.'

'Bartlett Road would never be the same,' Mrs Pritchard muttered. 'After all these years. I suppose you'd sell the place if she died. Sell it to some blacks and ruin the neighbourhood.'

Julia had not answered. The thought of her mother's death overwhelmed her. I don't want her to die. I couldn't bear to be alone.

For two weeks her mother had survived; a small, pale face on the hospital pillows, soiled nightdresses, a bowl of uneaten fruit. Her mind wandered, sometimes lucid but more often trapped in the past, in conversations with her long-dead husband, her beloved Ted, who was no more to Julia than a picture on the sideboard.

Clutching a handful of carnations Julia turned the corner into the ward.

'How are you today, Mother?'

'Julia!'

'Look, I've brought you some flowers.'

'It was the most beautiful thing you ever saw.'

'What was?'

'That dolls' house.'

'I don't remember it.'

Julia laid the flowers on the locker. 'Aren't they a pretty colour?'

'Nerveless, you were. He'd worked on it for weeks – an exact replica, even the wallpaper was right – but it wouldn't do. Not for you! You wanted a kitten. On to his knees in your yellow ribbons. Butterfly kisses he called them; you used to press your cheek against his and flutter your eyelashes . . .'

'Mother!' Julia's voice was loud in the quiet ward. 'I'm going to see if I can find a vase.'

'. . .Three days it took.' The story followed her down the ward. 'He bought you the kitten, took out the floors and the staircase, put in a cushion. Everything you wanted he gave you.

'It was dead in a month. Run over by a cab. You shed a few tears when we buried it. More than you shed for your father . . .'

The vase was too big; the carnations leaned out, skinny and forlorn. Her shoes squeaked on the linoleum. Her mother was weeping, a gloss of unwiped tears on her cheeks.

'I'm sorry, my dear. You've only just come and already I've said the wrong things. I'm just a foolish old woman.'

'Come on now. It's all right.'

Damp fingers snatched her hands. 'I'm dying, Julia.'

'You're not dying, Mother.'

There was a car in the drive. She stopped by the gate, trying to see into it without appearing to look. A man stepped from the shadow of the porch. She recognised the face from one of the parties of which Mrs Pritchard disapproved.

'Hello, Patrick.'

'I hope you don't mind me calling again.'

'Not at all.' She fumbled with the keys.

He stood in the hall, looming large as she carried her basket through to the kitchen.

'Have you been waiting long?'

He smiled. 'Ages. I think your neighbour was going to call the police.'

'Mrs Pritchard?'

'The one on the left.'

'That's her. She's all right, she's sort of taken charge while my mother's been in hospital.'

'How is your mother?'

'I saw the consultant this morning. He said I mustn't hope for too much.'

The kettle rattled under the tap. Suddenly there were tears on her cheeks, splashing down into the coffee cups.

Patrick took the cups from her hands. 'There, now.'

Her face was pressed against the blue anorak.

'I'm not crying for my mother,' she sniffed. 'I'm just crying for myself. I don't want her to die, but I couldn't bear to be trapped here, having to look after her.'

The anorak was soft and cool against her cheek. She

13

caught a hint of his smell, a slight tang of sweat and something else, the warm, intimate smell of the man beneath.

'I like a girl who doesn't cry too much.' He handed her a sheet of paper towel. 'If we were at home I'd have a clean handkerchief.'

Julia wiped her eyes.

The next day he took her to a restaurant near the hospital. Pink walls and white furniture. Beside their table was a tall potted palm. She touched the leaves.

'It's real, Patrick.'

'What is?'

'This palm.'

'What else would it be?'

'Plastic.'

'Plastic?' repeated Patrick. 'Why would they make a plastic palm tree?'

'So they don't have to water it.'

Patrick laughed. 'England is worse than I remember.'

'Don't they have anything like that in Africa?'

'Not yet,' said Patrick, smiling, 'so far we've made do with the real thing.'

Without asking what she would like to eat he ordered T- bone steaks and chips.

Julia ate part of the steak and put down her fork.

'What's the matter? Don't you like your steak?'

'I'm not used to eating so much.'

He grinned. 'You should come to Africa, I'd teach you to eat.'

When the meal was over he drove her to the hospital in his rented car. 'I'll wait for you.'

'Are you sure? I might be a long time.'

'That's OK. I've nothing else to do.'

'You could get something to read. There's a bookshop in the main building.'

'No,' said Patrick, settling back into the car seat. 'I'm not much of a reading man.'

14

Julia looked back across the car park. He was staring straight ahead, drumming his fingers on the steering-wheel.

I suppose they get out of the habit of reading, she thought. His Africa sounded romantic and beautiful. You wouldn't need books, she thought. There'd be so much to do.

She returned after an hour to find him sitting patiently in the car.

'How is she?'

Julia sighed.

'Are they going to let her out?'

She shook her head. 'Not for a long time.'

For a second she caught his eyes. They were clear blue, surrounded by tiny lines. His voice was sympathetic but his eyes were expressionless.

'It was kind of you to wait for me.'

He shrugged. 'I have nothing else to do.'

'Don't you have friends over here, people to visit?'

'Not really. Only the Thomases – they're parents of a friend of mine. They've seen enough of me already.'

'Why did you come to England?'

He nosed the car out into the traffic. After a moment he said. 'Clare Bowen suggested it.'

'Who is Clare Bowen?'

'One of the Ledorot wives. She mothers me a bit.'

'What about your own mother, where is she?'

He answered very quickly, as if he had expected the question. 'She's dead – and my father.'

Julia turned to look at him but he was facing the road. 'You poor thing,' she said quietly.

Patrick drove her home and carried in the bag of washing that she had brought from the hospital.

'Would you like some tea?'

He nodded. 'What shall I do with the washing?'

'Just leave it there, I'll deal with it later.'

15

He leaned against the wall and folded his arms.

'You shouldn't use an automatic kettle,' he said as she put the kettle under the tap.

'Why ever not?'

'The water boils too long.'

'What do you mean?'

'It should be just boiling when you pour it on the tea, if you leave it too late there isn't enough air left in the water.'

'I'd forgotten about you and tea,' said Julia, smiling. 'Somehow I just didn't make a connection between a tea estate in Africa and making a cup of tea here.'

'I shouldn't think there is much connection between what is in those tea bags and what we grow in Ledorot.'

Julia picked up the box of tea bags. 'It says that the bags contain a blend of the finest teas in the world.'

Patrick laughed. 'They're probably sweepings from the factory floor.'

'Do you make tea-bags in Ledorot?'

'Of course. We produce all grades of tea, but I can tell you, you won't find the locals drinking that stuff.'

Julia opened the larder and took out a tin of Earl Grey.

'This is mother's – she keeps it for her bridge parties.'

Patrick opened the lid and sniffed the contents. 'How long is it since the last bridge party?'

'You mean it's stale?'

He took the tin out of her hands and put it back in the larder. 'Let's stick with the tea bags. At least they don't taste of perfume.'

He warmed the pot with a swirl of water and put in a handful of tea bags. The roar of the kettle was just changing note when he pulled out the plug and filled the teapot.

'Now we'll leave it to brew for a bit.'

'It's going to be terribly strong,' said Julia.

He shook his head. 'That's flavour. If the flavour is there you can differentiate between teas just as you can with wine.'

The tea that came from the pot was like dark soup. Julia added milk and took a sip.

He watched her face. 'That's better, isn't it?'

She shook her head. 'It's too strong!'

He took a gulp from his own cup and ran it round his mouth like a wine taster. 'It's not bad,' he said after a moment, 'considering it's tea bags.'

He drank the rest of the tea black, unstrained; mother's china cup dwarfed by his thick, freckled hands.

Clumsy hands. They had been clumsy on the first date, the meal in the restaurant where he had slopped wine on to the tablecloth. His face had turned pink, a shade of his fiery red hair.

'I'm sorry. I guess all this business is making me nervous.'

'All what business?'

He didn't answer. His hands were clumsy again when he took her home; with the buttons of her blouse, with his own clothes. An unseemly rush that exposed tanned limbs, abruptly pale where shirt and shorts began; an impression of white against the sunweathered skin.

The bedroom was almost dark; she could see the cold square of the window and the cloudy twilight sky beyond it. Moving inside the circle of her arms, his body was hard and strong. The thought came into her mind that with this man she would always feel safe. Warm and safe.

It was over too soon, before her own body had begun. He raised his head and made a low, wordless sound. His body kicked hard against her and she held him close as he slumped, feeling the slackening muscles of his back.

'It doesn't matter,' she whispered.

He raised his head. 'What doesn't matter?'

'About me not . . .' She cast around for the right words, '. . . about me not being in time with you.'

'That's all right.'

'Where are you going?'

He was getting up, pulling on his trousers.

17

'I'm starving. Shall we have a take-away?'

He returned with two square paper carriers. She sat up against the pillows as he laid foil containers before her on the sheet. Fresh coriander sprinkled on yellow meat, crisp bhajia and glistening triangles of nan bread. She kissed his cheek.

'Do you eat like this at home?'

He smiled. 'Not quite like this – but my cook is pretty good.'

She speared a piece of meat and held it out to him.

'How many servants do you have?' she asked.

'Two. A cook and a houseboy.' He took the meat into his mouth. 'They have a soft time, cooking for one, *dhobi* for one, free electricity, leftovers.'

'Do you ever feel guilty about them?'

'Why should I feel guilty?'

'About exploiting them.'

He looked at her in astonishment. 'I don't exploit them. I pay them to do a job.'

Julia broke off a piece of nan and dipped it in the gravy.

'How did you find the servants?'

He waved his fork. 'You don't have to look for them, they come to you. There was a queue on the back step the day I arrived. I got through several before I settled on these two. The cook is a bit sassy and the houseboy coughs all the time, but they do the work and they don't steal my booze.'

'Is there a lot of disease out there?'

He shook his head. 'Much less than there used to be.'

'What about insects?'

'Insects? Hordes of them.' He took a forkful of steaming meat and breathed on it. 'All God's creatures. It's a wonderful country.'

'Do you find them in the house?'

'All the time!' He laughed. 'You'll find beetles in your slippers if you leave them on the floor.'

'Big ones?'

'As big as Morris Minors!'

'I'm serious, Patrick!'

'So am I.' Suddenly his voice changed and he grabbed her hand. 'Julia, if your mother . . .' His face was flushed. She answered the squeeze of his hand.

'Julia, when your mother gets better, will you come back with me?'

'To Africa?' She looked up in surprise.

'I need a wife . . .' He stared earnestly into her face. Light from the bedside framed his head, the fiery red hair was lit like a halo.

'But, Patrick, you hardly know me.'

'I know enough.' He leaned forward, grasping her hands.

'Patrick, you're hurting me.'

'What?'

'My hands – you're hurting my hands.'

He let go of her at once. His face creased with concern. 'I'm sorry, I'm so sorry.'

'It's all right.' She held her fingers. 'You're just stronger than you know.'

He rubbed his face in his hands. 'I still meant what I said, Julia. If I'm not too much of a roughneck for you.'

She smiled and touched his neck. 'Nothing that a shave wouldn't cure.'

'But will you think about it?'

She smiled. 'I'll think about it.'

The curry was finished. Julia had drunk little wine but the bottle was almost empty.

'What about your family?'

He shook his head.

'I know about your parents, but what about the rest? Where are they?'

He shook his head again. 'I'm the only survivor.'

She smiled. 'You make it sound like a dying breed.'

'It is, civilised man in Africa.'

19

He tipped the bottle to his lips and hiccuped when it was empty.

'Don't you have any brothers or sisters?'

'None.' He hiccuped again.

'What happened to your parents?'

He shrugged. 'It was a long time ago. They were farmers. The farm was sold to pay for my education.'

Julia wanted to go back, to ask how they had died, but he had turned the subject away. She let it go. She could ask another time.

'I was sent to boarding school.' He smiled. 'It was a good school then. They taught us to be tough.' He lay back against the pillows. With eyes closed he began to reminisce: Julia listened to tales of school, of rugby and cricket on hard, grassless murram, Marmite sandwiches in the dormitory, sharing the bathwater in the dry season. 'They've ruined it now, though.' He opened his eyes. 'After Independence they just opened the gates.'

'You mean it was all white boys when you were there?'

'Naturally. The blacks never had the money for schools like that.'

She looked at his face, his cheeks were flushed and his mouth slack with wine. 'Would you have shared your bath-water with a black boy?'

'Ha!' he shouted, raising himself from the pillows. 'What a question!'

'But they'd be no dirtier than you.'

'Don't you believe it, my love. That might be true here, where they've been civilised, but out there they're only just out of the trees.'

She looked at him again. He was still laughing. He didn't mean what he'd said. It was like the insects, as big as Morris Minors. He was teasing her, trying to shock her out of her narrow Finchley upbringing. She smiled back at him.

'What did you do when you left school?'

He lay back again, resting his arms behind his head.

'I got a job with Chaachi. That's the tea company. After a year they sponsored me to come and study Estate Management in England. I enjoyed myself but I didn't learn much. There isn't a book in the world that can teach you how to manage a team of kaffs.'

'Kaffs?'

'Sorry, darling.' He hiccuped again. 'Africans to you.'

'You mean the tea workers?'

'Pickers. But I don't manage them myself. We have foremen to do that.'

'Are all the pickers men?'

He shook his head. 'About half are women. They pick six hours a day, dawn to noon, and then sit in the shade on their arses. They could earn more if they worked in the afternoon, but we can't get them to do it. They'd rather sit about in the compound and drink.'

'Don't they need the money?'

Patrick shrugged. 'They earn enough to buy food and beer. Chaachi provides their housing and most of them have a patch of land to cultivate. Why should they work more than half a day? There's nothing they can buy in Ledorot anyway.'

'And where do you live?'

'In a house at the top of a hill,' he said, slowly. 'Surrounded by acres and acres of tea.' He smiled. 'It's a beautiful place. The most beautiful in the world. If you look out from the veranda, you can see the Rift Valley . . .' His eyes, which had been unfocused, looked at her again. 'That's if you . . . if you come to look.'

There was an expression on his face that she had not seen before, the way she imagined he would have looked all those years ago, a little boy bereft of his mother, alone in the world, as she might be herself before long. She pulled him gently towards her and put his head against her breast.

She hardly knew him. He was unlike any man she had ever known. He was so sure. So secure. She thought of

21

Africa, the Rift Valley, words on an atlas, the house on the hill. In her mind it was a magnificent place. Africa. She could go and be his wife, like one of the pioneer women, create a home for him, with children. She looked down. He was sleeping softly in her arms. Even in sleep his face was rugged as if he had lived all his life among men. She could soften his life, give him womanly things. It would be a wonderful adventure.

4

The lift doors clanged in the stairwell. Harry stirred. He shifted his feet on the desk and settled deeper into his chair. The lift gear hummed. He settled still deeper, striving to recapture his sleep, closing his eyes tight against the sharp splinters of sunlight on the blinds. It was no good. The gates on the landing crashed open. He heard the woosh-woosh of double doors that led into the passage outside.

''ello . . .' shouted a voice.

No reply came. Bare feet slapped along the parquet, accompanied by a loud whistle that faded as it reached the first of the labelled doors. Harry could hear them being deciphered.

'Accounts Department, Please Knock.'

'J. W. Uomu, Transport.'

'D. Muthaga, Export.'

His own door was second from the end. The feet stopped outside, a pause, his name painstakingly recited, 'H. Thomas, Export.' A tentative knock.

'Come in.'

A head came round the door, bright eyes peering anxiously into the shuttered room.

'Come in,' he said again.

The boy's face cleared as he recognised the man sitting behind the desk. 'Letter for you, Mistah Thomas.' He laid a square of paper on the desk. 'A man came on a bicycle. I tell him Office is shut, go away, but he says this is special fast letter for you.'

Harry picked up the cable and reached for his jacket.
'Share that with the bicycle man.'

'*Asante sana.*' The coins disappeared into a ragged pocket.

'You wanting office boy yet, Mistah Thomas?'

Harry shook his head. 'Not yet.'

'English more better every day.'

'Every day,' Harry agreed.

'You know I am speaking three tongues, Mistah Thomas.'

Harry had a mental image of three tongues waggling in the boy's mouth. 'First I am speaking my tribal tongue,' count one on the skinny fingers. 'Second, I am speaking Swahili,' count two. 'Third, English.'

Harry nodded at the eager fingers thrust towards him. He heard the same recital every day in the lift, it was timed for the sixth floor. Smile and the lift doors would open.

'Have a nice day, Mistah Thomas.'

The liftboy retreated down the corridor, whistling again, and jingling the coins in his pocket. Harry picked up the cable. It was eight weeks to the day. He inserted a pencil in the flap and flattened the page onto his desk.

The sections of print were stuck on crookedly:

WHITMAN TO THOMAS. LOVELY GIRL. WEDDING ON TWENTY-FIRST.

'I don't call that comfort.' Her mother's lips shook but her mind, like her words, was crystal clear. 'No television. You wouldn't be safe.'

'Of course I'd be safe, Mother. It's a civilised country.'

'What about all those black men?'

'They're just men, Mother, like other men. In any case there are lots of white people there as well.'

'You won't like them, Julia. They won't be our sort.'

'It would be an adventure.'

24

'An adventure! You can't marry an adventure, child. You'll need a home for your babies.'

'I haven't said I will yet. We're going to wait for you to get better.'

'I thought you said he was going back any minute.'

'He is, but I won't marry him until you're well. Until you don't need me any more.'

'Until I'm dead, you mean?' Her mother's voice was savage.

'I don't mean that, Mother. I really don't.'

'Ah, but it's what he means.'

By the weekend someone had defaced the sign outside the hospital.

PAKISTANIS ARE STRICTLY FORBIDDEN

'We're giving her something to help her sleep,' said the nurse.

Julia sat beside the bed and reached for her mother's hand. The palm rested in hers, upturned like an empty bowl. Naked, knuckle-thickened fingers, stripped of the gaudy rings that had scratched her during childhood hugs. She smoothed the fingers, flattened the palm, held the warm, slack skin against her cheek. Had she known the rings scratched? Worn them anyway? Gifts from Ted, the perfect father whom Julia could not recall – only the scrape of his cheek when he kissed goodnight and the smell of bonfires in his scarf; who had built the perfect dolls' house, a replica of his own, No 19, Bartlett Road.

She had found the dolls' house. It was on a shelf at the back of the garage, lying on its side with a scrap of withered cushion sticking to the inside walls. The cushion had been for the kitten. Its filling had gone hard, crumbled as she pulled it away.

The roof was on the shelf above, split along the ridge so that it lay flat under a box of flower-pots. She took

25

it out into the light to clean away the felted dust, like hoover fluff, that had preserved the colour of the roof tiles, oblongs of red, overlapping, showing the shadows, so finely painted that they sprang to life; a perfect reproduction, lacking only the terracotta peppering of the new tiles that had been put up in the years since he died.

He'd made the walls to support one another, clever dovetails that slotted like praying fingers into the base with its square of green, the painted rhododendrons and the cherry blossom against the window, just as she remembered it.

She could take the dolls' house to Africa. Someone there would mend the roof. Not Patrick, but someone else could do it. In Africa there would be someone with her father's deft hands.

A light was switched on in the ward, spilling a dull glow into the little room. Her mother's eyes were open, dark pools.

'You go, Julia.' The hoarse whisper cracked into the silence. 'Go and marry him. Go and be happy.'

Julia shook her head. 'I want you to get well, Mummy. I don't want to be alone.'

'I'm tired, Julia. I've only been waiting for this. It's not what I wanted for you but if it's what you want.' Her whisper became faint. 'I'll leave you in peace.'

Julia clutched her hand. Her mother had often talked of dying, always with impatience, as if she could not wait for heaven, a room she imagined, of infinite size, where the dead hurried in search of loved ones. Her fear had always been that she would miss him, her beloved Ted, be looking the wrong way when he passed.

Day began before the light, heralded by the rattle of trolleys and wheeled screens. A flat-footed orderly delivered a tray of breakfast. One glance at the patient sufficed for diagnosis.

'You eat it, Miss. Dis lady ain't gonna eat no breakfast today.'

26

'Oh, I couldn't,' said Julia.

'You eat or you be gettin' sick too and make even mo' work for dese po' feet.'

Julia took a bite of thin toast.

'If you want more, you come see me. Dere be many ladies not so hungry dis morning.'

Buttery water oozed from the scrambled egg. She ate the egg with a teaspoon.

At nine the ward sister found her asleep, her head on her mother's breast, restricting her breath. She hurried home, chastised and comforted by the woman's impersonal tongue. The familiar smell of the house drifted out as she unlocked the door, floor wax and old furniture, Ajax and dust.

She had barely taken off her coat when the telephone began. Loud jangling in the hall. 'This is St Peter's Hospital . . .'

Mother, dead. Julia was dry-eyed, numbed as though a limb she'd never used had been removed.

Mother dead. All that was left lying tongue-stilled in a refrigerator.

Mother dead. She caught the relief on Patrick's face. 'We can have the wedding the day before we go.'

5

Dust filled the tiny cracks in her skin, irritated her nose. Red-stained sweat ran in thin trickles behind her knees and between her breasts.

Patrick's arms were tanned, matted with fine hair the colour of the pale bush grass. His hands rested on the steering-wheel, his right elbow jutting out of the window. His body was loose and relaxed but his eyes were alert, frowning at the road.

They had started before dawn, leaving the city under a cold, black sky. The car doors had been freezing to touch. Julia huddled against the upholstery, clutching her hands between her thighs for warmth.

Dawn came. Long, shadowy streaks, fingers of light pointing across the sky. Land emerged from the darkness, colourless grass and crouching bushes, heaps of shadow beside the road.

They stopped under a baobab for breakfast. Patrick pointed to dark shapes that hung from the branches like large, misshapen fruit. 'Weaver nests,' he said, and even as he spoke she saw the movement, birds fluttering, growing yellow with the light

A cardboard box, described on the hotel bill as 'One Picnic Hamper', contained packets of sandwiches, a wedge of fruit cake and four bananas. Also on the bill had been 'Coffee For Thermos, 1 litre'. It was bitter and full of grounds, but she sucked it in like warm breast milk.

'Are you going to change or not?' He was pulling off

29

his sweater. Her shorts and sandals were laid out on the passenger seat.

She shook her head and spat the coffee grounds on to the tarmac.

'Come here.'

She had been in the shadow of the car, leaning against the engine cover for warmth. He took her hand and brought her out of the shadow. The dawn had progressed while she was eating, from a mere suggestion of red on the horizon to a yellowing ball of fire hovering at the edge of the plain. Warmth struck her face as she looked at it, not warmth as she had known in England but a sharp, direct blaze, dry and pervasive. She held out her hands to it and felt her cold skin expand and glow. It was like an enormous fireside.

'It's the lack of cloud,' said Patrick. 'Down here on the plain it's always cold at night, but in an hour we'll be sweltering.' He grinned as she started to pull off her sweater. 'Good girl.'

He surveyed the land while she undressed, sharp eyes sweeping over the low thorn bushes that crouched in the grass on either side.

He is strong, she thought, voicing the words to herself in a way that had become familiar even in the few days since the wedding. He is very strong. I will be safe with him. Words she might have used to recommend him to her mother. He is very responsible. He will look after me.

But it was her own voice that answered. Will it be enough, Julia? When you are used to being safe, will it be enough?

At ten they stopped again. She sat in the car while he strode off to urinate in the grass. She'd wanted to go with him but he shook his head.

'You'd be better off in the car.'

'But I could look out for snakes.'

He laughed. 'I think I'd see them before you, Julia.'

30

She watched his back, head bent, showing the streak of white skin where he'd had his hair cut for the wedding. He zipped his shorts as he walked back to the car.

Not much of a wedding. He had hired a suit, she had bought a new dress and a trousseau of summer clothes. The neighbours were scandalized, ('Your poor mother hardly cold in her grave!') and the girls from work couldn't take time off on a weekday. Even the best man couldn't get away in time. Patrick's friend from Africa, Harry Thomas.

Patrick showed her the cable.

SORRY CHAACHI HAVE CANCELLED PACKING MACHINES STOP NO FLIGHT HOME STOP MAKE SURE IT'S THE RIGHT TIN STOP BEST OF LUCK

'What does he mean about the tin?'

'It's just a joke,' said Patrick. 'Harry likes his little jokes.'

It was Harry's parents who witnessed the marriage, signed the book and kissed them both beside the taxi that would take them to the airport.

'Give our love to Harry, tell him it's his turn next,' said his mother. She gave Julia a carrier bag from Marks and Spencer. 'See if you can get this to him. I'm sure he can't buy any decent clothes in Africa.'

They opened the bag as the taxi sped along the M4. It was full of underwear, nylon briefs and nylon ankle socks. Patrick snorted. 'He'll get heat rash if he wears those out there.'

Julia stared at the clothes in the familiar green carrier bag. It was hard to believe that in Africa such ordinary clothes could give anyone a rash.

'I don't suppose there's a Marks near Ledorot?' she asked.

Patrick laughed. 'No, my love, there is not!'

She saw little of the coast. Their plane landed after dark and they left the city before dawn. What she saw looked ordinary enough; tall buildings, parks, shops.

Before leaving town they called at the Chaachi office and gave the carrier bag to a boy who was sleeping in the hall. He jumped as they knocked on the wide glass doors, grabbing for his janitor's cap. There was a sign beside the lift: 'Chaachi Tea Co. Ltd. Sixth Floor'. As they went back to the car she looked up. The building looked solid; square, blind windows reflecting the stars.

He waited in the car while she squatted behind a bush, feeling the wind and the soft stroke of grass on her buttocks. She was afraid of the insects, some crawling thing that would slither out of the ground and bite her exposed flesh.

As big as Morris Minors.

'I'm serious, Patrick!'

'So am I. Come back with me. Marry me.'

Make sure it's the right tin of peas.

Julia guessed Harry's meaning. She wished he had come to the wedding, that the best man's presence had not depended on the purchase of packing machines.

It shouldn't have mattered, it shouldn't have been important that the wedding was such a hasty affair, but the absence of even the best man had made her uneasy. She would have liked to have met him, to have seen someone else from Patrick's world, someone else who liked Patrick. She even wished she had taken him to her mother, to have witnessed his self-defence. But her mother had died and the best man could not come.

At dusk they reached the edge of the escarpment. All day it had advanced, at first no more than a pale line between bleached sky and grass, the division gradually darkening to emerge as land, breaking into ranks, grey becoming brown and green, rising from the plain.

Plantations replaced the bush on the lower slopes,

tall, dense sugar cane, stained red by the declining sun. She stared out, feeling her ears pop as the road climbed higher.

The twilight was swift; in half an hour it was quite dark, chilling the breeze through the open window.

She asked him to stop and let her unpack a jersey.

'No. There isn't time.'

'Please, Patrick. It won't take a moment.'

'No. I don't want to be late back. I have to be in the factory first thing tomorrow.'

'Patrick, I'm cold. Surely we could stop for a moment.'

He was silent, eyes fixed ahead, as if he hadn't heard, one hand moving automatically on the gearstick as they bounced up the steep road, already no more than a wide track cut into the escarpment.

'He won't take care of you, Julia.'

'You can't marry an adventure.'

They drove in silence, shut in by the darkness. From time to time he would glance across and smile at her, teeth shiny and white in the gloom.

A few miles further on he pointed to the left. 'Do you see the lights half-way up that hill? That's the Club.'

The Ledorot Club. Twenty-five white members and four blacks. She knew it by heart. Turf outside where they played golf, darts in the bar, bridge, snooker, 'Kojak' on the video. He had described it all.

'How many people live up here?' She knew the answer but needed to hear it again.

'Just twenty-five of us on this estate. Twenty-six now with you. You'll do fine here, Julia, they haven't seen a pretty girl in years.'

How many people, she had asked, not how many whites.

'Is there a school?'

'Only for the kaffs.'

'How many,' she hesitated, 'how many black people are there?'

33

'How many kaffs? I don't suppose anyone's counted them all. They breed so fast you'd need a recount every six months.'

They came to a plateau; the track was narrower than the spread of light from the headlamps, muddy and rutted, with deep drains on each side.

'It's been raining,' said Julia.

'It always rains at the end of the day. That's why the tea does so well, lots of sun and lots of water.'

Tea grew right to the edge of the drains, dense, fat bushes leaning busily into the light.

'Damn!' Patrick was braking, the car veering leftwards, bushes looming up. They slewed round, stopping inches from the drain. 'All this way without a single flat and we get one a mile from home.'

He got out and walked round to the boot. The smell of the tea filled the car, a strong, springy smell. She stepped out. There was little to see but dense bushes backing up into the darkness on either side of the track. The air was chilled and damp. She unpacked her jeans and a jersey and put them on while Patrick worked in the beam of a torch, pumping the jack to lift the car clear of the road.

The men came silently, appearing out of the darkness to stand beside the car. She jumped in fright as Patrick's torch picked out three faces. They greeted Patrick in Swahili and he answered like one of them, pointing to the wheel. Seconds before she had been changing her clothes in the torchlight. Had these men watched, waiting in the darkness until the show was over?

'Who are they?'

'Pickers,' said Patrick. 'They've come over from the compound to give us a hand.'

He spoke again and the men crouched beside him on the dirt. One held the torch while Patrick changed the wheel and then they helped him load the flat tyre into the boot. She saw him give each a coin before he got back into the car.

34

'Why did you pay them?' she asked. 'They didn't really do anything.'

'No, they didn't do much,' Patrick agreed. 'But they did come. If I didn't give them a tip this time, next time they might not turn out, and next time we might need them.'

'Are they always so willing?'

'Oh yes, willing enough when there's the chance of a few bob for a beer.'

'Do you know all the pickers?'

He nodded. 'Nearly all of them on this estate. They work in teams. You get to know the faces.'

The car rode easily over the murram, climbing and circling, the headlights swinging back and forth as the track twisted. There was nothing to see but tea.

'How are the pickers paid?' Julia asked.

'By weight. The foreman weighs the loads each day and we pay them in cash at the end of the week.'

'What happens to it then?'

'It goes to the factory. You can't see because it's dark, but the factory is just down there.' He pointed across her into the valley. 'The green leaves go through big drying machines and then they're graded and packed. The best stuff goes for export and we sell the chaff to the pickers.'

'How is it exported?'

'It goes to the Coast by road and then by ship to Europe. That's Harry's job, getting it out of the country.'

Harry. The almost-best man.

'Does Harry ever come up to Ledorot?'

'Four or five times a year. He comes up to check the books and see how things are. Usually he stays with me and we take a day out on the dam.' He looked across. 'I told you about the dam, didn't I?'

Julia nodded, smiling. 'It was one of your promises, fresh trout for supper.'

Patrick smiled. 'I like to get down there about once a week.'

'Does Harry like fishing?'

'Harry? No. He just sits in the boat. But we take a picnic and a few beers. It makes a nice day out.' He broke off to point to a glimmer of light atop a dark shoulder of hillside. 'That's it.'

A row of white stones marked a culvert over the storm drain. She braced her palms against the dash as the car bounced up and round a steep slope of long grass on to a flat lawn.

'Whatever is that?' A bundle of rags had moved in the lights. It unfurled as she pointed, revealing arms and legs, a face swathed in white cloth like a bandage.

'It's only the watchman,' said Patrick.

'Why has he bandaged his head?'

'It's not a bandage. It's just a rag to keep him warm.'

A swaddled arm saluted as they got out of the car. Patrick spoke in Swahili and the watchman bowed to Julia. She caught a glimpse of his face, shrivelled brown cheeks and rheumy eyes. Then he was gone, shouting, round the back of the house with a truncheon thumping against his thigh.

Patrick put his arm round her as they stepped up to the veranda. 'The boys didn't know we'd be back tonight so there isn't any hot water.' He was lifting her, hoisting her under his arm like a sack of vegetables. 'I'll just have to have you dirty, won't I?'

She was over the threshold, feet on the polished red floor before it occurred to her to be bride-like. His lips brushed her cheek and she reached out, but he was gone already, whistling under his breath.

She stood by the door and looked around. A stone fireplace ran the length of one wall, with a heavy sofa and two armchairs posted like sentries before it. The fireplace was empty, the mantel above it quite bare.

Patrick opened a door on the other side and she followed him past a long dining table into the kitchen.

'This is Mshoki, my cook.' A tall African bowed to her gravely. He wore a white jacket, neatly pressed trousers

36

and no shoes. She offered her hand and smiled at the flood of Swahili.

Patrick translated. 'He says he hopes you will be very happy here.'

'I hope I shall be.'

'They're good boys,' said Patrick. 'They've been with me a long time.' He turned to the other. 'This is the houseboy, Francis.'

The second man, much older than the first, bustled forward and took his turn to clasp her hand. His was slightly damp. Her fingers slipped a little as she looked up into his beaming smile, jagged teeth exposed to the brown roots.

At a word from Patrick the cook opened a cupboard and began picking potatoes out of a box.

'We'll get you settled in while Mshoki fires our supper,' said Patrick.

Shuffling ahead, the houseboy led them back through the house. It was spotless, with polished floors and gleaming paintwork, clean and featureless. He touched each piece of furniture as he passed, as if running through an inventory, like a seaside landlady.

The house appeared to have been built as a series of extensions from the living room. The dining room, kitchen and scullery retreated in single file, each a step below the other. The bedrooms had been built on at right angles. A door from the sitting room led to a dark passage that ran along the back of the house. Ceremoniously Francis showed her the bathroom, holding the door open while she stared at cracked pink tiles and a stained bath.

'Is the bath dirty?' she asked Patrick.

He grinned. 'It's not dirt, it's rust from the water tank. If you lie in it long enough you'll get a nice brown tan.'

The guest room had floral curtains and a faded patterned rug beside the bed. When they reached the last door Patrick pushed ahead and sent Francis back to fetch their suitcases from the car.

'This will be our room.'

The same floral curtains that didn't quite meet and a frayed mosquito canopy over a pair of iron beds. On the furthest pillow lay a pair of men's pyjamas, folded with military precision.

'Separate beds?' she cried, involuntarily.

Patrick grinned. 'Don't worry about that. In the hot weather you'll be glad of it. In any case, we can have as much fun in two as in one.'

Something in his expression made her recoil. He looked so keen, it was almost a leer.

'Well? What do you think?' He rubbed his hands.

She thought of the other rooms, of the shabby furniture and the rust-stained bath.

This? This was the house on the hill? All that he had promised? She sat on the nearest bed and felt the mattress roll back into the centre.

'Well?'

'It's fine, Patrick. Really it is.'

'Wait till you see the view in the morning, you'll say it's out of this world.'

Julia forced herself to smile. Out of this world. She had a feeling he spoke more truly than he knew. She clutched the bed, feeling the starched, unfamiliar sheet under her fingers.

'Is there anything else – I mean, apart from the view?'

'No.' Patrick beamed. 'That's the beauty of it. No shops, no traffic, just the view and the peace. You'll love it, Julia, after all that filth in London.'

'London isn't that bad.'

'It's a terrible place, just traffic and grime. When you've been here for a bit you'll wonder how you ever survived.'

Julia heard him in silence.

A deep, bronchitic wheeze announced the approach of the servant. He knocked on the open door. Patrick shouted something. The old man staggered in and heaved one of the suitcases on to a stand.

'They could stay on the floor until we've unpacked them,' said Julia.

'No, no.' Patrick waved the suggestion aside. 'We don't want the doo-doos getting in. Eh, Francis?'

The old man managed to shake his head.

'Insects,' said Patrick. 'Doo-doo is our name for all the little things that crawl and fly.'

'Our' word. His and theirs. The tongue she would have to learn and make her own.

6

The hills marked the edge of the Rift; green hills that stood proud of the plain. The tea grew between them, acres of green bushes, hunching and bustling in the breeze, spilling into every space and gap. The houses of the senior employees were perched on the hills, whitewashed bungalows, buttressed by lawns and trees, separated from the tea by the steep sides of the hills.

Patrick's house was the furthest, on the edge of the estate, turning its back on the tea to look out over the Rift Valley. Below the veranda was the garden, a well-watered lawn, like a hilltop table, green and lush above the long dry grass that clung to the hillside. Below the hillside lay the track, and below the track, thousands of feet down, were the plains of the Rift, a grassy flatland of gold silk.

Patrick had forbidden her to go further than the lawn.

'But it's only grass,' Julia protested, pointing to the tall, spiky undergrowth that hung below the lawn like a skirt. The rain had scooped away the earth at the edge so that it hung as from a hoop, swinging free, concealing the rise and swell of the hillside.

'You'll sprain your ankle. There are potholes down there, big dips hidden under the grass – and snakes.'

'Snakes! So close to the house?'

'There could be.' He pointed to the acacia that grew at the edge of the lawn. 'That's the edge of the garden, Julia. I don't want you to go any further than that.'

'But I can go for a walk, surely?'

'White women don't walk in Africa.'

'What do you mean?'

'White women don't walk. Walking is for kaffs. If you want to go anywhere, I'll take you in the car.'

'But what will I do while you're at work?'

Patrick looked up at her, nonplussed. 'I don't know. Whatever the other women do.'

When he had gone she walked across the lawn, scattering a flock of birds that had been feeding on the grass. Dust, disturbed by his car, was settling back on to the track below. She looked out at the view. 'There is game down there,' he had told her. 'Wildebeest, buck, zebra.'

She screwed up her eyes. She could see no game. The house was too high up to see anything but a vast sea of yellow. She had been watching the view since breakfast, a meal that Patrick ate alone, with Julia looking on, when it was barely light.

'Are you going so early?'

He nodded, swallowing the last of his coffee. 'The day starts at dawn out here, to get the work done before the heat.'

'Will you come home for lunch?'

He stopped. 'I usually go to the Club for a sandwich.'

'But you won't now, surely?'

For a moment he looked puzzled, then he smiled. 'No, of course not! Not now that I have a little wifey to come home to!'

She had been going to kiss him but the servant came in. Patrick said something and the boy began to clear the table.

Julia went out to the veranda. The view had looked the same then as it did now at mid-morning; only the colours had changed, from the blues and greys of dawn to a fine yellow haze.

She walked slowly around the house. Francis walked behind her with his hands up, as if waiting to be asked for something.

'I don't need anything,' she said. 'I just want to have a look.'

The servant stood still, his eyes on a point just to the right of her face. 'Why don't you get on with what you normally do?' She made a gesture of sweeping.

The servant put his head on one side. 'Don't you have to do any housework?' She ran her hand over the sideboard, as if to polish it.

The servant said something that she didn't understand.

She smiled at him, shaking her head. 'I really don't need anything.'

She sat on the sofa and looked out of the window. After a moment she heard his bare feet slapping away over the wooden floor. She stayed on the sofa, pretending to be absorbed by the view. Francis returned carrying a tray of coffee.

She smiled her thanks.

He put the coffee beside her and retreated. She was relieved, a few minutes later, to hear the clang of a pail and water roaring through the pipes from the outside tank.

Having finished her coffee she resumed her tour of the house. She went into the bedroom and was immediately aware of Francis following her. She felt the need to make a noise. She tried pulling the curtains; the metal rings squealed and stuck along the rail. Her sigh brought Francis forward.

She turned to him with a smile. 'They're sticking,' she said.

'Eh . . .' said the old man. It was not a word, merely a sound, a sigh in return for her sigh.

In the kitchen she found the cook kneading dough.

'You make the bread yourself?' she asked in surprise.

He inclined his head, a movement so neutral she wondered what thought it concealed, what response to her unnecessary question.

She opened the door of a large freezer. It was half

43

empty. 'Why don't you make a whole batch of loaves and freeze them?'

The cook stared at her.

She smiled. 'I'll have to learn your language, won't I?'

He smiled back.

When she had finished touring the house, she went out through the back door. Beside the kitchen was a lean-to scullery with a crazed enamel sink and an old-fashioned mangle. A water tank stood in the murram yard, like an enormous tin can, with wood glowing red in the fireplace beneath.

Behind the tank was the kitchen garden, as big as the whole plot at Bartlett Road. With a pang of nostalgia she remembered her mother's strawberry beds, the blackberries that grew along the trellis. Mshoki's garden was a grid of neat vegetable rows, divided by a path that led to the servants' quarters. She could hear voices, a radio playing, sounds that were not audible from the front of the house. There she could hear only the birds.

She went inside, found a notepad and pen, and started a list of things to do. She could fix the curtains for a start. When the rest of her luggage arrived she could unpack her china and pictures and make the place homely. It will be all right, she told herself, remembering her mother's expression: don't judge the book by its cover.

'A belated wedding present, my dear.'

Julia took the box from Mrs Ellis's outstretched hands.

'Thank you.' She smiled at the circle of faces. Nine women, smiling uniformly, except for the youngest who sat near the door and blew smoke rings towards the ceiling.

The invitation had come by mouth, mouthful to be exact; Patrick remembered it between forkfuls of potato at lunchtime. An invitation to the Ladies' Circle, a meeting of the wives that was held once a month in the Ledorot Club.

The clubhouse was a large wooden structure with

noisy floors, opening out on to a wide veranda that overlooked a balding patch of turf. An ancient doorman sat behind a desk in the entrance. A guest book was maintained but there were few entries; Patrick had introduced her with a flourish, not as a guest but as the newest member of the Club. The doorman smiled toothlessly as Julia signed the Members' Book.

The meeting of the Ladies' Circle was held in the Lounge, which was distinguished from the Bar by having leather armchairs instead of wooden stools, and a video set on a stand.

Julia looked at the coloured paper that covered the box in her hands. It had been used before, old Sellotape marks were visible on the pattern. Wrapping paper, like everything else, would be a precious commodity in Ledorot.

'Well, aren't you going to open it?'

They held their saucers in their laps, smiling at her over the brims of teacups.

Carefully she unwrapped the box. Inside was a wooden frame and a bag of coloured wools.

'What is it?'

'It's a tapestry set. We thought you'd like to have something to do.' The woman on her left patted her hand.

'It's occupational therapy.' The one in the corner interrupted her smoke rings, 'something to keep us from the bottle in the afternoons.'

The circle behaved as if she had not spoken.

'They sell very well at the Coast,' said another woman, loudly. 'The Anglican mission takes them for the fêtes at the Cathedral.'

Cathedral fêtes?

'Is there a charity for the local people?' She thought of the swollen-bellied infants she had seen clinging to the women who bent over the tea.

'You don't have to worry about the locals, dear. The Company looks after the pickers.'

45

The barman came in to remove the tea trolley. He wore white trousers and brown plastic sandals. She remembered Francis's bare feet. She would mention it to Patrick.

The conversation continued as the man walked back and forth, collecting cups and saucers. Nobody acknowledged him, just as if he were invisible. When he had finished Vera Ellis called his name. 'Joseph!'

Shortly afterwards he returned with a tray of drinks.

'It's almost sundown,' said Vera, brightly.

'Cheers, Julia!'

She was handed a tumbler half full of whisky. 'Thank you.' She turned to the woman on her right. 'How do I pay for my drink?'

'Don't worry about that, the Ladies' Circle has its own account. Our husbands divide the bill at the end of the month.'

Another woman, Clare Bowen, raised her glass. 'It's nice to have a fresh face up here, Julia.'

'Like meat,' said the one in the corner. 'A fresh kill to gloat over.'

'You mustn't mind Janyce,' Vera Ellis leaned close to murmur in Julia's ear. 'She has a difficult marriage. Dickie's a bit of a black sheep.'

Julia had already encountered the 'difficult marriage'. The Dickinsons were their nearest neighbours and had driven over on the second evening for drinks. For the first time Julia heard Patrick use the word 'wog'. As if a light had been switched on, everything was thrust into focus. Somehow, 'kaff' hadn't been important. It wasn't a word she knew. But 'wog' was a playground taunt, a bully's word, the girl at school who had tried to iron her hair.

'How are you getting on with your servants?' Clare Bowen's voice cut across her thoughts.

'Fine, thank you. They're very friendly.'

'Not too friendly, I hope?' The big woman raised her hand. 'Nothing wrong with being nice to the blacks, my

46

dear, nothing wrong at all. But remember to keep your distance. Particularly with the house servants.'

Julia sipped her whisky.

'And keep an eye on your pantry,' said Vera. 'If you show weakness they'll bleed you dry.'

'I'm sure Patrick's boys are honest,' said Julia.

Patrick's 'boys'. Francis was old enough to be her father. It was Patrick's word that had slipped from her tongue. Would she learn to use his other words, call them kaffs and bushheads?

Madeleine Waugh was speaking to her. 'Give it a year or two, Julia. Do as Patrick advises. He's been out here all his life. He understands the African mind.'

'You follow our example and you'll do very well, my dear.' Julia swallowed her whisky and smiled again, feeling their kindness and patronage spreading over her, like thin oil.

By the time Patrick arrived to take her home the huge measure of whisky was gone and her lips felt slightly numb. She walked carefully round the room, saying goodbye and trying to remember their faces. From Janyce Dickinson she got no response, she was asleep, her empty glass lying in her lap.

'They liked you, Julia.' Patrick grinned as they drove away. 'I told you they would.'

He had not asked if she liked them.

'They gave me a lot of advice.'

He nodded. 'You do as they say and you'll be fine.'

Do as they say. And they had said, do as he says.

'They were a bit stuffy.'

'Stuffy?' His eyes left the road to look at her. They had reached the place where the dirt track turned, commencing the long, winding ascent to Patrick's house.

'Watch out!'

As the car swung round the bend, a man in ragged shorts and singlet leapt off his bicycle and hurled himself into the storm drain.

Patrick was laughing.

'You nearly ran that man down!' cried Julia.

'Never!' said Patrick, still laughing.

Julia looked back. 'His bicycle is stuck in the drain.'

'Don't paff, Julia. He'll get it out.'

The car turned again, putting the man out of sight.

There were two books in the house: *Fly Fishing in East Africa*, and *An Illustrated Guide To English Stately Homes*.

The last bore an inscription: 'To Billy, with love from Emily, Christmas 1952'.

Billy and Emily, the story that he had not told, the tale that Clare Bowen, who came up to teach her tapestry stitches and asked for gin in the middle of the afternoon, told her with such grim relish.

'Didn't he tell you?' she cried in astonishment.

She had put down her tapestry and moved closer to Julia. 'Poor boy. I suppose he didn't want to frighten you away.'

'Frighten me?'

'He was only fourteen when it happened. I know the story because my Jack knew their neighbours.' She sipped her gin and laid a hand on the arm of Julia's chair.

'What happened?'

'Did he tell you they were farmers?'

Julia nodded.

'They were second generation. The grandfather had carved the farm out of the bush, made quite a go of it. They had a few hundred acres, mostly dairy.' Clare lit a cigarette. 'But it was very remote, way up near what is now the border. They sent Patrick away to school. He was the only son, so I guess they intended to pass the farm on to him. I know he didn't go to England, not until he was a grown man.

'Anyway,' Clare took a swallow of gin. 'There was a bit of trouble at that time. Cattle rustling that had got out of hand, skirmishes. The Colonial police were

48

doing what they could, but you know how it is with these blacks, they're such cowards you can never catch them. Anyway, things were getting worse, a couple of policemen were shot and, in the end, the Governor broadcast a message, recommending people to come off their farms and shelter at the Coast until the unrest was settled. Billy Whitman wouldn't budge. Frightened of losing his herd, I suppose. Old Billy bought himself a shotgun and said he'd stick it out.'

Clare paused to drag on her cigarette and tap the ash into a tray.

'What happened?' said Julia, impatient now to hear the end of it.

'Fortunately young Patrick was away at school,' Clare continued. 'Because when the trouble came it was more than his father could handle. He sent a runner, one of his own boys, to get help. The help came too late.' Clare shrugged. 'Who knows? Maybe someone paid the runner to walk.' She paused again. 'At any rate, they got there too late. Billy and Emily were hanging from a tree – and all their guts on the ground underneath.'

Julia put her hand to her mouth.

That night, when Patrick came home from the factory, she challenged him. 'Is it true?'

'Of course it's true.'

'Why didn't you tell me? Why didn't you tell me what happened?'

He yawned. 'What good would it have done you to know?'

'You brought me to this place, Patrick. I had a right to know.'

He spoke as if he was tired, yawning again. Julia wondered what emotion the tiredness concealed.

'It was a long time ago, Julia. Things like that don't happen anymore.'

'But didn't it make you hate them, didn't it make you afraid?'

49

'Of kaffs?' He laughed. 'You can't be afraid of a kaff, my love.'

'But you must have hated them.'

He shook his head. 'You wouldn't hate a dog.'

And there the subject was left. Billy and Emily Whitman, an inscription on a fly leaf, a farmer and his wife found hanging from a tree.

7

Mshoki's vegetables grew tall. Potatoes, carrots, runner beans, even asparagus thrived in the daily cycle of sunshine and rainfall. Every day, towards dusk, clouds would gather on the hills behind Ledorot, puffs that clung together, stringing out into lines that gradually encroached upon the retreating sun. The rain would begin abruptly, a drenching torrent that pooled on the grass and ran in jagged rivulets across the day-dried murram. Mshoki had carved channels between his rows of vegetables, a network of narrow drains that carried the surplus water away down the hill. He worked on the patch with his wife. Julia had seen her stooping over the rows, patting in cakes of manure that she carried up from the farm at the bottom of the estate.

An exercise book was kept in the kitchen, left open on the window-sill with a stub of pencil resting in the spine. Mshoki recorded every vegetable he brought into the house. Each day's consumption of potatoes and salad and tiny purple-skinned onions was weighed on the scales and listed on the dated pages. Patrick paid him for the produce, deducting a percentage from the market price – in lieu of rent for the soil and something he called 'sass' money.

'What is sass?' Julia asked.

'Cheek,' Patrick answered. 'Cheating.'

'Do you really think he cheats you?'

Patrick smiled. 'Of course he cheats, but only for the sass money.'

'Perhaps he wouldn't cheat you if you paid a fair price.'

Patrick shook his head. 'You don't understand, Julia. Africans don't think like that. If he didn't cheat me a little he'd feel he was cheating himself. So I charge him sass money and because he knows I know, he cheats for no more than it's worth.'

Julia shook her head. 'You should deal with him properly, Patrick. You should pay him a fair price.'

'I am doing! If I did it any other way he'd think I was going soft.' Patrick lowered his voice. 'You've got to keep the upper hand all the time, Julia. You've always got to show that you're smarter than they are.'

A path led from the house to the quarters, passing between the rows of vegetables and down the hill, into the tea at the back. She never ventured further than the rows of beans. It was somehow 'their' path, used by servants and their visitors, men on bicycles and women who came to gossip with Mshoki's wife.

Meat came from the same source as the manure. Patrick took her down to the small farm, perched on a slope between the last terrace of tea and the start of the sugar cane. A white disk hung at the entrance, 'Rift Valley Farm', but the house was derelict and sugar grew hard against the dairy shed.

Julia was left in the car while Patrick strode off to the cowshed. He walked as if he owned the farm, swaggering a little. When the black farmer appeared, wiping his mouth as if they had disturbed his meal, Patrick put his hand on his hip and shouted as he would to a servant.

The air in the car was hot and stale. She dabbed her neck with a handkerchief. Her eyes ached from the sun that glared back from the bonnet. She had closed the windows but already the car was full of flies, buzzing and whining about her head, crawling, thick-bodied, across the inside of the windscreen.

The cows were in the shade of the trees. The farmer poked them with a staff to make a path for Patrick. There was a long discussion. Julia listened to their voices drifting across the dusty field. Patrick wandered among the herd, slapping a few rumps, pointing to hooves and flanks. She thought of his father's herd, of Patrick as a youngster, dealing with the African farm hands, of his father, Billy Whitman, found hanging from a tree.

'You wouldn't hate a dog,' he had said.

The cow that he chose mistook Patrick's interest for friendship and stood between him and the farmer, chewing innocently while they argued over the price. Eventually Patrick took a wad of bills from his back pocket and the farmer shook his hand. He came back to the car, wiping his hands on the seat of his shorts.

'It won't be long.' He climbed into the car.

'What have we to wait for?'

'For the meat, of course.'

She glanced behind her and saw a sack spread out on the back seat. 'Do you mean he's killing it now?'

'Of course. Did you think it would come wrapped in cling-film with a sell-by date?'

A fly knocked against her face. 'You mean he's actually killing that cow at this moment?'

Patrick nodded.

'A whole cow?'

'You can't kill half a cow, Julia! Anyway, it's not a cow, it's a bullock.'

'That's not what I meant.' She swallowed. 'What I meant was, have we bought a whole one?'

He smiled and patted her knee. 'Don't look so worried. I've done a deal with Dickie; we're taking half the steer he bought last month – which the farmer has had hanging in that store over there – and I've paid for that one you saw, which we'll split with him when we're ready to eat it. We'll share out the best cuts and the boys'll get the offal.'

Mshoki and Francis were waiting in the garden. They

smiled broadly at the sight of the unwrapped carcass that lay, like the victim of an accident, on the sacks in the back of the car. For an hour the kitchen echoed with the squash and thud of cleavers. Mshoki was keen for her to witness his skill as a butcher but she couldn't stay, the sight of the blood and fat and bones on the table made her light-headed.

Patrick went through to the bedroom to change his clothes, discarding the shorts and shirt that had hugged the carcass as they pulled it from the car. 'Tell him to keep the best steaks,' he shouted. 'Harry's coming up at the end of the month.'

'Harry? When is Harry coming?'

'Like I said, at the end of the month.'

Her heart lifted. 'I'm so glad,' she said. It was as if he had announced the arrival of a gift or an old friend.

'Why, you've never even met him.'

'I know,' said Julia. 'But it's as if something has been missing. Perhaps because he didn't come to our wedding – I feel as though his coming here will somehow complete things.'

Patrick looked at her in surprise. 'You do say the strangest things.'

She watched him wash his face in the basin. 'Why didn't you tell me before that Harry is coming?'

He reached for a towel. 'I'm telling you now.'

He put the soiled towel on the side of the bath. 'Go and tell Mshoki about the steaks.'

Instead of obeying she followed Patrick out on to the veranda where Francis had already put out an open bottle of beer and a glass.

'Will he stay for long?' she asked.

'Just a few days. He wants to make a report on the packing machines at Kibwezi, and I hope we can get in some fishing.'

Julia walked to the edge of the veranda. Immediately below, in the flower bed that separated the house from the lawn, she had planted a cutting. It looked weak, its short, succulent stem lay almost horizontal on the soil. She had no idea of its name, only that the bush near the kitchen door bloomed continuously with a mass of delicate purple flowers.

'What is he like?' she asked.

'Who, Harry?'

'Yes. You know – why do you like him?'

Patrick shrugged. 'I've known him a long time. He was a friend to me in London and when he came out here we just carried on.' He took a long swallow of beer and licked the foam from his upper lip. 'Not that we agree about everything. With him being down at the Coast he's developed some pretty soft ideas.'

'Such as?'

Patrick's canvas chair creaked as he leaned back and put his feet out against the veranda wall.

'Like putting the kaffs in management positions – that sort of nonsense.'

'Is there anything wrong with that – if they're trained for the job?'

He turned to her with an ugly grin. 'I suppose you'd have them running the whole show?'

Julia sat in front of him, perched on the wall beside his feet. 'I think people should be judged by their abilities, not their colour.'

Patrick snorted. 'You'll get on well with Harry. That's the sort of rubbish he talks.'

'I think it's you who talks rubbish,' said Julia quietly. 'You behave as if this was 1930.'

Patrick pointed a finger at her. 'Don't you get sassy with me, Julia. These hills are the last place in Africa where you'll find peace. The only reason for that peace is that here everyone knows where they belong.'

Julia thought of the pickers, of a woman she had seen bending over the tea with a great basket strapped to her back and a small baby tied against her breasts. She thought of Kangeni, the smartly-dressed African who was Patrick's assistant, whom she had seen more than once, drinking alone at the Club, standing by himself at the end of the bar.

'What about people like Kangeni?' she demanded. 'Where does he belong?' She began to pace the veranda. 'You only tolerate him, you never make him welcome.'

'Kangeni's position is not of my making,' said Patrick. 'If it were up to me I'd have left him as a foreman. He'd be much happier.'

'Then why did you promote him?'

'We had to.' Patrick scowled at her. 'It was a directive from Head Office. We had to create a minimum of three black assistant managers and give them membership of the Club.'

'And was that such a sacrifice?'

'It was an abomination. How are we going to keep Ledorot civilised if we've got to let bloody munts into the clubhouse?' Julia turned away. Without another word she walked back into the house. The noise from the kitchen had subsided. Tentatively she put her head round the door. Mshoki was holding a meat cleaver. His apron was splashed with blood.

'Mshoki,' she began. '*Tafadhali* . . .' The strange words failed, as they always did when she tried to speak their language. She held up three fingers. '*Tatu* steaks.' Mshoki waved the cleaver over the table. He wanted her to point, to recognise the sirloin in the neat slabs of meat and bone. She swallowed and moved hesitantly towards the table. Francis came to her rescue, coughing loudly, he stabbed the meat vigorously with his forefinger. A gabble of vernacular spurted out between the coughs. Mshoki made a show of nodding to Julia.

'*Ndiyo*, memsahib.'

'Bwana Thomas is coming.'

Both servants nodded to her, repeating the name, 'Bwana Thomas.'

They know already, she thought. Patrick must have told them before he told me.

56

Mastering her annoyance she smiled at the cook. 'Thank you, Mshoki.'

He inclined his head and, as always, she had a feeling that he was laughing at her, a secretive, giggly laugh that would burst out when she had closed the door.

Her visits to the kitchen were always brief and unsatisfactory. She never knew if she had been understood, if it were chance or strategy when she did or did not get the meal she had ordered.

The servants had no need of her. They had kept Patrick's house for ten years without any memsahib to guide them. She had no confidence that she could do better. The house was spotless, the laundry without fault. Mshoki's cooking was plain, unimaginative, but no worse than she could have managed herself. The servants were polite, Francis even tried to be friendly, but they never referred to her, or asked for orders. She was simply there, Patrick's wife, as useless as the pictures and ornaments that she laid out so carefully on the day they arrived from England. Francis dusted them every day, systematically replacing each object slightly to the right or left of where it had been the day before, until the porcelain figures were spread along the mantelpiece like a parade of soldiers, a straight line that restored the austerity she had hoped to disguise. Francis listened gravely while she explained, day after day, that the figures were meant to be grouped, that they were for decoration. '*Ndiyo*, memsahib.' But the next day they were dispersed again, set out with mathematical precision in descending order of size.

So it was with the laundry. For ten years Patrick had been discarding his clothes where he stood, leaving a pool of soiled shirts and socks in the bathroom or on the bedroom floor. For ten years Francis had been gathering them up, making a little bundle to carry out to the scullery when the sweeping was done. Julia's clothes were treated equally; anything left out was gathered up, clean or dirty, and scrubbed with a Jumbo bar of green soap that sat on a saucer in the scullery. It was too soon, too intimate for her to bear the thought of his brown hands holding her underclothes up against the light, as he did Patrick's shirts, to see if they were clean. She learned to be tidy, hoarded her washing in a pillowcase until his day off when she could do it herself.

The sight of her clothes floating in the sink brought a lump to her throat. She felt busy, alive with the task; even the raw, green soap smelt active and useful. A bag of pegs hung behind the scullery door. She put it over her shoulder and, with the wet clothes in a tin bucket and a delicious feeling of busyness, she sailed out into the garden. The sun was warm. She hummed as she stretched up to the line. The clothes caught a little breeze and shivered with life as she stood back to admire her work. It was only when she turned to go, after one last glance at the dancing line, that she caught the wounded stare from the quarters.

With much encouragement from the other women, she began the tapestry, following all the advice she was offered, smiling. When it was finished, which was quite soon, for she had nothing else to do, Vera showed it around the circle.

The women clapped.

'I must say, this is very good work, Julia.'

'Have you done one before?'

'You'll have to do a more complicated one next time.'

I don't want to do another.

The words lay unspoken on her tongue.

'Why don't you design the next one yourself?'

'Are you any good at drawing?'

The questions went on and on, without a pause for her to reply. She had seen the same thing done to others, the sudden rounding of attention, turning like the vultures that circled above the Rift, diving in as one.

58

She drew a design, a single hibiscus flower with leaves on a shaded, grey background.

'Why, Julia! We didn't know you were an artist.'

'It's very good. Where did you learn to draw?'

'At school . . .'

'You must design some more. This will make a beautiful tapestry.'

'It really isn't all that good,' she managed to interject.

'But it is a great effort, my dear.'

'And that is what counts.'

So the truth was allowed to come through; that they were humouring her, encouraging her, just as they did each other.

Their praise was meaningless.

Julia longed for a radio. Patrick didn't own one. 'You can't get the World Service up here, only local rubbish. It's not worth listening to.'

Mshoki had a radio. She could hear it through the bathroom window that faced the back of the house; mostly pop music, African songs accompanied by electric guitars, endlessly repeated.

Mshoki and Francis had visitors every day, strangers who came in the afternoons to sit on the step. She heard their laughter, the radio turned up loud, but rarely saw the visitors, for they came up the back path and only ventured as far as the patch if there was to be a trade, a basket of beans for a clutch of eggs, or even a whole chicken, still alive in the owner's arms as they bartered. The path was a back route to the other houses, down to the township at the bottom, an artery for all the news and gossip and chatter of an illiterate society.

Patrick's fishing book was brittle with age. Yellowing pages tinged around the edge with red dust.

She read every page. Fishing was his hobby, she would learn to fish and go out on the dam with him.

He kept his tackle in a cupboard in the spare room.

She examined it all carefully, and selected a rod that looked less used than the others.

It took half an afternoon, poring over the book and fiddling with a transparent line, before she was ready to practise. Francis had been in and out, eyeing the book and the rod and the coloured flies set out in a box on the bed. When it was ready he followed her into the garden and grinned as the long stem of the rod whooshed through the air.

The hook caught in a bush beside the veranda. Francis went forward to unravel the line. She crouched beside him, hearing the faint rattle of his chest as he breathed.

Once again she walked out across the lawn and flicked the rod up as the book instructed. The line shot out like a whip, yard after yard snaking across the grass. She rolled it in and repeated the cast. Each time the line shot out, Francis chuckled, clapping his hands at the swooshing of the rod. She grew in confidence, raising her arm higher and higher until, having changed her position, she watched in dismay as a huge length of line hurled through the air and snarled itself in the acacia at the edge of the lawn. The line was barely visible against the leaves. Francis brought a kitchen chair and held the back while she stood on the seat, reaching up into the branches. When her arms began to ache he took his turn to stand on the chair. She held it steady, the sagging seat of his faded shorts was at eye level as he scrabbled uselessly among the twigs and branches.

'What the hell are you doing?' Neither she nor Francis had heard the car. Patrick slammed the door and strode towards them.

'I've been reading your fishing book,' she giggled. 'But I'm afraid we've had a bit of an accident. Francis has been helping me learn to cast out but I've got the line stuck in the tree.'

'For Christ's sake, that's my best rod.'

Patrick elbowed Francis off the chair and used his

penknife to cut the line free. He wasn't angry. He spoke as he might speak to a child, or a servant.

'There. Now, you mustn't ever touch my tackle again.'

'But I want to learn how to fish. So that I can come out with you on Sunday.'

'Women don't go on the dam, Julia.'

'Why not?'

'They just don't. There's bilharzia in the water and mozzies everywhere.'

'What's bilharzia?'

'Never mind that.' He spoke to Francis in Swahili and the servant hurried back into the house with the chair.

'Patrick.'

She reached for his hand. 'I didn't mean any harm. I want to learn to fish, I need something to do.'

'You can't come fishing with me.'

'But why not?'

'It isn't safe.'

'If it's safe for you . . .'

'Julia, don't argue with me.' He had stepped up on to the veranda and was looking down at her. 'You must try to settle down.'

'How can I settle down? There's nothing for me to do.'

'Can't you do what the other women do?'

'What do they do – except drink and gossip?'

'What about your tapestry?'

'I don't want to do the tapestry. I want to use my brain.'

'Fishing won't use your brain.'

'But at least it's something we could do together!' she cried.

He looked at her strangely. 'Isn't it enough for you, Julia? All this?' He gestured to the house and the garden, and out over the Rift.

8

Each day seemed to pass more slowly than the one before. She longed for Harry's visit – anything that would change the monotony of the hilltop. Every day was the same. From Monday to Saturday Patrick rose at dawn, ate his large breakfast and then left for the factory. He would return for half an hour at lunchtime and then leave her again, until the sun was slipping away and the rainclouds gathering overhead. On Sundays he went fishing on the dam.

'Do you go every Sunday?' she asked, watching him pack his tackle in the back of the car.

'Every Sunday in the season,' he answered. 'It's my only relaxation.'

'It's also the only day you're not at work. Perhaps we could spend it together sometimes.'

Patrick continued loading the boot.

Julia swallowed. 'Perhaps one day I could come with you.'

Patrick stopped to look at her. 'I've told you, I don't want you out on the dam.'

She turned away from him. 'Would it be such a terrible thing, to have your wife with you? Please, Patrick, I so want a change.' Her voice shook. 'There's nothing for me to do here.'

'I can't help that, Julia. You'll just have to find something to do.' He looked round helplessly. 'What about the birds? The birds here are fantastic. There are whole books written about them.'

Julia sighed. 'Why did you want a wife, Patrick?'

He frowned. 'What kind of a question is that?'

'It's just that I can't see what you have gained from it. You don't want my company. I'm useless to you.'

He closed the boot and put his arm around her. 'Of course I want your company. I look forward to the evenings, to having someone here for supper.'

'But why did you want a wife? You could have had a lodger.'

He smoothed a strand of hair over her ears. 'To warm my bed,' he said softly. 'And to give me sons.'

With a flash of anger she pulled away.

'What's wrong with that?' he asked.

She shook her head. 'I couldn't explain it to you, Patrick.' She sighed, letting her anger go in a long breath. 'You get me a book about birds then,' she said. 'I'll become an expert.'

A book materialised the very next day, with a visit from Vera Ellis. Julia wondered what Patrick had told her. The elderly woman kissed her cheek and presented an ancient guide book as though it were a treasured possession.

'I used to watch them, when I was your age,' she said. 'I brought this book with me from Ceylon. I was so homesick it was a relief to find the birds here. They weren't exactly what we'd had in Ceylon, but it was a comfort. You try it, my dear, it'll help you settle down.'

When she had gone, Julia took Patrick's binoculars from the sideboard and sat on the veranda. The book was a general guide to birds around the world and it was not long before she had identified a group of mousebirds, yellow and brown, with long tails, scuffling in the flower beds; and starlings, brighter than the English version, iridescent turquoise, pecking in the grass. High in the trees behind the house a pair of hornbills had nested. Their calls ripped the silence of the hilltop, but she rarely saw more than a stirring of branches, a glimpse of a huge curved bill.

Vera's book suggested that the smaller birds would eat

paw paw and mango. One morning, when Francis paused in his tasks to bring her a cup of coffee, she sent him back to the kitchen.

'Mango?' he frowned. '*Sasa*?'

'Yes please. Now. For the birds.'

He brought the fruit out in a breakfast bowl, carefully peeled and sliced, and laid it on the table beside her coffee.

'Would you put it under the tree, please.'

'*Huko*?' He frowned.

'Yes, please.' Julia pointed to the tree. 'For the birds.' He carried the dish across the lawn and put it carefully on the grass in the shade. As he straightened up he looked back at her, as if to say, 'Are you serious?'

'Thank you, Francis.'

He went back into the house and returned immediately with a bucket of water. The bucket clanged against the veranda door and again as he set it on the floor.

Julia trained the binoculars on the bowl of mango. Behind her Francis was squeezing out a cloth.

'What are you doing?'

'Windows, memsahib.'

Windows. Julia wondered what inner timetable dictated that today he must clean the windows? Or perhaps there was no timetable, only curiosity about the *mzungu*'s wife with her dish of fruit in the grass.

He gave the cloth a final squeeze and began to clean the french doors that led onto the veranda. He's better than a scarecrow, Julia thought. The wheeze accelerated as he laboured. The cloth squealed back and forth. She could see a pair of mousebirds watching the mango from the lowest branches of the tree.

When he had cleaned and buffed each pane of the french doors, he moved along to the bedrooms. She waited almost half an hour for him to reach the side of the house from where he could only see her by twisting round. She walked across the lawn and squatted under the acacia tree.

Yellow squares of fruit interrupted the pattern on the

dish. It was part of a set, one of her mother's 'good' things that had come by sea, in tea chests that were stamped with the Chaachi logo; her ornaments and cushions, the small paraphernalia with which she had dreamed of making a home in Africa.

The mousebirds shifted up a branch as she approached. She thought they might feed on the fruit if they could do so in peace, away from Francis's cough and the squealing cloth. She looked down into the long grass. Behind her the cloth faltered. She stood quite still. She was at the very edge of the lawn, the outer perimeter of all that Patrick offered her. After a minute the cloth began again, more slowly.

She meant to fling only the fruit but the dish slipped from her fingers, skittering out into the grass in a shower of mango squares. It landed intact, cushioned by a mat of knotted grass just below the ridge.

Two steps down. The polishing stopped. Sun-dried undergrowth scratched her ankles. A fly buzzed over the fruit, weaving between the stringy grasses, dipping into the residue of juice on the plate. She took another step, feeling the drop of the earth below the spring-bed of roots and grassy strands. Disturbed dust and pollen wafted up to her nose, a dry sneezy smell that matched the crackly dryness of the grass. She could see a small spider clambering up a stem of grass, eight tiny legs almost transparent in the sunlight.

'Memsahib! Memsahib!'

Francis was waving to her, the yellow cloth bright as a flag in his hand. She turned her back on him and reached out for the dish.

'Memsahib! Memsahib!'

His voice was pitched high with excitement. He waved the cloth, shouting and coughing from the safety of the lawn. She took a step nearer the dish. The ground gave way and she fell headlong, face down into a spiky cradle of grass. The dish was near her face. She hauled herself upright and picked it up. Through a mist of tall grass she could see Francis waving the cloth from the other side of the lawn.

'He snake! He snake!'

Snakes! She struggled to her feet. Her left shoe stuck in a tangle of stems. A spike of broken grass dug into her heel. She cried out, imagining poisonous fangs puncturing her feet. The grass seemed suddenly alive, swarming with slither-bellied reptiles. She scrabbled for a foothold and hauled herself, whimpering, back on to the lawn.

Francis was still shouting. 'He snake! He snake!'

A small crowd had gathered in front of the house. Mshoki, wiping his hands on his apron, his wife, two more whom she did not recognize. Francis stood in front, staring solemnly as she brushed grass and soil from her skirt and hobbled towards the house.

'Snakes, memsahib.'

The others hummed nasally in agreement.

'It's all right. Thank you, Francis.' She put the empty dish on the veranda table and limped, one-shoed, into the house.

Patrick laughed at her when she told him the story. 'You silly thing, I've warned you about the potholes down there.'

She had told him as soon as he came home, seeking reassurance and comfort. Instead he lectured her. 'You should learn to do as I say. You could have twisted your ankle in one of those potholes.' At supper he spoke to Francis in Swahili and the servant answered, nodding at Julia as he offered her the vegetables.

'He says he'll have to look after you, Julia.'

Julia managed to smile. Francis grinned back, without ridicule or malice, and was still grinning as he shuffled back to the kitchen.

'Couldn't we get some pickers to come and cut the long grass in their spare time?' Julia suggested when he had gone.

'It's hardly worth it.'

'I would be happier if we could get it cut.'

'There's nothing to be frightened of, Julia, so long as you keep away from it.'

'Please, Patrick.'

'It's a waste of time. Everybody has the same problem. You should see the Dickinsons' place. They've got a nice barbecue terrace up there, but if you go to the edge you look straight down into *bundu*. Dickie has cutters in every week but you'd hardly know they'd been.'

Three men came the next afternoon, wearing tattered overalls and carrying *pangas* over their shoulders. Julia heard Francis speaking to them and then they filed across the lawn, down into the long grass. At five o'clock Francis fetched her from the bedroom. The three men were waiting by the back door.

'What do they want?' she asked.

The men answered for themselves. 'Five shillings.'

She turned to Francis. 'Did the bwana not say he would pay them at the end of the week?'

Mshoki stepped forward. 'No memsahib, the bwana has not employed these men.'

The men were expressionless, standing in a row by the back door. One dangled his *panga* in the dust, the long blade swinging perilously close to his feet.

'Well then who . . .?'

'You are wanting the grass cutting. These men hear the news and come to be the first.'

At last she understood. They had not come at Patrick's bidding but in response to a rumour, an unspoken wish that had travelled the pathways of the estate. She went into the house and brought out three five-shilling notes.

'Thank you, please come again tomorrow.'

On the second afternoon one of them found her shoe and brought it to the veranda.

'Thank you.' A long spine of grass was still trapped in the buckle. She gave the man an extra shilling.

The grass cutters dropped slowly out of sight. By the end of the third afternoon they had almost disappeared, only the gleaming tips of the *pangas* and the silent showers of grass could be seen above the ridge.

On the last day of the week the grass at the top, that had been cut first, was beginning to turn green. After lunch Julia waited on the veranda, but there was no sign of the three men.

'Where are the grass cutters today?' she asked Francis.

The old man shook his head.

'Will they come today?'

Again he shook his head.

'Why?' asked Julia.

'Bwana Whitman *kusema*.'

Forbidden.

'Why did you tell the cutters not to come?' she asked Patrick when he had come home and settled down with a beer.

'Because those men are tea pickers.'

'But their afternoons are free, they can do what they like.'

'If they won't pick tea in the afternoons I'm damned if I'll pay them to cut grass instead.'

'You haven't paid them.'

His face flushed. 'Don't you get sassy with me, Julia.'

'I thought we agreed that we could have it cut.'

'I've changed my mind.'

'But I wanted to make it look nice for when Harry comes.'

'Why should Harry care about the grass?'

'I'm not saying he will!' Julia shouted, exasperated. 'It is I who care how my home looks.'

'But it looks fine,' said Patrick. He flung out his arm. 'With all this stuff.' He waved vaguely in the direction of the cushions.

'You've done a grand job.'

9

New wool arrived from the Coast, shades of the pure scarlet orange of her hibiscus flower.

She began the first leaf, an underleaf, not green but dark blue – a shadowy circlet that would throw the flower pattern into bright relief.

The afternoon was warm. Birds and insects hummed in the still air. She could hear Mshoki's radio and, occasionally, a burst of laughter from the quarters. The blunt needle passed in and out of the tapestry, pulling the wool in a zigzag pattern over the enlarged weave of the cloth. She had finished the first leaf and started a second, pausing to thread a lighter shade of wool into the needle, when the starlings suddenly rose from the grass, a whole flock rising as one into the air. She looked up, the mousebirds too had disappeared. Then she heard it, pounding feet, two-legged hooves on the hard earth.

'Memsahib! Memsahib!' A boy in ragged khaki shorts came into view over the rise, running, panting and spitting, up the drive.

'What is it?'

He shouted at her, a babble of English and Swahili from gasping, sweat-laden lips. She turned to call for Francis but he was already behind her.

'What is he saying?'

Francis murmured something and the boy babbled again. She felt a clutch of alarm as he pointed excitedly down the hill. A meaningless torrent poured from his lips. Something had happened down there. Something was wrong.

'Francis, what is it?'

The servant looked away. He had covered his mouth with his hand, as if to stop his words.

'What is he saying?' The servant was turning to go.

'Francis, wait!'

He paused.

'Tell me what he's saying.'

'Bartholomew,' he said. 'I come Bartholomew.'

I come. I will bring.

He shuffled away towards the back of the house. She made herself wait.

Through the french doors she could see the messenger waiting on the lawn. He was bending over, still breathless, resting his hands on his thighs and spitting onto the grass.

Julia picked up the tapestry from where she had flung it on the floor in alarm. She tried to calm herself. It would be nothing. Just someone sick in the compound. Or a snake found. Nothing to warrant such a panic. She dipped the needle into the cloth.

'Madam, you do not know me.'

The English was clear, almost stripped of the usual redundant vowels. A young man: tight denim jeans and a pink nylon shirt. He had come in from the back.

'Who are you?'

'My name is Bartholomew Wagirii. I am the son of your house-servant.'

The youth bowed to her. Wagirii? She had only known the houseboy as Francis. It seemed odd, incongruous, for him to have a second name.

'How do you do.' She did not shake the proffered hand. Francis crept in behind his son and together they stared at her. She saw the likeness at once; Francis's endearing vacuity reproduced as bland confidence on the son's smooth face.

72

'The running boy has come to tell you there has been trouble at the Office.'

She hadn't asked. She had forgotten all about the boy. 'Trouble?'

'Yes. Some men have come with guns. They have taken the wages.'

'Guns? What have they done? Is anybody hurt?'

'There are some casualties. But you need not fear, no white men have been wounded.'

'Are you sure no-one is hurt?'

'Oh yes,' said the son. 'One of the clerks has been shot. But he is a black man, nothing to concern you.'

'Of course it concerns me,' said Julia indignantly. 'What difference does his colour make?'

The youth smiled, fleshy cheeks pulling his mouth into a line. He looked past her, through the veranda doors. She followed his glance. The boy had moved into the shade of the acacia. She picked up her purse and went out to the garden.

'Thank you for coming to tell me.' She held out a shilling. Brown fingers closed round the coin like a trap. The boy backed away from her, down the drive. She watched him scamper down to the track and then he was gone, lost in the maze of paths that ran through the high grass. She turned back to the house to find Bartholomew waiting where she had left him, one hand on the back of the sofa, feeling the cloth. Francis had retreated to the kitchen, to stand beside Mshoki and watch through the open door. He was patting his chest, as if to forestall the cough that would prevent his hearing what was said. Mshoki stood beside him, motionless, muscular calves outlined against the light from the back.

She spoke to the youth. 'Thank you. Thank you for letting me know.' Another shilling lay heavy in her palm.

He inclined his head. He had seen the shilling.

'How did you know about this shooting?'

73

'News travels fast in Africa, madam.' Laughter twinkled in his eyes, changing his whole expression. 'What you call our bush telegraph.'

Julia smiled. 'Thank you again.' Once more he inclined his head and she felt his eyes rest momentarily on her breasts. Then he was gone, striding abruptly from the room.

Guns?

For an instant she had forgotten why he had come. Guns? Thieves on the estate? They could be running loose, looting. She felt afraid. Through her mind flashed the story of Billy and Emily. The precise image she had of the two figures hanging from a tree. She ran into the bedroom for her sandals. She wanted the company of whites, even Janyce Dickinson would do.

There was dust in her sandals before she reached the bottom of the drive, gritty friction under the balls of her feet. She had never walked out before. 'White women do not walk in Africa,' Patrick had said.

She tried to guess the distance to the Dickinsons' house. Half a mile? A mile?

The soles of her sandals seared her feet. Glare forced her eyes down onto the track, exposing the back of her neck to the fierce sun. The tea rustled, waist-high on either side. A whole army could hide in there.

Less than a mile. The Dickinson house came in and out of view, a copse of trees shading the whitewashed walls, a splash of green on the crown of their hill. She hurried along the track, carrying the last look of the servant's son in her mind. There had been a moment there, a look that had drawn her. Drawn and repelled, tripped her tongue against the impeccable manner which did not match the almost-insolence of his eyes on her dress.

She was half way, near the base of the next hill, when she heard familiar, noisy breathing and Francis was behind her, loping up in an arm-swinging, old man's run.

'Not walking memsahib!'

'Yes, I am going to the bwana Dickinson's house.'

'Not walking memsahib.' Waving his huge flat hands. '*Mbaya!*' He pointed at the sun.

'I must. I must know what is happening. Go back Francis, I will be all right.'

'Not walking!' He strode beside her, his white apron flapping in the sunlight.

'It's all right. It's not far, less than a mile.'

He kept up with her, breathing with difficulty in the flurry of dust thrown up by their feet. The dry murram settled on the cracked skin of his calves. She was looking down at them, at the pale meshy caste of dust like the bloom on chocolate that has been left in the sun, when a white Peugeot rounded the bend ahead at speed. Francis gave a shout and leaped into the ditch. The car braked hard, slewing round on the murram.

'Jump in, Mrs Whitman.'

Kangeni, Patrick's assistant, leaned from the driver's seat.

The car was in reverse, turning before she closed the door. She looked back as they pulled away. Francis stood in a cloud of dust, looking after her. The dust would make him cough again.

'You shouldn't have left the house, Mrs Whitman.' Kangeni was driving fast, swerving round the bends in fourth gear, letting the car hurtle downwards.

'Is anybody hurt?'

'You know about the shooting then?'

'Yes. A boy came up with a message. He said there were guns.'

'It was dangerous for you to leave the house.'

'I'm sorry.' Julia broke off. Patrick wouldn't apologise to an African – even this one, who belonged to the Club and, on occasion, came to the house for a beer on the veranda. ('But not in the bloody house. I'm not having any munts sitting down to dinner in my house.')

It was time for the rain. Thunderous grey clouds were

banking over the hills, obscuring the sun, creating a premature twilight.

The first drops hit the roof as they reached the centre of the estate where a stretch of tarmac gave unmuddied access to the low building known as the Office. Beside the Office was the airstrip and a lorry park where the loads of tea were registered for despatch to the Coast. On the far side a corrugated iron hangar housed tools and spare parts for the lorries.

'Wait in the car while I see what is happening,' said the African.

She watched him stride across the tarmac. The rain gathered force; she wound up the windows, closing herself in.

A group of workers in overalls crouched against the wall of the Office, sheltering under the eaves. While she watched, one of them, for whom there was no room, pulled his shirt up over his head and made a dash for the hangar.

Thunder joined the monstrous banging of raindrops on the roof. She huddled against the seats. The upholstery was leather, dried and split by the sun. On the back seat lay a brocade cushion, faded pink and gold. She stared at it. Kangeni's house was near the factory, in the no-man's land between the pickers' 'township' and the 'whites' houses. She recalled a broken wicker chair on the veranda, an impression of dust and chickens running loose. No hint of brocade cushions within.

Minutes passed. The windows steamed over. She felt chilled and uneasy, hidden in the strange car by the isolating wall of rain.

Suddenly there was a thump on the roof, louder than the thunder of raindrops, and then an arm, swathed in yellow, came up against the window. The door handle rattled. A thick-fingered, black hand, shiny with rain-water, knocked on the window.

She slipped behind the front seat and crouched down.

They couldn't get in. She'd locked the doors as Patrick had taught her. If she kept very still they'd try one of the other cars.

Two fists banged against the glass and through the noise of the rain she heard a voice.

'For God's sake open the door.'

Kangeni.

Heaving herself onto the back seat she reached up and cleared the mist from the inside of the glass. His broad, black face loomed beside her.

She pulled up the inside lock and the door swung open, letting in a rush of water. Kangeni thrust himself into the car, almost rolling on top of her in his rush to pull the door closed behind him.

The yellow plastic sheet slipped to the floor. His white cotton shirt and shorts clung obscenely to his body and rain hung in droplets from his hair.

She reached for her handbag and offered him a crumpled tissue. 'I think it's clean.'

'No. You keep that. Little bit of rain hurt no-one.'

'Did you tell Patrick I was here?'

'Of course. He wants you to come into the Office. He's on the phone to the Coast.'

Kangeni held the plastic sheet above their heads as they dashed across the tarmac and into the Office. Patrick's hands were cold against her cheek. 'You should have stayed in the house. I sent Kangeni to check on you.'

'I couldn't.'

'You might have been attacked on the road.'

He turned back to the phone. He was speaking to Harry at the Coast, reporting the theft.

A turbaned Sikh sat behind a desk in the corner, head down, making entries in a ledger. The back of one of the men sheltering under the eaves was visible through the window.

Patrick pointed to them as he put down the phone. 'Bloody heroes, those boys.' Bleddy eerows. His accent had grown sharp. 'Turned on them. Unarmed. Got one too.'

'How much did they take?'

'A full week's wages. That's why the pickers got so mad. They were due to be paid today.'

The rain was stopping, the thunder on the roof reducing to a rattle, the downpour ceasing as quickly as it had begun. The men outside moved away towards the hangar. Yellow flip-flops washed clean as they squelched through the puddles.

'Were any of the thieves caught?'

'Yes.'

The Sikh set a waste bin between his knees and began to sharpen a pencil with a small knife.

'Where is the one they caught?'

Patrick looked away. Rainwater rushed along the gutters outside.

Kangeni put his head on one side, hunching his shoulder against his cheek, as if to speak caused him pain. 'These are simple people,' he said slowly. 'They do not understand the niceties of trials by jury.'

'What did they do to the one they caught?'

Kangeni looked away. The Sikh ceased scraping his pencil. She was suddenly conscious of what was being said. Behind her back her hands grasped hold of one another.

It was Patrick who spoke, his voice deadpan. 'They chopped his head off with a *panga*.'

Here?

She moved towards him and stared into his face.

'Here? Did they do that here?'

His pointing finger was steady. 'Just over there, behind the hangar.'

10

Outside the Club the car park was full. Patrick pointed to the overflow of vehicles parked near the storm drains.

'They've come all the way from Kibwezi. The news must have got round very quickly.'

'How far away is Kibwezi?' Julia leaned on his arm as she picked her sandals across the gravelled path.

'It's the most northerly estate, a good fifty miles away. The Kibwezi people don't use this Club much, it's too far to come and the road is terrible after the rain.'

They had come straight to the Club from the Office. Her wish to return home to reassure Francis had been waved aside.

'Don't paff, Julia.'

'But the boys will be waiting for us, they'll want to know what happened.'

'They'll know it better than we do by now,' said Patrick. 'Mshoki will have sneaked off to the beerhouse to get all the details.'

Kangeni had offered to run her home but Patrick interrupted before she could accept.

'No thanks. She's coming with me to the Club.'

Kangeni nodded. 'Good idea. We all need a drink after this business.'

'You weren't thinking of going to the Club yourself?' Patrick's voice was sharp.

Kangeni stopped. It was obvious that he had, and for a moment he looked confused. Then Patrick's meaning became clear and he looked away. 'I'll see you tomorrow,' he said shortly, and climbed into his car.

Julia was furious. 'How could you talk to him like that, Patrick?'

'Why not?'

'He has every right to go to the Club.'

'Don't be naive, Julia.' He had smiled, putting his arm along the back of her seat as he reversed the car out on to the road. 'The kaffs know exactly what their membership means. They can come in for a drink, play billiards, golf, whatever, anytime they choose. Except when the white members would prefer them to stay away. It doesn't need to be spelt out. Kangeni knows, just as the others know, when they're not welcome.'

'And why shouldn't they be welcome tonight?'

'Because we want to fucking talk about them!' Patrick exploded. 'How do we know that Kangeni didn't organise this wage snatch?'

'Don't be absurd!'

'Don't you be absurd. You know absolutely nothing about these people. When you've been here as long as I have you can come to your own conclusions. Until then we'll do as I say.'

Julia clenched her fists in an effort to stop the tears that had started down her cheeks. She sniffed. After all the terror of the day she wanted comfort, not anger.

Patrick stopped the car and handed her a handkerchief. 'Don't cry now, Julia. You know I don't like a girl who cries too much.' Clumsily he patted her knee while she blew her nose. 'Come on, we'll go and have a good few and forget all about it, eh?'

The roar of voices could be heard before they opened the door of the clubhouse. Patrick received a special gap-toothed grin from the old man who acted as doorman and a shout of welcome went up as they pushed into the crowded Bar. Julia was quickly separated from the hero, surrounded by a detachment of women who took her into the Lounge.

'You must tell us what happened.'

'Your Patrick is quite a celebrity.'

'Why did you try to walk?'

'How many were there?'

Julia put her hands up to her ears. 'I'm afraid I can't answer. You'll have to ask Patrick. I didn't get there until it was over.'

The women crowded round her, most of them were strangers, more planter wives, she guessed, ladies from Kibwezi. She recognised Clare Bowen sipping gin at the edge of the group, and Vera Ellis pushing through to stand beside her.

'You should have stayed at home, my dear.'

The others murmured in agreement. 'Sitting duck if they'd come along the road.'

Madeleine Waugh fitted a cigarette into a long ivory holder. Julia had never seen one before, outside a museum. 'They must do something.'

'It's no use waiting for the police,' said another woman. 'We've just got to be firm with these people.'

'I knew something was afoot.' Vera Ellis joined in. 'My Joshua has been behaving oddly for over a month.'

'Your Joshua wouldn't steal a spoonful of jam,' said Janyce Dickinson scornfully.

'They're all as bad as each other.' Madeleine lit her cigarette. The ivory tube and the white cigarette stuck out like a great tooth from her tight, painted lips. 'I've been suspicious for a long time. It's the ones who come up from the Coast that make trouble among the pickers – put all sorts of ideas in their heads.'

Julia looked for Patrick.

He was near the bar, well on his way to having his 'good few'. She could see him signing a fistful of bar notes, double whiskies in exchange for his deteriorating signature. He would argue when the bill came; it had happened the week before, papers spread across the dining table while she tried to eat. Patrick had sworn and shouted, accusing Joseph, the barman, of forging the slips that bore his own, unmistakable scrawl.

He was standing under the dartboard. The blackboard flaps carried the scores of an abandoned match. She could hear his voice above the roar of gusto and unease that filled the room. 'I swear they were not our boys,' Patrick shouted. 'I know all my pickers and it wasn't any of them.'

'Nah, this was an outside job. A gang up from the Coast, maybe. The boys round here wouldn't know one end of a gun from the other.'

'There's nothing for it. We've got to clamp down.'

'What about the police?'

'I phoned the substation at Ledorot,' said Patrick. Heads turned to listen. 'It took twenty minutes to get through and they said that the Officer in Charge had gone out. "That's a bloody contradiction in terms," I said. "If he's gone out he's no longer the Officer in Charge." "Call back in a little while," they said. And I said, "There's a bloke here with his . . ."' Patrick stopped. The room was quiet. The men round him looked unhappily into their glasses; the beheading was not common knowledge among the wives.

Dickie broke the silence. 'We can't just rely on the police.'

'Those monkeys – they'll do bugger all.'

'Probably them at the bottom of it.'

The wives clung to Julia.

'You should have stayed in the house, dear.'

'Sitting duck if they'd come along the road.'

'I didn't feel safe at home.'

'But my dear girl,' Vera Ellis put a thin hand on her arm, 'you didn't even know if Dickie would be there.'

'It wasn't Dickie I was going to. I wanted to see if Janyce was all right.' The lie came conveniently, she had not thought of Janyce's safety, only of her own. She wanted a white face, anyone would have done. Now she had white faces all around her, looming, pink in the heat of the clubhouse. She felt no comfort in their presence.

'Well, that was very generous of you, dear.' Clare Bowen raised her voice. 'Did you hear that, Dickie? Julia tried to walk to your place just to see if Janyce was all right.'

'I call that jolly brave.'

There was a murmur of agreement. Clare Bowen turned back to Julia. 'But this is Africa, and white women do not walk out alone.'

More nodding. The men parted to let her through. One patted her back as she passed. 'I must say, Julia,' he said, spitting a little, 'I think you're a brave girl. Darn brave.'

Patrick smiled, his face blotched and slack. She put a hand on his arm. 'Patrick, I think one of the boys might know something.'

He smiled, pinkly.

'That's my girl.'

Her voice was lost in the din around the bar. Jack Bowen had started to tell a joke. As the whisky-shot eyes turned on him, Julia edged closer to Patrick. She tugged at his elbow.

'Patrick, Francis's son knows something.'

'Good girl.' He patted her hand and bent into the group to catch the punch line of the joke.

'Patrick,' she said again, louder. 'I'm sure the boys know something about the robbery.'

Jack Bowen lost his audience as half a dozen pairs of eyes swung round to watch her lips.

'Who knows something?'

'What's this? Julia knows the *mwivis*?'

'No. I don't know them, but none of you has asked me why I tried to walk to Dickie's. How I knew what had happened before Kangeni came up in the car.'

The rustle of bar slips was suddenly audible in the silence. Julia found herself watching the barman's lips as he counted, the black head framed between heads and shoulders that had gathered in to hear her story.

'Who told you?'

'Who was it?' She was about to tell them, to give the name of the houseboy's son, to re-direct their accusing eyes, but her mind swung back to the wide, archless feet shuffling the dust beside hers. 'Not walking memsahib!' Panting to keep pace with her, the old black face wrinkled with concern.

'Someone who came to the house,' she said.

'A kaff?'

Julia hesitated. 'Yes.'

'When?'

'Some time after lunch.'

'And did you know him?'

'No.'

Patrick's voice was stern. 'Julia, did the boys know who he was?'

'I don't know. I don't think so.'

'Well I'll be damned,' said Dickie. 'Some bloody munt came all the way out to reassure Patrick's wife. What's so special about you? Why not Janyce, why didn't they warn my wife?'

'Sounds bloody odd to me.' Clare Bowen's voice drowned the others. Nobody turned to look at her, all eyes were on Julia. 'You've not been here long, Julia. I expect you haven't quite understood the ground rules.'

'Are you sure you don't know who it was?' Jack Bowen spoke less sharply than his wife.

'Yes, of course I'm sure.'

'Can you explain why he chose to tell you, and not the rest of us?'

'It's no use taking sides with these people, Julia.'

The voices converged on her.

'I haven't taken sides,' she shouted. 'How should I know why this boy came?' She felt cornered, absurdly guilty. What did they suspect her of doing? Bartholomew's face hung in her mind's eye, smiling. 'I've no idea who he was or why he came. Perhaps he thought Patrick would be at home.'

'But he would know Patrick wouldn't be home. He was down at the Office paying the wages, and there isn't a worker on this estate who wouldn't know that.'

'Well I'm sorry, I can't explain.' Their hostility frightened her. She had meant to tell Patrick about both the boys, the one who had run up the drive and the houseboy's son. But they all seemed so angry, even Patrick's face was flushed and suspicious. She wished she'd said nothing, it was out of all proportion.

'Come, come now.' Vera Ellis moved to the centre of the group. 'I think we've all got a bit overheated. Of course Julia knows nothing. She's only been in Ledorot five minutes, poor lamb. I expect it was one of the pickers' boys.'

'I gave him a shilling,' said Julia. 'He was terribly out of breath.'

'You did all right, my dear.' Donald Ellis patted her arm, nodding his grey, fatherly head. 'As Vera says, it was probably one of the pickers hoping to earn a few cents by being the first to tell you.'

So the truth slipped away. She had shielded herself, and in so doing shielded Bartholomew, the servant's boy. She remembered his quiet voice, his look as she had come towards him with the shilling, an attempt at hauteur and, breaking through it, the fear that she would belittle him. He had smiled, no, beamed when she put it away. She remembered the smile and was glad.

The veranda light was on, a pinprick of yellow on the hilltop. The night watchman unfurled himself to salute as they came up the drive. It was late and cold and he stamped his feet and rubbed his hands meaningfully as Patrick locked the car.

'Must remind Francis to make him some tea,' Patrick muttered, solving, in one breath, the mystery of the empty jar that was left on the veranda step each morning. The watchman's tea. Naturally they would give him a jam jar to drink from.

Mshoki and Francis were sitting on the old hardbacked chairs inside the kitchen door. The table was laid, fish pie and peas drying in the oven.

Patrick opened a bottle of beer and poured a little into Julia's glass before filling his own. When they had eaten he called both servants from the kitchen.

'Who was the boy who came with the message?'

Mshoki answered with a question. 'This one who came this afternoon?'

'Yes, the boy who ran up to the memsahib.'

'This boy. This was a boy from the estate. Karanja's boy.'

'Who is Karanja?'

'A picker,' said Mshoki.

'He wanted a tip, eh?'

'*Ndiyo*, bwana.' Francis spoke for the first time. Yes, the boy ran up to get a tip.

Patrick laughed. 'Bloody long way to run for a shilling.' The servants watched him laugh and after a moment, they joined in.

He was still chuckling as they undressed for bed.

'Will you tell the others?' Julia climbed into her bed, pushing hard with her feet to force a passage between the tightly tucked sheets. 'They seem to suspect me of something.'

'Of course I will. They didn't mean anything. People get a bit excited after a beer or two.'

She heard the sheet catch on the bedsprings as he pulled the covers off and squeezed in beside her. She reached out to turn off the bedside lamp and he locked his arms about her pulling her against him. The bedsprings moaned as he struggled to pull up her nightdress. He smelt of stale smoke and whisky and fish pie. She turned her face away, wondering how she had ever dreamed that she could change him, that in Africa he would be different. The sweat between their bodies sucked noisily. When he had finished he rolled off her and went into the bathroom. He came back a few minutes later, holding up her packet of pills.

'Are you still taking these things?' She was. It hadn't occurred to her to stop.

'Well, what am I wasting my time for?'

She turned over and closed her eyes, pretending to sleep while he fumbled with the pack. The pills made a soft plopping sound as they dropped into the toilet. There were no more. Janyce Dickinson had already informed her, with a certain malicious glee, that the mission clinic did not stock contraceptives.

The pipes shuddered through the house as Patrick pulled the chain.

Francis brought tea at six. Slapping bare feet in the corridor, a clink of china and then a single knock, elbow to the door.

'Come.' It was always Patrick who shouted.

'*Jambo*, bwana. *Jambo*, memsahib.'

He put the tray down on the dressing table and tied up the mosquito canopy before bringing the tea to the locker between their beds. It was the same china teapot he brought every morning, the same hot water jug, milk, the sugar bowl with the chipped edge. 'Thank you,' said Julia. He bobbed his head and backed away.

'Francis.' Patrick's tone broke the routine.

The servant stopped, facing towards the passage, as if the summons had come from there and not from the bed behind him.

Patrick was half sitting, his pyjama buttons undone, exposing the distinct 'V' neck of his tan and an expanse of pale chest. He spoke quickly in Swahili, too quickly for Julia to understand.

Francis's answer was brief, followed by a long affirmative sigh. 'Eh . . .' His face collapsed into mournfulness.

'What did he say?' Julia asked when Francis had gone.

'The one who was shot. The clerk. It looks as though he might lose a leg.'

'Have they taken him to hospital?'

'All the way to the Coast? No, the clinic can cope. They're pretty tough, these people.'

They drank their tea in silence. Patrick drank his like a taster's brew, without milk. She was sure that one day he would forget where he was and spit it out with a fast, hard aim on to the floor.

She stayed in bed while he went into the bathroom. She heard him humming and the clank of the pipes as water travelled to the shower from the outside boiler. The water would be brown, coloured by rust from the outside tank.

'You'll get a nice tan if you lie in there long enough.' Patrick often repeated the joke.

11

Ledorot looked peaceful enough from the air. The tea lay like a green furrowed carpet over the valleys. On the hills the bungalows gleamed like white sentry posts, and at the bottom the brown-red corrugated roofs of the pickers' houses merged with the dust.

Kangeni was waiting by the windsock. Harry could see him, standing apart from the group of factory hands who waited to unload the cargo.

He waved as the Beechcraft taxied down the strip. When the steps were in place he held out both hands to Harry, one to shake and the other to take his bag.

'Patrick sends his greetings. He is detained at the factory but asked me to take you up to the house.'

Harry shook his hand. 'It's very kind of you to come. Is Patrick having trouble?'

The African shrugged. 'Nothing serious, just one of the driers playing up.' He put Harry's bag on the back seat of the car and walked round to hold the passenger door. 'The mechanic has taken it apart but you know how it is with Patrick, he can never trust a black to fix something by himself.'

Harry smiled. 'You know he doesn't mean any harm.'

'I know it, but do the others?' Kangeni started the engine and steered the car on to the road.

Harry sat back. 'Has there been any more trouble – since the shooting?'

'No.' The African shook his head. 'Not since the shooting. But these *mzungus* should learn to be more cautious. The pickers are not deaf. They hear the things that are said. So do the servants.' He shrugged. 'Things get around.'

Before Harry could ask what he meant Kangeni changed the subject. 'If you don't mind, I'll drop you up there and drive straight home. I'd like to be in the dry before the rain comes.'

Harry looked at the sky. Clouds were building in the east, patching the land with shadow.

He turned his attention back to Kangeni. 'Have you met Mrs Whitman?'

'Yes. I showed her round the factory when she first arrived – and we've met once or twice at the Club. Have you met her, Harry?'

Harry shook his head. 'What's she like?'

The African smiled. 'You know, Harry, we have different ideas about women. For me, she's a little bit thin, a little bit pale, but such a lady. She puts the rest of the *mzungu* wives to shame.'

Harry chuckled. 'Have they made her welcome?'

Kangeni shrugged. 'They have tried. She does not confide in me, but I would say that they are not her kind.'

'Has she changed Patrick at all?'

Kangeni shook his head. 'I wish I could say yes, but you know, he's worse. I think she tries to make him justify himself and it makes him angry because he can't.' The African waved his free hand. 'I don't hate him, Harry – you know that. I think he is a good manager, he is even a good man in his own way but eh . . .' Kangeni sighed. 'He is so blind.'

Harry listened in silence. He liked Kangeni. They had always spoken freely and he valued the African's confidence.

As they climbed the hill Kangeni continued. 'It gets worse up here, not better. I used to think that they would come round gradually. That in time even these planters would wake up to Independence. Now I think they never will change.' He turned intense dark eyes on Harry. 'You should hear them in the Club, that Dickinson, and Jack Bowen – they sound like a bunch of Boers. Since the shooting, they've been talking about having vigilantes, a little private army to protect their families from the savages!'

Harry sighed. 'I thought they might overreact. But they'll calm down, you'll see.' He spoke with more assurance than he felt.

'Apart from that, how have things been?'

'Quiet enough. As you know, they got one of the thieves.'

Harry nodded. Patrick's telephone call had been followed by a written report, a bald account of the beheading and a passing mention of the clerk who had been shot in the leg. In the same paragraph was a request for supplies of stationery and the reassurance that 'everyone is all right, it was only a munt that bought it'. His colleague, Muthaga, had read the report first, black lips curling in distaste as he dropped the paper on Harry's desk.

'Have the police done anything?' Harry asked Kangeni.

Kangeni shook his head. 'What can the police do? They have four officers for the whole Ledorot area. It's like the needle in the haystack, or – what would you say? – the nigger in the woodpile?'

Harry was silent for a moment, then he said, 'I've suggested to Head Office that the clerk should be given a pension if he cannot work.'

They had reached the track that led up to the Whitmans' house. Kangeni stopped the car and switched off the engine. He twisted in his seat to face Harry.

'But he is working,' he said. 'Patrick has given him a new job, manning the petrol pump by the Office.'

'I thought he was a clerk?'

'He was.'

'Why doesn't he go back to his old job in the Office

– surely it's easier to sit at a desk than hobble round a petrol pump?'

Kangeni shrugged. 'But Mr Thomas, the boy has lost a foot – you know we kaffirs keep our brains in our feet.'

Harry looked across at the African. 'Seriously? Patrick won't give him his old job?'

Kangeni started the car and turned onto the track. 'The truth is the boy was no good as a clerk. He is barely literate. Patrick just took the opportunity to get rid of him.'

She was standing on the veranda. Taller than he had expected, slender. As she stepped down on to the lawn she tucked a loose strand of hair behind her ear, a gesture of diffidence carried through to the quick smile, the shy turn of her head as she offered her hand. She was pale, skin like glazed china, and fine bones, perfect but for the slight jut of the chin, upthrust, just short of obstinate.

Harry held out his hand. Hers was cool.

She smiled. 'I'm so pleased to meet you at last.'

At that moment they heard Patrick's car, an exchange of horns as he passed Kangeni on the track below. The car appeared over the rise in a swirl of dust. He called his apologies as he climbed out of the car.

'I hope Julia's been looking after you.' He came across, shook Harry's hand and put his arm around his wife, tucking her bare shoulder against the sweatstain of his shirt. 'Here she is then.' He beamed. 'All that a man could wish for.'

His hair seemed darker, its sharp red colour heightened by the thundery light. Harry looked at Julia.

She was smiling, at least it looked like a smile. Another yard between them and Harry would have believed that it was.

'Well? What do you think?' Patrick demanded, patting her flank like an auctioneer.

Harry ignored him and directed his question to Julia. 'How do you like Ledorot?'

Her face suddenly loosened. Harry could see the white indentation where her teeth had been sunk in her bottom lip.

'I think it's very beautiful,' she said.

Her words were followed by a loud clap of thunder. The first huge drops of rain scattered across the grass.

'Come on!' cried Julia.

Harry ran with her into the house, with Patrick following and behind him the servant, carrying Harry's bag.

Once inside Patrick announced that he was going to take a shower. 'I'll have to leave Julia to entertain you,' he said, laughing. 'I'm dirty as a kaffir.'

'Did you manage to fix the drier?' asked Harry.

Patrick called from the passage. 'I had to fix it myself. It was only a welding job but the bloody mechanic would have had it out of action for a week.'

Harry followed Julia into the familiar guest room.

'I expect you've used this room before,' she said.

'Many times.' He smiled, looking around. 'But it never looked as nice as this before.'

'Thank you,' said Julia. 'Patrick has so little idea of comfort, I found it all terribly bare at first.'

'But you've settled in, now?'

His question was ignored. 'I was sorry you couldn't come over for the wedding. I'd have liked to have met you before I came out here.'

'I was sorry not to be there,' said Harry.

'I'll leave you to unpack your things,' said Julia. 'Please have a shower if you'd like one. Patrick will be finished in a minute.'

He smiled. 'Thank you, I will.'

'You know about the water, don't you?'

'The water?'

'It's brown. It's not dirty, it's just rust from the tank.'

'I remember it well,' Harry said, smiling.

'Supper will be ready in an hour. I've asked the boys to do some steak.'

She was lovely. To Harry's eyes, weary from the Coast, she was as lovely as an alpine day; as fresh as the flowers he found beside his bed, the posy of roses that filled the gaunt room with sunshine. She had fixed the curtains. In all the years Harry had been visiting, the curtains in the guest room had never closed properly, the rings had always jammed half way, leaving a band of darkness, glimpses of the watchman passing in the night. Someone had polished the rod, and loosened and re-gathered the material so that now they closed, tight against the night.

Patrick had needed a wife. The house had ached for a carer, for the flowers and the pictures and the delicate ornaments ranged along the mantelpiece; he had needed a companion, a friend who would laugh with him, throw back his absurdities, help undo the knots of fear and prejudice that ruled his life. A woman who could take on Ledorot, cope with the other women and not mind how her skin would look in a year or two.

But not this woman; not this pale Julia against whom the whole garden seemed vulgar, the bougainvillea as brash as a circus tent; not this woman, this wisp of a girl with her brave little chin, pretty as the morning glories that clambered on the pillars of the veranda.

At dinner he found her watching him, pale eyes on his hands, making him suddenly conscious of the way he held his knife. Conscious too, of the noise that Patrick made as he ate, the pant and gulp as each forkful reached his mouth.

When she spoke he had an impression of a tide of words, straining to break through her careful remarks.

She had put down her knife and fork. 'Harry, what is bilharzia?'

'It's a type of flatworm, I think,' said Harry. 'A parasite that you can pick up in tropical waters.'

'Can you die of it?'

'Sometimes. More often than not it just debilitates you. Parasites don't normally kill their hosts.'

'And is there bilharzia in the dam?'

'Probably. What do you think, Patrick?'

'Almost certainly. But you don't have to worry, as long as you never go into the water.'

'Is the dam pretty?' asked Julia.

Harry smiled. 'Why, it's a magical place. The birds are astonishing – fish eagles, cormorants, herons, kingfishers. Why don't you come out to the dam with us tomorrow, Julia?'

'She doesn't want to go,' said Patrick, answering for her. 'Too many mozzies, eh love?'

'Keep away from the water!'

She waited on the veranda while they loaded the car. The dawn breeze whipped her housecoat against her legs.

'We're not likely to drown,' Harry laughed. He was helping Francis heave a large cool box into the boot.

'I was thinking of the bilharzia. Don't wade in.'

'Don't you worry about that, Julia.' Patrick sat in the driving seat. 'We'll find some boys to push us out.'

Francis banged the boot shut and gave a thumbs up sigh. *'Bahati njema,'* he shouted. Good luck.

Harry looked round at the canvas cases of rods and tackle lying on the back seat. The dull gleam of metal caught his eye.

'Why the shotgun?'

'I carry it all the time.' Patrick's face was grim.

'Since the shooting?'

Patrick shrugged. 'I guess it started about then. These days there's a bad atmosphere up here. You don't feel you can trust them any more. Even the boys at the house, something in their eyes.'

They reached the bottom of the escarpment and turned right past the estate of pickers' housing, the 'township', that had been built on a terrace below the road.

'Bloody palaces.' Patrick pointed to the flat-roofed dwellings laid out symmetrically on the murram.

'I wouldn't call them palaces,' said Harry. The houses

95

had no gardens, just tiny, wire-fenced enclosures where chickens scratched in the earth and stands of mealies struggled for the light. A shanty had grown alongside, a huddle of tea chests and scrap, spilling into the township like a persistent weed.

'Thirty years ago there was nothing there at all,' Patrick observed. 'Just mud and straw and cattle boys wandering after their herds.

'You ask Vera Ellis, she's been here since Day One. The munts had nothing but their mangy cows and what they were given. Old Vera used to dole out medicine from her back door. It was either her or the witch doctor and probably not much to choose between them.' He chuckled.

'Are they better off now?' asked Harry.

Patrick glanced across.

'Of course they are. There's a bloody sight more of them so we must be getting something right.'

'Have you ever been down there?'

'To the township?' Patrick shook his head. 'Kangeni goes down there from time to time. I gather it's pretty raw – especially round the toilet blocks.'

Harry smiled. Patrick had called them 'bloody palaces', but he had never been there. Too raw for a white man.

A mile further on they turned on to a track of flattened vegetation that led down to the lake. Patrick was silent for a while, fighting to keep the wheel straight as they bumped and shuddered across the tangled grass.

He parked on a patch of dried mud overhung by trees that grew right to the edge of the water. Flies swarmed in clouds above the ruts, rising to irritate their bare legs as they climbed out of the car. They loaded the fishing gear and the cool box into a fibreglass dinghy that had been pulled high on to the dry mud beach. Patrick locked the shotgun into the boot of the car and Harry waited in the shade while he walked along the shore in search of some fishermen. The sharp cries of fish eagles filled the air. The noise was continuous, a cadence of query and answer, high pitched and plaintive, like small children in distress.

Patrick returned with two men. Tiny droning flies had detached themselves from his companions to swarm around his head. The men helped load the boat and when Harry and Patrick had climbed aboard, they pushed it out through the reeds, staying with it until the water was chest deep. Patrick gave them a shilling each and promised two more if they would come back and pull them in at the end of the day. The flies followed the fishermen back to the shore.

Patrick rowed strongly and the fibreglass boat slid easily across the water. The lake was like a sheet of glass, throwing back the glare of the sun-yellowed sky. At intervals dead trees broke the surface, marking the contours of the drowned land. Cormorants crowded on to leafless branches, their oversized young clinging fiercely to the edge of the nests.

When Patrick finally pulled in the oars the shore was a brown blur against the skyline. There was no shade. The boat circled gently in the water. Patrick opened the cool box. The ice packs had softened but the chicken legs and samosas were still cool. They helped themselves to the food and Patrick handed Harry a bottle of beer, slippery with condensation.

They ate in silence and when the food and beer were finished, Harry lay back, using an empty canvas bag as a pillow. He was no fisherman; it had become a tradition that though he came out on the dam it was Patrick who did all the fishing. Harry settled his head against the canvas. Patrick stood in the stern. As he whipped his rod back and forth the boat barely moved, and only the faint whoosh of the rod and the occasional noise of a fish breaking the surface disturbed the silence. Harry slept and when he woke an hour later there were three large trout lying in the lid of the cool box and Patrick's shirt was draped over his chest, protecting him from the sun. Small fish foamed around the boat as Patrick gutted the trout over the edge.

'Harry, my friend, I just don't know.' Patrick spoke softly, as if to himself, resuming the conversation they had begun in the car. 'I think we'll have a little Rhodesia up here one day.' He was threading weights on to the second line, his freckled fingers bunching over the delicate task. 'Mine-proof cars and electrified fences.' He spun the reel against his hand. 'It's these outsiders that come up from the Coast, stirring up the pickers, demanding contracts, union recognition. It rubs off on the house servants. Causes trouble on both sides. The munts get the idea that they're being exploited and the whites get so jumpy they'll shoot their own watchman if he walks differently.

'I've always treated my boys fairly. They get the legal wage, leftovers, free electricity. I look after them if they get sick, send their wives to the clinic. But I get no thanks for it. Just this new, shifty-eyed look and them wanting a tip if they work on a Sunday.'

The line sang out over the water.

'The pickers don't give a damn by themselves. It's these slick city buggers who come and stir them up.'

Harry didn't answer him. He was thinking of Julia, of her clear blue eyes watching him across the table. He wondered how she saw her surroundings. Was it through the eyes of her husband? Or had the closed, archaic world of Ledorot given her the same breath-taking shock he had known when first he came up to the hills?

The sun was low, a hazy yellow glow on the water, when Patrick finally laid down his rod. They packed up the tackle and Patrick rowed them back to the shore. There was no sign of the fishermen when they reached the bank.

After a few moments they shouted, setting up an echo of bird cries.

'Ah shit,' said Patrick. 'Never rely on a munt.'

They called again, in unison. The trees on the shore cast long shadows over the water. They had begun to argue about who should wade in, each insisting on taking the risk, when the men appeared at the water's edge. Harry couldn't tell whether they were the same men who had helped them in the morning.

'It's nearly bloody dark,' shouted Patrick. 'Couldn't you hear us, thickears?'

The men waded into the water and grabbed the sides of the boat. In silence they hefted it up onto the mud and waited under the trees while Harry and Patrick loaded up the car.

'I suppose they want a bloody tip,' said Patrick.

Harry pulled two five-shilling notes out of his pocket and gave the fishermen one each. There was no acknowledgment. The money was taken from his hands and the two men retreated into the darkness.

'That was stupid,' said Patrick. 'Now they'll want ten bob every time I come down here.'

'It's not all that much,' said Harry. 'Less than a pint in London.'

'It's a hell of a lot to them,' said Patrick. 'They hardly earn that much for a whole day's fishing. This is what causes all the problems, giving them too much money. It'll be the death of this country, prosperity.'

Harry's legs were peppered with insect bites.

Seeing him scratching, Patrick said, 'Get Julia to give you some Caladryl. She's got some in the bathroom.'

They got into the car. 'Has she been suffering from the mozzies?' asked Harry.

'Not a lot. They probably get put off.'

Harry smiled. 'What puts them off?'

Patrick's voice was suddenly bitter. 'Even the mozzies know when something's too good for them.'

They drove home in silence. The bites on Harry's legs had started to bleed.

12

It was early afternoon. Harry had been gone four days and already it was as if his visit had never occurred, the brief glory of it burned out by the sun that seared the grass, by the routine of the view and the silence. The servants had visitors; a drone of voices, punctuated by laughter, and the smell of roasting maize drifting on the warm air.

She was sunbathing.

'You must be the whitest woman in Africa,' Patrick had complained.

'But I never go brown, Patrick. I just go red and peel if I sunbathe.'

'Not if you do it properly. You should spend at least half an hour in the sun every day. At least you'd stop looking like a piece of china.'

'The other women don't lie in the sun.'

'They don't need to. Most of them are tanned already.'

Like old walnuts, thought Julia.

'The sun will dry out my skin.'

'Nonsense. A little bit of sun is good for you.'

So she dug out her swimsuit and waited for the servants to go off before she pulled the deckchair on to the lawn. She wouldn't get a tan. By evening she would be pink and blistered. But she could try. It was little enough, to try to please him.

Her arms and legs itched, her back became slippery with sweat against the canvas. Twice she went back into the house, the first time to fetch her straw hat and the second time for a can of aerosol to ward off the whining army of mosquitoes that hovered overhead. She was leaning over the chair, spraying her legs, when a voice spoke to her from behind.

'Good afternoon.'

She dropped the spray can on the grass.

'I am Bartholomew, madam. Remember me?'

Francis's boy, the one who had told her about the shooting. He was standing by the veranda, his shadow dark on the grass.

'What are you doing here?' She tried to sound authoritative, feeling vulnerable, naked in the swimsuit.

He was silent.

'Are you visiting your father?'

He waited for a moment and then folded his hands like a priest, moving forward to stand directly before her. His eyes were on her legs, travelling upwards from her knees to the high cut of the costume.

'I have not come to make trouble for my father.'

'No,' said Julia.

'But I come to visit him from time to time. My father and the others here. To see if they are well. If anything is needed.'

'Good. I am sure Francis is very happy to see you.'

She wanted to be dismissive, to end the conversation, but he moved closer. The sharp smell of his sweat crossed the space between them.

'He is getting old, my father. Sometimes it is difficult for an old man to understand his son.'

Julia sat down on the deckchair.

'His cough is very bad now.' Bartholomew picked up the spray can and handed it to her.

'I know. I am trying to get him some medicine.'

'I am grateful to you, Mrs Whitman. He told me that you sent him down to the clinic, gave him the morning off when he complained of pains in his chest.'

'The clinic doctor had nothing to give him, but I have ordered a linctus to be sent up from the Coast.'

'I am grateful to you. This is not what the other ladies would have done. They would have just given him aspirin – from a special pack they keep in their kitchens, away from their own medicines. I have come to say thank you.'

She smiled. 'It's nothing.'

'It is very important to me.'

She nodded, unsure, feeling that the conversation should be brought to an end.

'I hope I may consider you to be my friend, Mrs Whitman.'

She noticed his use of her name. Previously he had called her madam, the new word from the capital that had replaced 'memsahib'. Calling her by name was a step further. Patrick would call it sass.

'I do not think you will object,' he continued, smiling blandly. 'I believe you are more, shall we say, more modern than your sister expatriates.'

Expatriate, another city word, *mzungu*, white man, expert, welcome only for the knowledge to be sucked from him.

'I don't know what you mean,' she said, finding a bite on her leg to scratch though it did not itch.

'I think you are a modern woman, Mrs Whitman, I do not think you will snub me because of my colour or the position of my father in your house.'

She stood up. Clare Bowen would have slapped his face; the son of a servant offering his friendship.

He made a little bow. 'I must pay my respects to my father.'

'One thing before you go.'

He stopped.

'Will you tell me why you came here that day?'

'Which day?'

'The day of the shooting.'

He inclined his head. 'Why not that day?'

103

'It is hard to believe your visit was just a coinci-
dence.'

'Do you think I had something to do with the shooting?' He put his hand on his heart. 'Me? But I am an
educated man, Mrs Whitman, not one of your picker
boys. However, since we do not know one another
well, I will forgive your suspicions.'

Sass. Plain sass.

'Do you know who they were – the thieves?'

He shrugged. 'Nobody knows. Men from another
tribe, a gang from the Coast maybe. They were not
from these parts.'

'Do you think they will try again?'

'I am sure they will not. Even a savage likes to keep
his head.'

He was chuckling, holding out his hand.

She stood above him on the step. He waited a full minute while she fiddled with the strap of the costume, and
then looked out across the Rift, as if at last she had found
something of interest to look at there, before, finally she
was drawn to look at him, to stoop and shake his hand.

He smiled up at her, open-eyed. Involuntarily she
smiled back. He was still smiling as he walked away,
back around the house, denim swishing between his
thighs.

Patrick was irritable when he came home, slamming the
car doors and stomping towards the house. Julia went
outside to greet him.

'What's the matter?'

'Nothing, nothing.' There were circles of sweat on his
shirt. For a moment she wondered if he had heard, if
the pathways of gossip had already carried news of her
conversation with the servant's boy.

If he had, it was not the cause of his anger. 'One of
the bloody machines has gone down. We've no spares.
How many times have I told the bloody mechanic to
keep a stock? I've been on to Harry all afternoon but he

says we'll have to wait until next month. It means we're depending on just one machine. If that goes down we'll have to take every bloody leaf over to Kibwezi.'

Patrick poured half a tumbler of whisky and drank it neat. 'I'm going for a shower.'

He stripped off as he went leaving a trail of sweat-stained clothes. Francis followed him, gathering the washing into his arms like something precious. Ten minutes later Patrick re-appeared with a towel wrapped round his middle, pink and smiling.

'And what have you been doing, little lady?'

I've had a visitor. It was almost said. The words ready on her tongue, but he had turned away, calling to Francis to bring him a cold beer.

'I'd like a beer, too,' said Julia.

'No, no.' Patrick dismissed her request. 'We can't have you drinking beer this early.'

'It won't do any harm, Patrick. I'm just as hot as you are.'

'Don't argue with me, Julia.'

'But I've been lying in the sun all afternoon.'

'Whatever for?'

'You said I was too pale.'

He came closer and peered at her face. 'You've got a blister on the end of your nose.'

She turned away. 'I told you that would happen.'

'Then why did you do it?'

'To please you!'

He looked up in surprise. 'Why should I be pleased for you to have a blister?'

Bartholomew came the next day, and the next, almost every day that Patrick worked. Hesitantly at first, clutching his hands behind his back, waiting for her to speak. The third time she offered him a chair on the veranda. He smiled, a shy satisfied smile as he settled himself against the canvas. He had chosen Patrick's favourite chair.

She asked him if he worked in Ledorot.

'Not exactly, Mrs Whitman. But I am living here for the present.'

Was the evasion deliberate? She had not asked where he lived.

'But are you working?'

'Yes.' He spread his hands, a gesture of confidence from his newly won place on her veranda. 'I am working all the time. Mine is a universal task.'

The slowly blinking eyes held hers, forbidding her scorn.

'And what is that task?'

'To educate the people. To bring light.'

'Are you a preacher?'

He shook his head, smiling his bland, secretive smile.

'A missionary then?'

He nodded. 'Something of the kind.'

Julia did not pursue her questions. She tried to guess his age. Twenty-five, thirty perhaps. It was hard to tell, so smooth was his face.

His visits settled into a routine. Julia would wait for him on the veranda after lunch. He never came too soon, never arrived when Patrick was at home or before the servants had gone to the quarters for their lunch. As if he watched from some secret place in the garden, choosing his moment. Julia kept her tapestry box beside her chair. It became a habit to leave it there, untouched, reaching down to pick up the frame only when all was quiet and she was ready to welcome him. He never mentioned the signal, if he saw it. She liked to think that he did, that if one day she should fail to pick up the tapestry he would stay away.

He grew more at ease with her, settling himself into the canvas chair without invitation. He told her he had been to London.

'For a visit?'

'No, I was a student there.'

'Were you?' She couldn't keep the surprise from her voice.

He laughed. 'You are wondering how the son of a houseboy became a student in London?'

Julia nodded.

'I was lucky. And clever.' It was a serious boast. He looked at her gravely. 'It makes a great difference, to have a father who earns, even as little as mine.'

'Where did you go to school?'

'St David's. The same school as Mr Whitman. I was one of the "kaffir" boys who invaded the place after Independence.'

Julia was intrigued. 'What was it like?'

'Beastly.' He smiled, the schoolboy word sounded absurd. 'We black boys won scholarships. After Independence they had to open up the school to all races. It changed overnight. The *mzungus* couldn't take their boys away fast enough.'

'Then you went to England?'

'Yes.' He smiled again.

'Francis must be very proud.'

'Not any more.' Bartholomew shook his head. 'It has made us strangers. I am just another white man to him now.'

Julia was silent. He looked so subdued. She could see the harm it would do, the houseboy's son alone in London, acquiring the tastes of a white man.

'What did you study?'

He had been staring out at the Rift, his thoughts miles away from her. The question was meant to bring him back, like pulling a string to make him look at her.

'Economics. The dispersal of wealth.'

'Do you mean the distribution of wealth?'

'I mean what I say!'

A pause while he lit a cigarette. Then he smiled again, wide-mouthed, eye-to-eye. 'Excuse me. I did not mean to speak sharply.'

The next day he brought her a book, *The Politics of Race*, left it in a brown paper parcel on the table. 'Something for you to read.'

Was it a loan or a gift? He didn't say. She put it on the shelf beside Patrick's two books. Unread.

13

He came on Sundays, too, when Patrick went to the dam. She grew impatient for the afternoons, forgetting to ask Patrick to drive her to Vera's or Madeleine's or Clare Bowen's house; delighted to forego the Ladies' Circle.

One evening they drove to the Club to watch a film on the video. The film was a comedy that Julia had seen before.

'I'd rather stay at home,' she told Patrick.

'Why?'

'I've seen the film before.'

'I know,' said Patrick, 'but it'll stand a second viewing – and anyway, it would do you good to see some of the other women.'

'What do you mean?'

'You haven't been mixing as much as you should.'

'And how much mixing should I be doing?' Julia demanded. 'Is there a prescribed dose for new wives?'

Patrick patted her hand. 'They like you, Julia, they come to the Office and ask me where you are.'

She could see from his face that what he said was true, but it was hard to believe.

'Who, in particular?'

'Well, Vera for one. She's worried about you being alone up here all the time.' Patrick took her hand. 'You come on down to the Club and talk to her.'

When they arrived at the Club, Vera made no pretence. She took Julia's arm and steered her into the

Bar before the film had even begun.

'We're all very worried about you, Julia.'

'Worried about me?'

'Yes. You know, nothing is a secret in Ledorot. I am afraid we all know all each other's business . . . perhaps more than we should, sometimes . . .' She pulled two bar stools together and signalled to the barman.

'Joseph, will you get us two whiskies?'

She turned back to Julia. 'I know it's none of our business but people have been talking about you, Julia. All sorts of things are being said. You must realise that there are certain things that a white woman just doesn't do.'

The arrival of the whiskies saved Julia from making any reply. Vera signed the bar slip and raised her glass.

'Cheers, Julia. I hope we at least can be friends.'

Bursts of laughter filtered through from the Lounge. Julia could hear Patrick and Dickie Dickinson laughing at every other word.

'They seem to be enjoying the film,' said Julia.

Vera sipped her whisky. 'There is so little entertainment up here, it is important that we share what there is, and don't get distracted by the wrong sort.'

Julia nodded gravely, suppressing a smile at the consternation on Vera's face. Vera was afraid of Julia's friendship with the black boy; that she had found something in Ledorot which they could not have, a source of happiness from which they had shut themselves out. She could imagine them all, Clare, Vera, Madeleine, all the others, clacking together, encouraging their servants to exaggerate the stories that drifted along the paths of the estate.

Did Bartholomew exaggerate, embellish the tale? Go back to the township and talk of 'his' white lady? She shrugged the thought away. He was her friend. He walked up from the township in the hottest part of every day to see her; returning down the drive, instead of the

110

quicker route down the back path, stopping frequently to look back at her and wave.

The door to the Lounge swung open on a loud burst of laughter. Through it came Janyce Dickinson, holding an empty glass.

'Hi Julia!' she called. 'Hi Vera!'

She weaved towards the bar. Julia felt the woman beside her stiffen.

'You're having a little talk with Julia, are you, Vera?' Janyce's words were slurred. She poked a finger towards them. 'Is she giving you a little lecture about the woggy boy, eh?' Clinging to the bar, she leaned towards Julia. 'You stick with him, Julia. They've got bigger ones than white men.'

Despite Vera's protests, Janyce persuaded the barman to refill her glass, and lurched back into the Lounge.

'I know,' said Julia, before Vera could speak. 'She has a difficult marriage.'

Vera sighed. 'Dickie is a difficult man. You're very lucky to have Patrick.'

Julia took a swallow of whisky. Her glass was almost empty. She was surprised at how quickly she had grown used to the large measures.

'Would you like another drink?' she asked Vera.

The older woman shook her head. 'I shall go and watch the last bit of the film.' She put her hand on Julia's arm. 'I've said all I can, my dear.'

Leaving Julia alone in the Bar, Vera went into the Lounge. Another wave of laughter burst out as she opened the door.

Bartholomew's visits continued. He was charming, friendly, harmless. All she had to do was listen.

He told her of his childhood, his mother and sisters on the family *shamba*. They had two goats, a patch of mealies and a steady income from Francis, money from the white man's house.

'Did you have any brothers?'

'One, much younger. That's why my father is still working, even though he is an old man. My brother didn't win a scholarship, his schooling has to be paid for.'

'Out of Francis's wages?' she asked.

Bartholomew laughed at the incredulity in her voice. 'Not entirely. He has borrowed from my uncle, and my two sisters are working at the Coast, sending money for the school.'

Julia shook her head, wondering how it could be done. How much would it cost to send a son to school?

'Where is the *shamba*?'

'Away.' He gestured towards the Rift. 'Away' as he had first meant it, in another place, not here.

The glass left a ring on the table. He wiped it clean with the sleeve of his shirt.

'Does your father never go home?'

'For two weeks every year. It is the statutory minimum holiday for domestic servants. Mr Whitman is very kind, he pays for the bus fare.'

Two weeks a year?

'And does his wife – your mother – does she ever come here?'

Bartholomew shook his head. 'He is not allowed to have visitors to stay. There is not enough room in the quarters.'

'But Mshoki has his wife there.'

'Mshoki is the cook, much more important than the houseboy; he has the larger room.'

'Perhaps your mother could become a tea picker, then they could be together?'

Bartholomew shrugged. 'And let the weeds grow tall on the *shamba*?'

'But the pickers here are very contented.'

His answer was swift and sharp.

'And you, you would know that, Julia?' Raising his voice for the first time. 'Omniscient white woman, you would see into their hearts and know they are content?

112

You, who have never exchanged one word with them, who can calmly look on the swollen bellies of their children? What would you know of their contentment?'

She kept her face turned towards the Rift. He had used her first name. Shouted at her, called her Julia. Could they hear him in the quarters? Could she ever explain it to Patrick?

After a moment's silence he sat forward, blocking the view with his face.

'I meant no offence.' Smiling again, irresistibly.

She took a gulp of lemonade.

'And where was your family *shamba*?' he asked.

She smiled, remembering the house in Bartlett Road, the rose trees with little mounds of mulch at their feet, blackberries on the trellis fence that hid the dustbin. 'Did you ever go to Finchley?' she asked.

Bartholomew clapped his hands. 'Northern Line, Barnet branch!'

'You know it?'

'No. It was just a place on the map. Tufnell Park, East Finchley, Finchley Central. So, I remember it all.' He looked serious again. 'And your father, he has a big house in Finchley?'

'Had. He is dead. And it wasn't very large, no.'

'So . . . And your mother?'

'She died just before I came out here.'

He put his head on one side. 'How sad.'

Conventional words. The minimum, no less nor more than Patrick had offered.

'So Julia is an heiress?'

She laughed. 'Not exactly. There was a bit of money in the bank. And the house, of course. Would you like to see the house? My father made a model of it for me when I was a child, it's a perfect replica.' She hurried inside and pulled down the suitcase from the top of the wardrobe. The model lay flat in the bottom, carefully concealed under her winter woollens.

'But what in God's name do you want to bring that

113

for?' Patrick had said, the day before the wedding.

'It has sentimental value, Patrick.'

'We have a weight limit, you know. We can't have you filling the cases with junk.'

'It's not heavy.'

'And what will you do with it when we get there?'

'I'll find someone who can mend it.'

'But it's a toy.'

'It's not a toy.'

'It's just rubbish, Julia. It'll be in the way.'

'You'll never see it. I'll keep it packed away, but I must take it with me, Patrick. It is all that is left.'

It was wrapped in newspaper, as small as she could make it, in the bottom of the suitcase.

She carried the package out to the veranda.

'Here it is.' She held out the flat sections of painted wood.

'See, it fits together like this.'

Bartholomew helped her slot the sides into the base, the long black fingers unexpectedly deft.

'But this is enchanting.' He held it aloft. 'Such an English house! And were there twenty others just like it, side by side along the street?'

She nodded.

'I feel as if I know this place. It is so perfect. Such craftsmanship!'

'But look, the roof is broken. Here, along the ridge, it needs a piece to support it.'

He put the model down on the table and walked around it, like a giant surveyor, humming to himself. 'I could mend the roof.'

'Could you?'

'I could fit a joist here, and a beam to support the other end. It would be a simple task, a pleasure.'

Someone in Africa, she had known there would be someone here who would mend it.

She helped him dismantle the walls and found a piece of string to make a parcel for him to carry.

114

He brought it back the next day, already erect, carrying the open base across the garden like a cake on a tray. The roof was complete, assembled with a tiny wire hinge so that it would still pack flat. Another wire was fitted to the front door so that it swung open as if it were hinged. He held it out.

'Bartholomew, thank you! It must have taken you hours.'

'Not so long. It was one of the things they taught at St David's, woodwork. I was the best in the class.'

She smiled at the boast.

'I should like to give you something in return. What would you most like to have?'

There was a pause. A brief, embarrassed silence while he sat very still, watching her hands fluttering in her lap. With the merest movement of his face, he lifted an eyebrow.

She changed the subject, offered him biscuits; chocolate cookies still warm from the oven. He crunched them loudly, washing them down with sips of lemonade. A froth of crumbs gathered around his lips.

'The cookies were excellent,' he said, when he had eaten them all.

'I'm afraid I didn't make them.'

'It doesn't matter, Julia.' Using her name again. A small but irrevocable leap into intimacy, pronouncing it slowly. Julia. He crouched beside her chair. She glanced at his eyes. They were on her dress, staring deliberately. She stood up. Avoiding the table, with the dolls' house so proudly displayed, she walked to the edge of the veranda.

'I think it's going to rain.'

He laughed. 'You English with your weather. Of course it's going to rain.'

His chair scraped the floor. He was close behind her. It was possible to imagine his breath on the back of her neck.

'Have you seen the tracking station?' Julia shook her head.

He pointed out into the Rift. 'There, to the North.'

Julia stared hard. She could see nothing but endless scrubland.

'Look again. They use it to keep track of the game.' His arm stretched out to guide her eyes. 'There.'

'Oh, yes. I see it.' Seeing nothing, wishing and not wishing to touch the outstretched arm.

'Julia.' His voice was low, pitched for the hush of the garden as it waited for the rain.

She looked down at his hands, encircling, almost touching her, his nails were long and yellow, not quite clean. She meant to move away, not right away, just clear of the circle, but she missed her footing and stepped heavily into the soft band of soil that separated the veranda from the lawn. When she straightened up he had gone. Francis stood in his place, empty-faced, holding the biscuit plate.

The next day he didn't come. Or the next. She waited all afternoon but there was no sign of him.

The weekend came. Patrick went fishing on the dam with Jack Bowen and she was left at home with Clare.

'We don't see a lot of you at the Club these days, Julia. You should come more often.'

'I'm not very keen on that sort of thing.'

Clare tapped her cigarette on the brim of an ashtray. 'Neither am I, my dear. Neither am I.' She leaned close. 'But we women must stick together. In such a small community it's essential.'

Julia sipped her coffee. From the kitchen came the sounds of Mshoki preparing their lunch.

'I suppose Patrick painted a rosy picture of Ledorot for you,' said Clare.

Julia looked up, too quickly, betraying her answer.

'Yes, I thought so. My Jack did the same twenty years ago. I couldn't believe it when I got here. I was expecting something out of Somerset Maugham: parties, nightlife, punkah wallahs in every room. There was nothing but the view. It was two years before I forgave him.'

Julia put down her cup. 'And do you like it now?'

'Now? Well, I've grown used to it. I suppose I'm quite at home here. There's a lot more in Ledorot than there was twenty years ago. You ask Vera, she'll tell you about the time when there wasn't even the Club and she was the only white woman for a hundred miles.' She stubbed out the cigarette with a firm, stabbing gesture.

'But we are still a very small community, Julia. We all depend on each other. Remember the shooting? We must keep together and not allow ourselves to become isolated.'

'I'm not isolated,' said Julia. 'There are people here all the time, Mshoki, Francis, they won't let me look over the ridge without coming to see what I'm up to.'

'I don't mean servants, dear. You need to have friends about you.'

'I have a friend,' she wanted to say. 'I have a better friend than you'll ever be.' But the words were cheap and the meaning too rich for the face that looked at her across a coffee cup, its nose turning pink in the steam.

After lunch Clare fell asleep in an armchair. Julia waited on the veranda, listening to her thin snore and wondering if he would come, hoping that he would and fearing that he might; the worst and the best that could happen. She would not send him away. Clare Bowen could think her thoughts, spread such tales as she would of the servant's boy who sat in Patrick's canvas chair.

But he did not come. At dusk Patrick returned with Jack Bowen and a cool box brimming over with fish. She went to bed early, pleading a headache.

Tomorrow he would come. She hugged herself under the sheet. She would ask Mshoki to make some more cookies. He would hear of it and know that she wanted him.

14

'Hello, Bartholomew!'

She could not keep the gladness from her voice. Mshoki had baked the cookies in the morning and here was Bartholomew, the midday meal barely cleared away, striding boldly across the lawn.

'Good afternoon.'

'I thought you had gone away.'

'Where would I go?' Smiling, taking Patrick's chair without invitation. 'Besides, I have work to do here for now.'

'You have a job?'

'Not a job as you would call it. Shall we say, a task?'

'I see.' Not seeing, conscious that she had asked these questions before, but unable to pursue them. It wouldn't do to pester him, not now that he had come.

'Would you like a cold drink?' She fetched it herself, detouring through the bedroom to check herself in the mirror, pleased that her nose was no longer peeling, that she was wearing her favourite sundress.

He will like me better like this. Surprising herself with the thought, and the skip of her heart as she went back out to find him in Patrick's chair, one leg slung across the other. He had put on a pair of sunglasses. The lenses were mirrored, when she looked at him she found her own reflection looking back from his eyes. How small she seemed, with her face upturned to his, how close.

'They need another teacher in the school,' he said, taking a sip of lemonade.

'The pickers' school?'

'Yes. The headmaster wants the senior girls to have a separate class.'

'Why?'

'Because they are too big for the lower forms. These are girls who can already read and write. Father Dominic has ambitions for them, he wants them to be prepared for jobs outside Ledorot.'

'Won't they become pickers?'

'He hopes that some of them will escape. They're not the poorest girls, they have a chance of getting away, maybe finding jobs at the Coast; he wants them to make some use of their lessons.'

He put a cigarette in his mouth and struck a match. 'Would you like to be a teacher, Julia?'

'I've never taught anyone.' She shrugged. 'Besides they'll want someone qualified.'

Bartholomew smiled. 'You'd make a good teacher, Julia. You're wasted up here.'

'Am I?'

'You know you are. Come on, I'll show you where it is.'

'But the school is miles away.'

'Only one mile if you go direct.'

'It's further than that, Bartholomew, I've been past it in the car.'

'Yes, it is miles by road, but not if you go on foot. There's a path. We can cut straight down to the bottom without going through the estate.'

'But white women . . .'

'. . . don't walk in Africa!' he finished for her, laughing. 'I know, you told me. But since when have you been one to obey the rules?'

She looked at him for a moment, looked at her twin selves looking up at him. What harm could there be? He could show her the path, she needn't go right down. She could just have a look and still be home before Patrick.

120

'I'll get my shoes.'

The path was a branch off the track, a gap in the long grass, plunging steeply down the side of the hill, part of the secret web that crossed and re-crossed the land like creases on a piece of silk.

Bartholomew went first, guiding her over the ruts and dips in the ground. She felt suddenly gay, liberated by the petty defiance. Women do not walk in Africa, but here she was, walking out, as safe as could be, with a guide who knew, even better than Patrick, the way it should be done.

The house was quickly out of sight. She followed his back, watching where he put his feet, the print of her sandals fitting inside the larger print of his plimsolls in the dust. Occasionally, where it was very steep, he held out his hand. She did not take it, clasping instead at the branches and long grass that overhung the path. Half way down they reached a section of flat land, like a pause in the hillside, and Bartholomew led her off the path to a small plateau of rock.

'We can rest here.'

The rock was too hot to touch, even through her dress. 'Is there any shade?' she asked.

'Over there.' He pointed to a corner that was in shadow. A bush had grown up where the rock sloped into the ground. He sat beside her and leaned back, pushing aside the leaves to reveal a cool bed of earth.

The hillside was quiet, the grass towered around them, cutting off the view. He had stretched out, lying almost flat with his legs on the rock and his back resting on the bare earth. He put his hands behind his head, releasing the sharp, sour smell of his sweat.

'You could do it, Julia.'

'What?' Feeling his eyes on her back, the almost touch of his legs lying beside her.

'You could teach them. They would like you, they could learn a lot from a pretty white lady.'

She remained upright, uncomfortable, brushing at the

flies that buzzed around her face. He was silent for so long that she thought he had fallen asleep.

She had come too far. Sitting in the secrecy of the grass with him, out of sight, out of earshot. This was not the walk she had consented to. It occurred to her that he had chosen this place, chosen the time too, knowing more of her life than she realised. When to come, when to stay away; keeping her waiting for a week and then coming at the smell of the cookies. She should go back, follow the path up to the track and go home. She started to plan how she would sneak away, now, while he appeared to be sleeping. It was her own fault, not his. He had misunderstood her just as she had misunderstood his invitation. She should leave immediately, creep away from this hot, silent rock and Bartholomew's body, too close for excuses.

But he was sitting up, turning to her.

Frantically she cast around for something to say, anything to distract him, to change the look on his face.

'I forgot the biscuits!' she cried. 'I asked Mshoki to make some this morning.'

It was too late. Too late to retrieve the veranda, the safe exchange of talk and chocolate cookies. His hands were on her. Her arms, breasts, quick now, elastic ravelling on her legs. She made no sound, there was none to make, no cause to scream. She had come to the place he had chosen.

'Please, Bartholomew, don't.'

The glasses were gone. His eyes close against her face. 'Are you ready for me now, Julia?'

'Of course not.' The answer came involuntarily, surprised from her tongue.

He let her go, so suddenly that she fell back hard against the rock. Her head jarred, catching a sliver of tongue between her teeth.

He was sitting up, unexpectedly dressed, still in his shirt and jeans and plimsolls. It was only the buttons of her dress that were open, only her knees caught in a twist of elastic. Only a schoolboy's touch then, not a rape.

He was getting up, brushing the rock dust from his jeans. 'Will you still let me show you the school?'

She shook her head.

'I'll take you home then.' He held out his hand to pull her up. 'Don't look so puzzled, Julia.'

Unsmiling, he stared into her face.

'One day you will be ready for me. I can wait for that.'

She followed him like a child, picking her way up the path in his footsteps.

At the join of the track he stood aside to let her pass. 'You'd better go quickly, it will be raining soon.'

15

The rain was late, still falling steadily at half past six. Julia and Patrick sat together on the veranda, waiting for darkness. Bartholomew's cigarette ends lay in an ashtray on the table between them.

'I saw Clare Bowen today,' said Patrick.

Julia was half-listening, her ears tuned to the gathering chorus of crickets as the rain eased.

He had said, 'Are you ready for me?' and she had said, 'Of course not.'

Of course not.

'She said they need someone down at the school.'

'Do they?'

She looked at Patrick. Was he teasing her? Did he somehow know of her outing with Bartholomew – of the walk that had begun so innocently? His face betrayed nothing. He stared out into the darkness, chewing a piece of skin at the edge of his fingernail.

'Someone to teach the senior girls' class,' he continued. 'They've asked if one of the wives would help out.'

You could do it, Julia. They would like you.

The twilight was fading. Behind them in the darkening house, Francis was closing the curtains. The rings rattled easily along the newly polished tracks, closing the house against the approaching night.

'Clare suggested you,' said Patrick. 'She thought it would suit you.'

'Why?'

'It would give you something to do. She says you're bored up here.'

'She says I'm bored?' echoed Julia. 'What did you do? Have a conference at the Club? Is this job another of their prescriptions?'

Patrick shrugged. 'It's their suggestion, not mine. I don't see why you need a job.'

'But the Ladies' Circle thinks I do?'

'They think it might be better than the way you spend your time at the moment!'

Patrick stood up, his face was charged with pink under the carroty hair. He held the ashtray aloft. The metal edge caught a flash of the fading light.

He is going to throw it at me! She shrank from him, covering her eyes against the pile of ash dust and crushed filters, the guilt and outrage that he would throw in her face. Nothing came. She opened her eyes to find him crouching, banging the tray against the step, the debris tossed far out into the dusking garden.

When he spoke his voice was mild. He held out his hand.

'Come on, love. It's time for supper.'

As they sat at the table he began an anecdote about the factory. The story lasted for the entire meal, allowing no space for any other conversation. Julia barely listened to him.

Are you ready for me, Julia?

Of course not.

Not yet.

Have you ever had a black man?

Of course not.

Not yet.

Clare Bowen called the next morning to drive her down to the school. It was near the township, a muddle of low buildings, whitewash daubed red and brown by mud splashing up from the playground.

The headmaster was a priest, a little man in a dusty

126

black suit who leapt from his chair as the white women entered, upsetting a box of drawing pins on to the concrete floor. He shook Clare Bowen's hand first and then turned to Julia.

'Mrs Whitman, this is so kind. Yesterday when they told me you would come my heart leapt for joy.'

Yesterday? Someone had told him yesterday that she would be a teacher. Before she knew it herself. Bartholomew, or Clare Bowen, or both?

'I am thinking at last we shall have a nice white lady to teach the senior girls.' The priest clapped soundlessly, opening and closing his hands as if an invisible spring separated the pink-brown palms.

'I'll leave you to it, then,' said Clare.

'Must you go right away? Why don't you stay and see around the school?' Julia tried to sound cool, as if she did not feel, inside, like a little girl being abandoned. She saw Clare's eyes gleam.

'No, my dear, you'll get on much better here without me.'

Father Dominic, who had bent down to gather up the drawing pins, raised his head. 'Thank you so much, Mrs Bowen, for bringing Mrs Whitman this morning. It was most kind of you.' His hand waved uncertainly above the desk, clutching a fistful of pins.

Julia bent down to help him. They knelt side by side on the floor.

'These girls must learn the ways of the City and get good jobs.' His voice was muffled by the desk. The drawing pins rattled back into their box. When the last one had been retrieved the priest stood up. 'We are so unsophisticated here in Ledorot. It will be most appropriate. Most kind of you to help us in our difficulty.'

She would not take a salary. Twenty-five shillings a day had been mentioned.

'Put it into the school fund.'

'Oh, this is most kind, Mrs Whitman. Our school is so poor.'

There was no way of knowing if he did, or what it would have bought for the school. Perhaps there was no money to pay her at all; it was offered only to tempt her, to give her the means to be generous, and so draw her in.

The priest was proud of his school. She was shown the chapel; a shed with a black 'Our Lady' painted on the wall and a white sheet over an altar of up-ended tea chests. The classrooms were filled with chanting pupils, crammed together at old wooden desks. There were no books in sight, and not much paper, only the blackboards and chalk and a Bible on the lectern for the guidance of the teacher.

She was to teach the senior girls. Their mature, heavy bodies overflowed their school desks. They stood up in silence as she entered and the priest-headmaster wrote her name carefully on the blackboard.

'Good morning Mrs Whitman,' they chorused, like a class of primary children.

She had brought a piece of card from the house, the back of last year's calendar from the kitchen wall.

'This morning we shall draw a plan of the classroom.' She held up the card. Father Dominic was outside. She glanced through the window and he waved, holding up his thumb.

You could do it, Julia. They would like you.

She cleared her throat and looked at the class. They stared back, sixteen round, brown faces like upturned chocolate puddings. How would she ever tell them apart?

'I'm going to draw a box for each desk and I want you to come forward and write your name in the box that corresponds to your desk.'

Her felt tip squealed in the silence. She looked up and smiled. 'Now, start from the back.' She pointed to the girl in the corner, fuzzy hair cropped so short she was almost bald. The others turned to look but the girl remained seated.

'I don't know your name.' Julia spoke gently. 'If you write your name in the square it will help me to remember it.'

The girl put her hand to her mouth and giggled.

It was Francis's gesture, an embarrassed giggle that meant he didn't understand. She spoke again, more slowly. 'Please come up to the front.'

The girl squirmed in her chair, the giggles like small sobs behind her spread fingers.

A hand shot up at the front of the class. 'Excuse me. We do not understand.'

Julia cleared her throat again and repeated herself, still more slowly. 'I want you to come up here and write your name in the square.' There was a sigh, like a small rush of wind, and the girl at the back rose. Not a girl, a woman, sixteen or seventeen; squeezing her hips between the rows.

The others followed, queuing to write their names in the blank squares. Hope Njori, Mary Kamau, Galilee Njoma. Missionary names hitched to the tribal patronymic, baptised and scarred, deep diagonal slashes from lip to cheekbone. The exercise dispersed the tension, melting it into laughter as each pupil made the journey to the front of the class, the fatter ones squeezing along the aisles, to write their names laboriously on the plan.

She learned, after another false start, that it was her English that they could not understand. Theirs was a language apart. English learned from Africans who had themselves learned it from a black tongue; extra vowels to end every word, sing-song inflections, Father Dominic's 'most' a favourite word. It was the language of the land, of shop keepers and radio broadcasts. She had heard it from Francis, from Mshoki's radio, from Kangeni, even Bartholomew.

Are you ready for me, Julia?

Patrick collected her at noon. He smiled indulgently as she recounted the morning.

'And are you happy now?'

'Oh yes,' she said. 'This is something I can do.'

'Good.' And he slowed the car while she waved to the girls walking home along the track.

Bartholomew arrived soon after lunch, hurrying across the lawn. 'I just came to see how it went.'

For the first time he wore shorts. White, drill cotton, cut high. Hair clung to his legs in tight black curls.

She offered him the tin of biscuits. 'Why don't you take them home?'

He ignored it. 'They like you, yes?'

'Yes, I think so. They had trouble with my English.'

'It will do them good, to hear English spoken as you speak it. It was one of my problems as a student, no-one in England understood what I said.'

He chuckled. 'I used to carry my O-level certificate in my pocket. "Look," I wanted to say, "I have a certificate." I never showed it to anyone. I just learned to speak again, tape-recording the BBC and practising in front of a mirror.' He shrugged. 'It was a lonely business.'

She tried to imagine him in London; staring around Victoria Station, amazed by the sight of all those white people carrying their own suitcases.

Her days were suddenly filled with activity. Going out with Patrick in the early morning to the shabby huddle of classrooms, returning at noon, when the school day ended against the heat, bursting with all that she had achieved and the praise that Father Dominic heaped upon her.

She made a collection of teaching aids: her pocket calculator, an ancient filing cabinet filled with old files from the factory, a picture of a photocopier torn from a magazine at the Club.

Gradually the faces became distinct, the names on the squares linked to the eager smiles and the deep cuts, lip to ear, that scarred them. Initiation rituals were confused

130

in their memories with the ceremony of baptism. 'I was blessed with the water and the salt and then the father took a hot knife to make the mark of my blessing.'

She set them essays to write. Two pages on any aspect of Ledorot. She took the results home to show Patrick.

'You should read these, they're amazing.'

'I should think they are if a bunch of kaffir girls wrote them.'

'No, look. The English is quite good. It's what they say that I want you to read. It's as if they're talking about somewhere else. This isn't the Ledorot that we know.'

She selected one of the essays and put it in his hand.

'Ledorot is a very nice place,' he read in a sing-song voice. 'I live here with my mother and father and two brothers and my younger sister. My mother and father have been here for many years. We have no *shamba*. My mother is a picker. She goes at sunrise to the place where she is told. The Company have given her a red apron to protect her from the poison in the tea –

'Doesn't say what father does,' Patrick interjected, 'probably sits in the bar all day.'

He picked out another essay and continued to read aloud.

'I was born in Ledorot. I have three brothers. We were all born in the house in the township. My father sends me to school. He wants me to go to work at the Coast to earn money to pay the school for my brothers. If I do not get a job, my father will send me to be married to make more room to sleep at night.'

Patrick tossed it aside. 'You're wasting your time, Julia. Next year she'll be bending over the tea with a *mtoto* on her back.'

She showed the essays to Father Dominic. The little priest blew his nose loudly while he read them. 'Well, Mrs Whitman, now you know something of our Ledorot.'

Julia nodded. 'They are teaching me more than I am teaching them.'

The priest took her hand. 'There is something to be learned from every soul.'

'But what can I teach these girls, Father?'

He shrugged. 'I have taught them to read and write, and simple arithmetic. Now it is up to you to teach them the things I do not know.'

'But will they all just be tea pickers?'

The priest's pinched face filled with passion. 'I hope not, Mrs Whitman. How will we go forward, if we are to be a nation of tea pickers? I want these girls to be ready for a different life. For those who have the opportunity to leave to have the confidence to go.' He squeezed her hand. 'You can teach them more than you know.'

They were willing to learn whatever she tried to teach. Together they moved the desks to form a table in the centre of the classroom. She brought knives and forks from home, plates and glasses, almost the entire contents of the sideboard. She taught them how to lay a table, which implements to use for each course. Father Dominic attended the lessons, entranced.

'Excellent, Mrs Whitman, most excellent. From me they have learned spelling and arithmetic but you, you make them into ladies.' The class joined in the praise, marvelling at the china, black fingers tracing the ugly pink flowers. Mother's china. She would turn in her grave.

Patrick grumbled at the fetching and carrying, waited in the driving seat while the girls struggled with heavy boxes of crockery. 'You could go too far with this, Julia,' he said as they drove away.

She ignored him.

'What good will it do them to learn white table manners?'

The same good it would do you.

She swallowed the words. 'I can only teach them what I know, Patrick.'

When they reached the house he smiled at her. 'As long as it makes you happy.'

He stayed to lunch and then lingered on, opening another bottle of beer, keeping her on a knife-edge wondering whether Bartholomew would come before he had gone.

He appeared just as the car pulled out of sight. She had given no signal, not yet reached down for the tapestry, but he was there before she had lowered her arm, still waving at the dust of Patrick's departure.

He held out a yellow rose. 'A present for the teacher.'

'Bartholomew! You shouldn't bring me gifts.'

'But it's not a gift.' He grinned at her. 'It's not a gift because it's not mine to give.'

'You stole it?'

'I borrowed it. Dear Mrs Ellis will not miss a single rose from the great bush that grows at the bottom of her drive. She cannot even see it from her house.' The rose perfume was sweet, cloying in the warm air. Julia pinned the flower to her dress.

He was still standing. 'Well?'

'Well what?' She looked away, turning her head from the unwavering gaze.

'Is it time for a walk?'

A walk. Another outing to the rock. Women do not walk out in Africa. With good cause. It was clear in his face. This time she would be ready.

'I'd rather not, Bartholomew.'

He sucked his breath through his teeth. 'One day you will.' He reached out to touch the flower and put his hand on her breast. It felt as if he had burned her.

The rose was still pinned to her dress, drooping a little, when Patrick came home in the evening.

He had brought an old telephone set. 'I expect you could make use of that in the classroom.'

Julia kissed him. 'Can you spare it?'

He nodded. 'It doesn't work.'

The class clapped at the sight of it. Her difficulty was not to hold their interest but to restrain them.

'Dial slowly,' she taught them. 'Release the dial when

you reach zero and let it return freely. Be sure you do not hold your finger there while the dial returns.'

They vied with one another to obey exactly, poking out a finger to turn the ancient dial and then withdrawing as if it had stung.

''Ello . . ., 'ello.'

''Ello, 'ello. . .' Over and over into the silent handset.

16

'To the Coast?' Julia almost squealed with delight.'Of course I'll come with you. I'd love to.'

'I thought with all this teaching you'd be too busy.'

'No,' said Julia. 'I'm sure Father Dominic will let me have a couple of days' leave. When are you going?'

'Thursday morning, probably. We'll drive back on Sunday.' He pointed a finger. 'But I won't have time to take you about. I'm going down as a favour to Harry.'

'Will he be there?'

'No. I've told you already. He's gone to London. The reason why I have to go down is that he wants me to check on something while he is away.'

'Couldn't one of the local people do it?'

Patrick shook his head. 'This is something he couldn't trust to a kaff.'

Julia felt as excited as a schoolgirl.

'Are there lots of shops? Can we go to a cinema?'

Patrick laughed. 'You're like a big kid, Julia. It isn't London, you know.'

'I know!' she cried. 'But there must be shops. I'm longing for a new dress.'

'All the good stuff is imported,' said Patrick. 'Things like dresses are terribly expensive.'

Julia shook her head. 'I don't care. I've got plenty of money to spend, I haven't touched what I brought out with me yet.'

At the mention of her money, Patrick's expression altered.

'I hope you haven't been bragging about that money. I don't want people thinking I can't keep my own wife.'

'I haven't said a word about it, Patrick. I wouldn't.'

The prospect of the visit filled her with delight. She imagined herself walking among the stores, sitting at a pavement café, doing all the ordinary things that were not possible in Ledorot.

Her excitement was infectious.

Father Dominic clapped his hands. 'Of course you must go, Mrs Whitman. You must see our great City.' He put his head on one side and peered at her. 'Will you visit the Cathedral?'

'I expect so,' said Julia, though she had not thought of visiting a church.

'Could you possibly collect something for me – just a small thing?'

'Of course, Father.' Julia smiled as the little priest's eyes lit up.

As word of their trip crossed the estate, the number of errands grew. Clare Bowen wanted a dress length. 'Anything will do, something with flowers would be nice.' Julia needed no further description. All the Ledorot women made their own dresses. Printed cotton shifts that looked almost identical. At least I'll be able to buy something different, thought Julia, no matter what it costs.

Vera Ellis wanted place mats and Janyce Dickinson wanted lipstick. Julia made a list, smiling at every request, at how they came forward when she had something to offer, the same women who had so recently veiled their eyes when she came into the Club.

The class shared her delight. She asked how many had never been to the City and was astonished when more than half put up their hands. She asked how many had never been away from Ledorot and at least a quarter of the hands remained.

No wonder it was all so precious, thought Julia, her ugly patterned china, the broken telephone. Hers were treasures from another world. Did they think she held the key to it, with her classes in Office Practice and the uses of a gravy boat?

The few who had been to the Coast strutted a little, and took the stance that she should be warned of its dangers.

'They will steal from you in the bazaar.'

'There are men who will take your purse.'

'Men who will try to trick you.'

Laughing, Julia held up her hand. 'I'm sure it is no worse than London.'

'But in London you are familiar, in our City you are a stranger.'

'We have read of these things.'

'And Father Dominic teaches us that great places are full of wickedness.'

At the end of the morning one of the girls stayed behind when the class had gone.

'My brother is in the City,' she said.

Julia smiled. It was Hope, the one who had been so shy on the first day. She knew their names now, the sea of brown faces had become individuals with names and characters.

'Does he live there?'

The girl nodded. 'My father keeps his address in a book.'

Julia wondered where the conversation was leading; an errand perhaps, something to be delivered?

'Would you like me to take something to him?' she offered.

The girl looked down, half shy, half sly. 'Please, is there room in your car for me?'

The question was so unexpected Julia was caught off guard.

'Of course! I mean, I expect so.'

She dreaded Patrick's response, but he was less angry than she expected.

'Isn't it enough that you teach them for nothing? Are we operating a free taxi service now?'

'I didn't think it would be a problem. She wants to visit her brother and we've plenty of room in the car.'

'And I suppose next time there'll be a whole crew of them with brothers to visit in the City. Have you ever smelt them close up, Julia? Have you ever had a kaffir in the car with you?'

One lay beside me on a rock.

He smelt of sweat and maize.

No worse than you.

Patrick looked up, as if the words had been spoken. 'Give me that cloth.'

She handed him a rag from the dash and waited while he wiped the dip-stick clean. 'Just this once then. Tell her to wait by the school at eight o'clock.'

There was no smell; hardly any baggage. The girl sat in the back, tight against the passenger door, as if to minimise the space she must occupy.

They drove overnight, sharing the road with the tea lorries that crawled, heavily laden, down the escarpment, and empty tankers, hurtling back to the Coast, their trailers perilously swinging as they overtook on the narrow bends.

Hope slept as they approached the city, her face pink-brown in the red light of the sun coming up over the sea. Julia leaned across the seat and shook her arm. Her skin was like ice. She had worn nothing all night but a thin cotton dress; her bare arms were dimpled with cold.

'Where does your brother live?' Julia asked.

The girl yawned and gazed dumbly through the window at the city.

138

'Where does he live?' Julia asked again.

She fished a scrap of paper out of her *kikapu*. Julia read the address aloud.

'But that's miles out,' said Patrick. 'It's one of the estates on the way to the airport.'

Julia remembered them. The first sight of the city, moonlit acres planted with rows of concrete boxes, a larger version of the township in Ledorot.

How many would share such a house in the city? With how many would Hope sleep on the concrete floor that night?

She asked, 'Where does your brother work?'

'He is in the Post Office.'

'And what does he do there?'

'He is in the Post Office,' Hope repeated.

'Yes, but what is his job?'

'In the City the Post Office is larger than in Ledorot,' the girl said slowly.

'She probably doesn't realise there are different jobs,' said Patrick.

The Post Office at Ledorot had a staff of one. Julia recalled the bare wooden counter, divided along its width by a shield of rusty mesh and the rows of metal boxes opening on to the step outside. Post boxes were for the use of Chaachi executives. Pickers and house servants could use their employer's box number, but with the sure knowledge that what mail they received would be scrutinised.

Julia remembered the first time Patrick brought home a letter addressed to Mshoki, its envelope shamelessly torn. She had been outraged.

'It's not right, Patrick! You don't own these men, they're entitled to privacy.'

The memory was vivid. The first few weeks in Ledorot, a time of plunging disappointment; Patrick in his own place, not the man she thought he'd be.

He had waved the letter at her. 'You wouldn't say that if you read one of these. Look at this – some nephew

139

complaining about the women on the *shamba*, and look, another one needs shoes for school. They want Mshoki to pay. Twenty-five shillings!' He thrust the letter into her lap. 'Read it.'

She couldn't. It was one of Mother's cardinal sins, reading other people's letters. She replaced the tidy, childish script in its envelope. Mshoki was summoned from the kitchen and Patrick spoke to him in Swahili.

Mshoki nodded, bringing his hands together for a fraction of a second. A thank you gesture.

'What did you say to him?'

'I told him I would pay for the new shoes.'

'But that's ridiculous.'

'Why?'

'Because if they know you're going to read the letter, they can exploit you, knowing that you'll pay what they ask.'

Patrick's smile was ironic. 'We have learned something about Africans, haven't we?'

Julia felt herself flush. 'It's not just Africans, anybody would do it.'

'And so they do,' said Patrick. 'They know I'll read the letter, but they also know I'm not a fool. I will send them ten shillings.'

'But they say the shoes will cost twenty-five shillings.'

'That's the point. They know and I know that a pair of kaffir shoes costs ten shillings.'

They had reached the end of what appeared to be the main road. Patrick pointed to a red brick building with banks of mail boxes along its walls. Africans were collecting letters and small parcels, box keys dangling casually from their fingers. She saw Hope looking at them, at the women on the pavement. Unconsciously the girl smoothed her dress.

Patrick pulled into the bus station and paused on a yellow line. The girl's expression did not change as he explained that she would have to catch a bus to her brother's house. Without a word she climbed out and hefted the *kikapu* on to the pavement.

'Sunday morning,' he said. 'At eight o'clock sharp.'

Julia looked around. The bus station looked new but already the dust had taken over, flurrying around the men and women who crowded the benches or sat on the floor. There was constant activity, elbowing and pushing; the dirty, overflowing buses were piled high with bundles, rolled mattresses, even bicycles that slipped and bounced as they hurtled around the station.

'We can't just leave her here,' said Julia. 'She doesn't know which bus to catch. She probably doesn't have any money.'

'Of course she's got money,' said Patrick. 'I bet she has a great wad stuffed in her bra.'

Pointless to say that she didn't wear a bra. Julia looked back as they turned out of the station. Hope was standing just as they had left her, motionless in the crowd, holding the *kikapu*, her empty hand stuck out to counterbalance the weight.

Harry's house was in the suburbs, a shabby bungalow standing in a flat, overgrown garden. His servant unlocked the door, and showed them the house, made dreary by wire window mesh that kept out the light.

'I thought it would be better than this,' said Julia.

Patrick shook his head. 'Rents are very high down here. Harry's lucky he's got a house to himself.'

The furniture was old and had the spiritless, broken air that characterises rented property. In the dining room someone had used the table as a desk; the wood was scratched and blotched with ink. She wished Harry had been there to greet them, offering his hand to her on the veranda in place of the sloppy-footed servant who brought bottles of unchilled beer in finger-marked glasses.

'But he could at least decorate the place,' she said, as they sat down to a meal of tinned ham and potato salad. She looked around at the darkened room, windows

141

closed tight behind the mesh. 'A bit of paint would brighten it up.'

Patrick smiled. 'Are you nesting for Harry too? I'm sure he likes it just as it is.'

'What do you mean, nesting?'

'Homemaking. Like you've been doing in Ledorot. All the pictures and so on. Francis has never seen anything like it.'

'Do you object?'

'Not at all. I've told you, that's what you're there for. To be my wife and make a home.'

He reached out for her but Julia shied away, turning the conversation to her shopping expedition.

After lunch they drove back to the centre of town. Patrick dropped her off at the bank.

'You can change your sterling in there. Then the main shops and the market are that way.' He pointed backwards with his thumb. 'The Cathedral is down there near the docks.'

'What are you going to do?'

'One or two things. I'll be calling into Harry's office. Then I'm going down to the depot to try and get a proper supply of spares for the factory.' He patted her knee. 'You enjoy yourself, love. Buy yourself something nice.'

In exchange for her sterling, a wad of notes she had withdrawn from her mother's savings, the bank cashier handed her a bundle of coloured paper. The thin, worn notes were the wrong size for her wallet.

She turned north and wandered up Government Road. The pavement was wide and planted with trees. On either side were tall, modern buildings; tinted glass and the hum of air conditioning. A roundabout marked the end of the thoroughfare. Beyond it the concrete and glass gave way to a parade of flat-roofed shops. The street divided into a maze of alleyways. On the corner a sign said Herji's Bazaar; a low building, with windows almost entirely obscured by burglar-proof metal shutters.

The smell of the sea, fish and decaying seaweed, drifted on a warm breeze that shuffled dust along the pavement. Through a doorway she saw bolts of brightly coloured cloth piled right to the ceiling, and at the back, two elderly Indians hunched over treadle sewing machines. She went in and chose a dress length for Clare Bowen. 'All the cotton is locally made,' the shopkeeper told her, proudly.

Next door was a 'Gentlemen's Outfitters'. She peered into the windows, at rows of cotton shirts, suits displayed on metal coat hangers. She walked on, past a confectioners, perspex trays of coloured sweets displayed under a greasy glass counter. A fat Asian youth dozed by the till, undisturbed by the flies. Beside it was a shop selling antiques, a huge carved mirror filled the window. She started at her own reflection; a girl in a straw hat and sunglasses, a woman in Africa.

Vera had told her to 'look for Habari Park. It used to be Livingstone Park – a proper park with grass and swings for the children. Now it's a dirty African market but you should find some place mats there.'

The market was easy to find. A noisy, stone-walled enclosure surrounding a warren of stalls that sold everything from lettuces to carvings.

The narrow lanes between the stalls were crowded with tourists, haggling in loud voices. Julia watched a strident American conduct a pantomime by a stall of carvings.

'Forget it. It's too expensive.' He pretended to walk away until the vendor called him back, shouting his compromise.

She watched another man beat a boy down to a quarter of the price he had asked for a carving of an elephant. The difference was fifteen shillings, enough to feed the boy for a week. The man was triumphant.

She couldn't see any place mats. The stalls overflowed with carvings; masks, animals, small figures. She glanced twice at a collage of dried banana leaves, a *bibi* tilling a field, but the vendor's persistence drove her away.

Reaching the other side of the enclosure she followed an exit sign and found herself on a dusty pavement with the city behind her and ahead the docks and the tall spire of the Cathedral.

'*Asante sana*, memsahib,' a voice wheedled in her ear. She had given nothing, not even looked up, had only an impression of rags in the corner of her eye. Rags and deformity. '*Asante sana*.' Thank you.

A split-skinned black claw touched her arm.

Without looking at her wallet, she pulled out one of the coloured notes.

'*Asante sana*.'

Involuntarily she raised her eyes, and met the beggar's one eye, bloodshot but bright as a bird's, and a weeping, bulbous scar where the other had been.

He was gone before she could react, hobbling rapidly across the broken pavement. His movement alerted a horde of others, deformed, limbless, materialising from alleys and doorways; one, truncated to the hips, propelled himself along the gutter on a makeshift skateboard, shrieking in English, 'Yes madam! Yes madam! Look at me!'

There was no escape. She had to raise her head and walk through them, pity swamped by revulsion, striding to outwalk their hobbling, limping progress.

They followed her to the Cathedral, the beggar on the skateboard and two small boys. Runny noses and stick-thin legs. Could her tapestry help any of these? The Cathedral was vast. A grey stone cavern in an acre of car park. The beggars scattered as she reached the gate, as if the Cathedral grounds were somehow forbidden. Then she saw why; at intervals along the perimeter stood security guards armed with truncheons. She climbed the steps and went inside. The building towered over her. She stood at the back, dwarfed by the fluted pillars that supported the soaring roof. Her arms and legs were streaked with coloured light from diamonds of glass set into the walls. Incense mingled with the dust, rising in swirls through the shafts of colour. The noise of the city drifted in through the open doors; car horns and squealing tyres, shouts and the hiss of airbrakes.

A placard announcing a Saturday fête was nailed to the door. 'Grand Draw, cake stalls, second-hand clothes, toys, handicrafts.'

Handicrafts. Money for good work, tapestries from the ladies of Ledorot.

A sacristan walked past her up the aisle, blue plastic sandals poking out beneath the hem of his gown. The altar was a distant marble slab, draped with lace.

'Excuse me.'

The sacristan paused.

'My name is Whitman. Mrs Julia Whitman, I have come from Ledorot.'

The young man looked blank.

'Father Dominic asked me to collect something from here.'

The dark eyes flickered. 'You have come for his collar?'

Julia smiled. 'He didn't tell me what it was. Just that there was a parcel to be collected.'

'Follow me, please.'

He led her to the communion rail, pausing to genuflect before turning aside. 'Wait here please.'

He left her standing by a statue, flanked by huge displays of flowers. Their sweet scent mixed with the other smells, polish and incense.

'Here it is.' The sacristan held out a shallow cardboard box. The lid was transparent. Inside lay a pair of white clerical collars with short black bibs.

'Father Dominic has been waiting for these a very long time,' said the sacristan.

'Surely they could have been posted to him?'

The sacristan shook his head. 'It is not the post, it is the shortages. Only now is it his turn to have a new collar.'

Julia shook her head. 'The Cathedral is so big.' She gestured around, at the coloured glass and the great display of flowers.

'It looks so rich.'

The young man sighed. 'It was built by rich men. But the rich men have gone. Like so much of our wealth in Africa, it is an illusion.'

Avoiding the beggars, Julia returned to the city centre. There were few shops of the kind she had expected, no department stores, just a handful of expensive boutiques that sold imported clothes at prices that would have paid for a second-hand car. She wondered who bought them, who would wear such a dress in the midst of the beggars? She returned to the bazaar and bought a dress length, similar to the one she had chosen for Clare Bowen. She would become what Patrick wanted, a woman of Ledorot.

'So what did you think of our capital city, Julia? Were you impressed?'

He was swirling his glass in his hands. It was almost empty, the ice clacked against the sides like a slow castanet.

'Yes.' She hesitated, watching the ice. 'It was just a short visit, but I did enjoy it.'

Bartholomew took a sip of coke. 'And did the passenger behave?'

Julia nodded. 'Yes, it was fine. She was no bother at all.'

'But she was sick on the way back?'

'You heard about that?'

'Naturally. Everything is known to everyone in Ledorot.'

Julia shook her head. 'I haven't told anyone. Anyway, it was nothing. The poor girl was simply carsick. I don't suppose she's used to travelling at speed over the potholes.'

Hope had been waiting where they had left her, at eight o'clock, just as Patrick instructed. Transformed, her head a mass of tiny ribboned plaits, a new dress, and underneath, unmistakably, a bra.

They stopped for lunch just before noon. The girl sat on the verge with her back to them. Like the children who hawked mangoes from the side of the road, she ate her fruit without inhibition, folding back the peel and burying mouth and chin in the moist yellow flesh.

In less than an hour it came back, jolted out by the potholes and tedium into the lap of her new dress. Patrick swore nastily and made her hold the skirt like a bowl while he fetched a can of water from the back. They waited in the car while the girl cleaned herself. She stood behind the car, sponging her dress. Water slopping from the can on to her skirt moulded it against her thighs. Julia saw Patrick's eyes in the driving mirror, watching the girl.

It was dark when they reached the township. Hope's dress had dried long since and smelled only a little as she said goodbye and stood shyly in the headlights beside her *kikapu*.

'Thank you,' she said to Patrick. 'See you at school, Mrs Whitman.'

'Will you be all right walking from here?' Julia called.

Patrick slammed the door and the car pulled away before Hope could reply. 'Christ, I'm tired.' Rubbing his eyes. Not seeing. Possibly, probably, not seeing Bartholomew, ten yards up the road, his round face gleaming in the light of the stars.

He emptied the ice into his mouth and began to crunch it loudly.

'Did you get all the things you wanted?'

Julia nodded. 'Except Vera's place mats.'

'Vera's place mats,' he repeated, nodding. 'And did you get anything else, something you didn't want, some knowledge?'

Julia frowned. 'What do you mean?'

'Did you learn anything, Julia? Did you see the beggars?'

She nodded. 'I was appalled.'

His eyebrows rose. 'Appalled?'

'By the poverty – and the wealth. All those fine buildings surrounded by filthy beggars.'

'Was it their filth that you objected to, Julia?'

'What do you mean?'

'I think some of you white people mind dirt more than poverty.'

'Surely one leads to the other.'

'Ah, but which leads to which? Are we poor because we are dirty, or dirty because we are poor?'

Julia sighed. 'I cannot answer you, Bartholomew. All I can say is that I went to buy an expensive dress and I came away with a length of cheap cotton.'

Bartholomew clapped his hands. 'We will make you a local woman yet!' He stood up.

'Are you going already?'

'In a moment.' He leaned towards her. She could smell stale smoke on his breath.

'Are you ready now, Julia?' His voice was soft.

'Bartholomew, no!' She tried to push him away. Reaching out, blindly, her floundering hands landed in his mouth.

He took hold of her fingers and put them back in his mouth, sucking them in between his lips. The sensation made her feel weak.

17

'Long time no see, Mistah Thomas!'

The liftboy beamed as Harry parked his car.

'Raining in England?'

'Yes, it was.'

The boy took Harry's bag and followed him into the lift.

'You looking very white, Mistah Thomas.' He grinned, waiting for Harry to catch the joke.

In his office he peered into the mirror behind the door. His skin looked slack and grey. The trip to London had been exhausting, and the long flight back had left him parched and tired.

Muthaga knocked on the open door. 'I see you are back, Mr Thomas.'

'Yes.'

'We managed quite well without you.'

'I'm sure you did.'

'I gather you let someone use your house in your absence.'

'Yes, the Whitmans stayed for a weekend. Why?'

Muthaga shrugged. 'No reason, I drove past one night and saw the light on.'

'Do you know Patrick Whitman, from Ledorot?'

'I know of him, Mr Thomas. But I did not think he would welcome a visit from me.' He pointed to Harry's desk. 'You will see that Mr Whitman has left you a note.'

Harry looked at his desk. At the top of the pile of

papers was a torn envelope fixed to a page on which was scrawled:

'I looked in to your office. The monkeys are doing surprisingly well in your absence.

Thank you for the loan of the house – Julia thinks you need a wife, or at least a can of paint!'

Harry felt himself blush as he read the note.

'I took the liberty of reading it,' said Muthaga. 'You will see that he reports that we monkeys are doing well without you.'

'Yes,' said Harry, in a strangled voice.

'There was, however, one small problem.'

'What was that?' Harry looked up in alarm. It would not be beyond Muthaga to manufacture a crisis in his absence.

'This problem arose after Mr Whitman's visit.' Muthaga smiled. 'Some Customs forms were completed incorrectly. It has caused a delay. Last month's consignment is still in store.'

'What about this month's?'

'I made a decision in your absence, Mr Thomas.'

'A decision?'

A smile grew slowly on Muthaga's face. 'I decided that as we could not export the tea it should be sold locally.'

'But we could have stored it somehow!'

'But I could not see how, Mr Thomas. You were not here to guide us. The supermarkets were very pleased to buy it. Export grade tea is not often available for the local market.'

'When did you decide to flog it?'

'As a matter of fact it was yesterday.'

'Yesterday? But you knew I would be back today.'

'Yes, Mr Thomas. But, as they say,' the African smirked, 'time and tea waits for no man.'

When he had gone Harry put his arms on the desk and cradled his head. Piles of paper had accumulated in his absence; letters to be answered, forms to be completed, inquiries, circulars from London. Mrs Holu, his secretary, had done nothing but open envelopes and distribute the contents between two wire trays. It would take him weeks to catch up. He picked a page from the top. It was a copy of a contract with Joshi Warehouses Ltd. The carbon was so faint he could scarcely read the price. A percentage had been added for packet labelling when no labelling was required, but they'd forgotten the delivery charge.

'Are you all right, Mr Thomas?' Mrs Holu smiled at him. 'Here's your coffee. I put in two sugars because you've grown so thin in England.' She wagged a finger and put the cup and saucer on to his desk.

A moat of coffee surrounded the cup. Catching his look she waddled round the desk, picked up the saucer and tipped the contents back into the cup. A large drop fell from the saucer and spread, making a brown, wrinkly stain on the Joshi invoice.

'Thank you, Mrs Holu.'

She smiled benignly. 'All the girls are very pleased for you to come back.' She bustled to the door and peered out into the corridor. 'Mr Muthaga's been giving us a bad time.' She wagged her finger again. 'I'm serious, Mr Thomas. Never have an African for a boss, he is the worst kind.'

Muthaga's rank was exactly equal to Harry's. They received the same salary and were supposed to co-operate in all matters. The Company had created the two posts deliberately in the belief that it would satisfy both the political requirements of Africanisation and the commercial requirements of the Company. But the Company, with its remote personnel department in London, had not taken account of personalities. Though Harry had tried to befriend him, Muthaga sustained an implacable hatred of all white Chaachi employees. For Muthaga there was no place for Harry in Africa; by occupying his post he deprived a deserving African of the chance of promotion. The fact that Chaachi had tried to recruit locally, that Harry's two predecessors had been Africans, made no impression on Muthaga.

'It was the fault of the colonials,' he claimed, when Harry asked what had happened. 'The first was a mission boy. He had not been properly educated.' Muthaga pointed a finger at Harry. 'Your people kept us down, you know. It was not considered necessary to provide education beyond primary school.'

'But that was years ago,' said Harry. 'Things have changed.'

'Not in time for this man,' said Muthaga. 'The paperwork was too much for him. He had not been taught how to deal with the great white Chaachi bureaucracy.'

'And what about the second man?'

Muthaga sneered. 'He was doing fine. But he took it into his head to tour the estates. He drove up to Kibwezi, to Ledorot. I am sure you can imagine the welcome he received at the Ledorot Club. Your friends – Bowen, Ellis, Whitman – they did not even acknowledge him. He was left to the little puppet they have up there, their token African, I forget his name.'

'Kangeni?' suggested Harry, wearily.

'The same. Unfortunately your predecessor was not so tolerant as Kangeni. He minded being called a monkey and being snubbed by the big white bwanas of the Ledorot Club.'

'So what happened?'

Muthaga shrugged. 'He resigned.'

Harry looked at Muthaga. 'Was that the real reason? He resigned because he didn't like the estate managers?'

'It was – how would you say? – the last straw.' Muthaga clicked his fingers. 'That and the advertisement he saw in a copy of *The Times*.'

'What was it, a better job?'

'No. It was his own job that Chaachi was advertising.'

'The advertisement that I answered?' asked Harry in dismay.

'The same,' said Muthaga.

18

Shadowed by the mosquito mesh and a flowering frangipani, the tiny bathroom window let in little light. Julia stared at herself in the mirror. Even in that dim light she was cloudy-eyed and pale.

With her head swimming and a singing in her ears that drowned the noises of the garden, she perched on the side of the bath and tried to count the days. Patrick had thrown away her pills. She winced at the memory. 'What am I wasting my time for?' Wasting his time, making love that he did not feel, of which no word had ever passed his lips. In England she had believed that it did not matter. In England he had talked of Africa, of the house on the hill where a woman would be content. In England she had imagined his love as a silent thing, a deep, quiet knowledge of each other that would grow with the years.

Steadying herself against the bath, feeling the chipped enamel under her fingers, she clenched her teeth against a wave of nausea.

She had not thought it through, had not recognised that the first stage of love is kindness, gentleness, not the unrefined heaving of her bed, the indifference to her needs, to her boredom.

Had he not driven her? Abandoned her in an empty house, scorned her teaching, driven her as surely as if he had pushed her physically, into Bartholomew's arms. It was his doing; if he had listened, if he had only heard her, if he had only asked a single question, he might have prevented it. But he had never asked, never listened, never inquired where or how she spent her long, empty days.

He knew. Of course he knew! The women would have competed to be first with the news, each with her own story, her own weasel smile of understanding, repeating the lies that flowed along the pathways, rivulets of spite from quarter to kitchen. I heard from my Joshua, my cook tells me, Samson heard that . . . put a stop to it, Patrick, before any harm is done.

Too late. She had let him be her friend, the kaffir boy; her guide, her bringer of flowers, the one who, with deft hands, had mended her little house as Patrick could not have done.

A beetle crept across the bathroom floor and paused by her feet. Its coat was hard and black, broken into shiny sections like the button of an overcoat. Its feelers tickled the edge of her sole. Her eyes sharpened and dimmed as if a piece of gauze were waving in front of her face. The beetle became a dark spot, black and menacing as a drop of blood on the tiled floor.

Her head felt light as air. Boom! Boom! Her eyes cleared. The singing in her ears ceased as if the power supply had been cut. Boom! Boom! The same noise, the thump of a fist on the bathroom door.

'What's the matter with you in there?'

'I don't know.' Her voice sounded faint and hollow.

'Are you sick?'

'I feel faint.'

'Have a cold shower or something. If you don't come people will think you're snubbing them.'

He drank beer from a bottle while she struggled into her clothes and pinned up her hair.

'I don't want to go, Patrick. I feel ill.'

He patted her bottom. 'You'll be fine when you get there.'

At the Bowens' house Clare greeted her with a swift embrace and a kiss carefully aimed at the air beside her cheek. 'You don't look well, Julia. Come and sit here.'

Julia sat beside her, conscious as usual of the guarded looks of the other women, of pursed lips and elbows nudging one another. Only Janyce Dickinson grinned at her. Julia realised with a shudder that she had acquired an identity. Like Janyce, she had become a 'black sheep', part of a 'difficult marriage'.

Somebody poured her a glass of beer. She ignored it, keeping her eyes away from the full glasses around her, and the loaded buffet table in the corner. She concentrated on the conversation; the men were swapping kaffir stories.

'Did you hear what happened out on Kibwezi?' Jack Bowen took a swallow of beer. 'They found a youngster roaming about the factory car park in the dark. He couldn't account for being out so they made him get into the car.' He wiped foam from his upper lip on to the back of his hand.

'I don't know what the boy said but I guess the lads had had a beer or two. Anyway, they cuffed him around a bit. Nothing too serious; an eye swollen up and a bruised jaw.' Bowen took another draught of beer. 'It turned out he was one of the foreman's boys, a little bit simple but quite harmless.'

Dickie interrupted, 'How could they tell? They're all bloody simple.'

Jack Bowen guffawed. 'You're right there! The foreman came up the next day, started threatening to go to the police and I don't know what else. Old MacKenzie wasn't having any. He told the foreman if he wasn't back at work in fifteen minutes there'd be a new foreman. That sent him scuttling. The kaffir has six children younger than the idiot boy, all sitting in the compound like nest chicks with their mouths open.'

Their voices grew faint. Patrick was laughing with the others. Open mouthed, showing his teeth.

They'd been white in London. Straight and white,

gleaming against his tan. It was only later – when the solitaire was safe on her finger and the one-way ticket tucked in his wallet – that he told her he'd had them polished for the trip. Three sessions with a dentist at the Coast, at great expense and some discomfort. An occasion not to be repeated, part of the cost of getting a wife.

Now his teeth were brown again. Their colour was a measure of the time she had been there. The stain of the tasting table. Part of the life.

Clare was shouting for the servants to fill everyone's glass.

'Why, Julia! You haven't touched your beer. Would you like something else? How about a nice sherry?'

Julia shook her head.

'Had a bit of a night of it, did we?' Janyce Dickinson winked. 'Patrick giving you a hard time?'

Julia looked away.

Clare Bowen put a glass of sherry in her hands and smiled down at her. 'How is the teaching going, Julia?'

'I'm enjoying it.'

'But are the niggie girls learning anything?' asked Madeleine Waugh, pausing to fit a cigarette into her long ivory holder. 'I mean, anything useful?'

With an effort Julia turned to face her. 'I'm teaching them Office Practice. On Monday I shall be showing the class around Patrick's office.'

'Over my dead body,' said Patrick.

'You've already said I can bring them,' said Julia quietly. 'It will only take an hour.'

'The office isn't a circus.'

Julia sat up and at once all the women raised their heads, other conversations ceased.

'How else will they learn to use a proper telephone?'

'I don't care, I don't want a bunch of kaffir women tramping around. You're going too far with this teaching business.'

Julia took a deep breath, fighting a wall of dizziness. 'It's important to me, Patrick.'

156

The other women stared.

'But what good will it do?' asked Jack Bowen. 'You're teaching them to want things they can never have.'

'They might. They won't all stay in Ledorot. Would you want them to go to the Coast without knowing how to use a telephone?' Julia said. The speech left her breathless and weak.

'What I want is kaffirs who can pick tea,' growled Patrick.

Clare was taking the covers off the buffet table. 'Come and eat,' she cried.

Julia stood up unsteadily, and followed the other guests to the table. Her eyes roamed hazily over dishes of cold meat, ham, beef, pressed tongue; bowls of salad, smoked trout with the eyes still in place, a platter of chilled curry with a layer of rice over the top. The other guests surged about her. She pressed her fingers onto the white cloth, conscious of a cold mist of sweat on her face.

A servant brought out a basket of bread, soft rolls piled into a high pyramid. The guests swarmed round him. Donald Ellis and Madeleine Waugh reached simultaneously for the top roll. The servant stepped backwards. His foot caught against the leg of a chair and as he struggled to right himself the bread basket tilted, scattering rolls over the patio and down into the flower beds.

'Really, Donald.' Vera dug her fingers into her husband's arm.

Julia returned to her chair.

The commotion had brought the Bowens' cook out on to the veranda. He stood near the door, waiting for orders, smoothing the stiffness of his apron. Her dizziness receded. The servant was close to her chair. She noticed thick, knotted scars that stood out on the backs of his hands.

'Did you burn your hands?' she asked. Jack Bowen shouted something in Swahili and the cook moved forward to help the other servant gather up the rolls. Then he turned to answer Julia's question.

'He tipped boiling water over himself, a couple of years back. You should see the rest of him. All down his chest. We had a hell of a caper – six weeks before he could walk and poor Clare making do with a youngster from Kibwezi.'

The cook went back into the house. Julia caught sight of his scar again. The skin had gathered, creased like the trunk of an old olive tree; in some of the creases cracks had appeared, exposing pink, raw skin.

'It must still give him a lot of pain,' she said. 'Perhaps it would have healed better if he'd had plastic surgery.'

'I don't think Doctor Patel runs to plastic surgery.'

'In any case,' said Vera, 'they probably don't feel it as much as we would.'

Behind her the other servant was fishing rolls out of the flower bed with a long barbecue fork.

'No point in doing plastic surgery on a black skin, eh?' shouted Patrick. 'Too bloody ugly to start with! Ha! Ha!'

Their faces rose in surprise as Julia sprang up. Vomit was spilling from her lips as she lurched towards the bathroom. Leaning over the toilet pan she thought she would turn inside out. Beer and morning tea and then nothing except wild racking heaves. Over and over she pulled the chain, and then collapsed, bathed in sweat on the bathroom floor.

'Let me in, Julia.'

Clare's arms were cool, a gentle embrace as they shuffled together into her bedroom. Julia lay on the bed, resting her face on green candlewick. Clare unbuttoned her skirt and pulled it down over her legs. She took it outside. Julia could hear the servants murmuring in the passage. Clare spoke to them from the doorway, her plump figure oddly comforting against the light from the passage. She returned with a damp face cloth and gently wiped Julia's face and neck.

'Were you knocking it back before you came over?'

Julia shook her head. 'Only morning tea.'

'Tea and a little sherry got you this sick?' She walked over to the window and opened the fanlight. 'I don't believe it. You want to start counting, my girl, and get yourself down to the clinic.' Returning to the bed, she smiled. 'We haven't had a baby up here for years.' She pulled the bedspread over Julia's legs. 'You have a little sleep now. You'll feel better later on.'

Julia dozed. Through the window came the sound of laughter and the clink of cutlery on plates. Soon she began to feel hungry but it would seem a shame to ask for food. Sleepily she rolled onto her side. The green candlewick was soft against her cheek. Clare Bowen had been kind, she thought, like a mother. For a second she was back in Bartlett Road, feeling her mother's embrace, the hard rings on her fingers. She put her hand on her stomach, it felt flat and empty. The idea of a child was remote. How can I be a mother, she thought, when I still need a mother of my own?

The sun had moved round, casting a square of light across the bed that slipped down onto the floor like a fallen scarf. A tray had been placed beside the bed. A jug of fresh lime juice under a white, beaded cloth and a plate of wafer-thin sandwiches. Julia ate them hungrily, closing her teeth on the soft, white bread.

They'd cleaned her skirt; it hung on the wardrobe door, freshly pressed. The bathroom, too, was pristine. The white tiles gleamed. All trace of her sickness had been cleaned away. She washed her face in the basin and dried it on towels that were stiff with unrinsed soap, just as Francis left them.

The women had gathered in the shady part of the veranda. Their glasses were full. A tea trolley waited untouched by the door.

'There you are, Julia,' Vera Ellis cried. The others smiled at her encouragingly.

'Sit down my dear. I'll get the boy to bring you some

159

fresh tea.' Smiles, more friendly than they had ever been.

Madeleine Waugh patted her hand. 'You are a lucky girl.' Leaning across, she whispered in Julia's ear. 'Janyce and Dickie have been trying for years. A baby would have solved all their problems.'

Julia looked at Janyce Dickinson. She was sitting away from the group, her legs spread wide apart, sleeping with her mouth open.

A net had been strung between two trees on the far lawn. Patrick stood by it, shirtless, shouting instructions as the others tussled for possession of a ruptured football.

'How do you like our volleyball court?' asked Vera Ellis.

'They seem to be having a lot of fun.'

'But you won't want to join them, Julia. You'll stay up here with us.'

She stayed with them, returning their smiles, observing how all their disapproval had evaporated. The baby will be like a passport, she thought, it will make me part of their society.

'I bet you can't wait to tell Patrick,' said Madeleine, removing her cigarette holder to smile at Julia.

She told him that evening. She lay on her bed, waiting for him to finish in the bathroom.

'Sickness all gone now?' he asked as he came in rubbing his hair with a towel.

'Patrick, I may be having a baby.'

'A baby!' He threw the towel into the air. 'Clever girl. Well done! When will it be?'

'Clare thinks it will be January.'

'January you say?' He left the towel on the floor to comb his hair before the mirror. 'It'll be too hot at the Coast at that time of year.' He turned from the mirror, grinning. 'We'll have him up here, make him a real little African, eh?'

160

He buttoned his pyjamas and got into his own bed. 'You'll have to do as the other women tell you, now. No gadding about.'

Julia smiled. 'It isn't even confirmed yet.'

'That's just a formality. Clare Bowen knows what she's talking about. I'll drive you down to the clinic tomorrow and we can get old Patel to tell us it won't be twins.' He punched his pillow into a comfortable wad.

'We can't go tomorrow.'

'Why not?'

'The visit to your office is tomorrow.'

He raised his head from the pillow. 'Well that's off for a start.'

'I mustn't let them down, Patrick.'

'Forget the school, Julia. You're having a baby.'

'Might be.'

It hadn't sunk in. She couldn't think of a baby, only of the eager brown faces in the morning, the borrowed dresses and newly plaited hair. 'Couldn't they come anyway? Kangeni could show them round.'

'Julia, I said forget the school! This baby is more important than a bunch of bloody picker girls. You're having my son.'

'It doesn't make me an invalid!'

'No, but you've got to rest. This is the tropics. You can't go gallivanting around in your condition. In any case,' he settled back, rearranged the pillows once more and turned away from her, 'you might throw up in my office.'

The clinic was next to the general store. A long brick building with a raised veranda, where a line of patients queued; a man with his arm in plaster, another with a huge ulcer on his leg; women with small, bandy-legged children, their tiny swollen bellies echoing the bulge of their pregnant mothers. The queue began to move along the bench, to make room for Julia at the end.

'No, no.' Patrick propelled her from behind. 'You

161

don't have to wait out here, Patel will deal with us straight away.'

Julia glanced at the people in the queue, wanting to apologise. None would meet her eyes.

The doctor was a plump, smooth-voiced Indian. He shook Julia's hand.

'I am so pleased to meet you, Mrs Whitman. Please,' he gestured to the armchair beside his desk, 'wait for me here. I will finish dealing with this patient outside.' A man had been standing in the corner of the room. He hobbled out after the doctor. Julia glimpsed an infected wound on his leg.

'We could have waited outside, Patrick. We've no right to push in front of all those people.'

'And have you queue up like a kaffir woman?' Patrick thrust his hands in his pockets. 'Next time I'll get him to come up to the house.'

Patrick stayed in the surgery while Patel examined her. The doctor's hands were cold but he smiled kindly at Julia and asked his questions with delicacy.

'The beginning of February, I should say, Mrs Whitman,' he said when the examination was over. 'Will you stay in Ledorot for the confinement?'

Patrick called across before she could speak, 'Would the baby do better at the Coast?'

'Probably not. It will be cooler in Ledorot.' Patel scribbled a series of notes. 'Provided there are no complications it might be easier to stay up here. We'll consider it nearer the time.'

They had been in the clinic for an hour. The tree under which they had parked no longer shaded her side of the car. Patrick spread an old towel over the seat to protect her from the burning upholstery.

Surprised by his sudden gallantry, Julia smiled. 'Thank you, Patrick.'

He shrugged, looking at her for a moment with a kind of gruff tenderness, a look that she hadn't seen since they were in London.

He drove a hundred yards and pulled up beside the general store. 'I won't be long.'

'Where are you going?'

'I want to get one or two things. We'll have to take good care of you from now on.'

Now that there was a child.

She waited in the car. A fly was caught inside the windscreen, buzzing back and forth, hurling itself against the glass. From the valley came the sound of a stick on a dustbin lid, the school bell, a sharp clanging sound coming and going in the breeze. After a few minutes a group of schoolboys came along the road, all ages and sizes, shouting and laughing. They looked into the car as they passed. The girls from Julia's class were behind them. Brightly coloured frocks and shiny plastic shoes. Dragging their feet in the dust, all the disappointment of the morning written in their wide brown faces.

They too looked into the car. She smiled at them but their faces were still, looking at a white woman sitting on a towel. No-one they knew.

He was carrying a box, balancing it in the crook of his elbow as he unlocked the boot. She got out of the car.

'What did you buy?'

He grinned broadly and opened the flaps of the box. 'Presents for the little mother.'

The box was full, rows of canned fruit, condensed milk, bottles of orange concentrate, dusty tins of baby powder, tissues, Vaseline; everything the shopkeeper stocked piled a foot deep into the box.

'But I don't need all that, Patrick!'

'Of course you do, I want my son to have a good start.'

19

She grew big. At the Club, in other people's houses, her condition became a topic of conversation. Clare Bowen would relate how she had known it.

'I just took one look at her and I knew straight off.'

The other women smiled and nodded. They had all felt the foetus kick, taking it in turns to lay curious hands on her belly, smiling knowingly.

'Motherhood will be the making of you, my dear.'

'You'll be fulfilled.'

'One of us.'

Dr Patel probed the swelling with cool brown fingers. 'Everything is progressing normally, Mrs Whitman.'

He said the same on each of his weekly visits, listening to his stethoscope and nodding to himself.

Clare Bowen made a set of cotton maternity dresses, comfortable floral sacks for Julia to waddle in.

'Doesn't she look a picture?' Clucking, patting the lump. 'It's put some colour in your cheeks, Julia. I knew pregnancy would suit you.'

The thought crept in unexpectedly, Vera Ellis's own words. 'I'm sure Donald would insist on a white doctor if it were me.'

And she imagined her own mother's voice in her ear. 'How can you think of it, Julia? A black man's fingers touching you there. It isn't right!'

Patrick had no doubts about Doctor Patel. 'He knows his job, Julia. He's one of the Chaachi facilities. Look at all the little bushheads you see running around. They look well enough, don't they?'

Bartholomew brought her flowers.

'Birds of paradise.' He laid them in her arms. 'For a most beautiful lady.'

Long green stems enfolded beaks of flame-coloured petals, the stamens thrust forth, dancing. For a moment she was lost, blushing.

'They're lovely, Bartholomew, I'll go and find a vase for them.'

Awkwardly she rose from the chair, conscious of her swollen body and his eyes on her face, smiling.

'Tell me one thing.' He stopped her.

'Yes?'

'Do you think I stole these flowers?'

'Why, of course not.'

'Honestly?' Teasing her. 'Honestly?'

'I did wonder where they came from.'

He chuckled. 'Mr and Mrs Bowen have a large number growing in their garden. One armful will not be missed.' He paused to light a cigarette. He smoked the same brand as Clare Bowen, cheap local tobacco, thinly rolled.

'And now I want something from you.'

'Yes?' She felt suddenly uneasy. Something in his face warned her. As if the role he played, sitting casually on the veranda chair, had subtly altered.

'I have a friend. He is far from home. There is no work for him in his village and so he works here on the estate, picking the tea.'

'I see.' Julia wondered what was coming.

'He has been here for two years and in all that time he has not been home.'

'Two years is a long time,' said Julia carefully.

'Now he has heard that his mother is dying but still he may not go home.'

'Why not?'

'The fare is two hundred shillings.'

Ten pounds. Bartholomew's look was steady.

'That's a lot of money.'

He continued to look at her.

'Perhaps I could lend it to him,' she said. 'He could pay me back when he has had time to save up.'

She went into the bedroom and took the money from the wallet in her handbag. I should not do this, she thought. I should not give him money. She stayed in the bedroom, holding the notes and watching herself in the mirror. The bulge of her stomach looked grotesque.

What would he do if I did not give it to him?

Through the open doors of the house she heard his cough. A false, impatient cough.

She hurried outside and laid two bright green notes, one hundred shillings each, on the coffee table.

Bartholomew smiled.

'They make them in England,' he said.

'What?'

'The bank notes. The quality is excellent, don't you think?' He pocketed the money, the soft paper rolled in his fingers, like old linen.

She arranged the birds of paradise on the dining room table. At supper the tall flowers towered over their plates.

'Do you like the flowers, Patrick?' she asked, determined that he would not ignore them.

'I'd like them better out of sight. How can I see you through that forest?'

'I think they're pretty.'

'I don't want flowers on the table.' He picked up the vase and dumped it on the sideboard behind him. 'They could be full of insects. We can't have you feeding doo-doos to my son.'

My son. The lump in her lap. 'His' son. Patrick shouted to Francis, a stream of Swahili; the servant scuttled away with the vase.

20

Tied to the house, denied her classroom, time stood still. The only progress in the world was in her swelling womb. The boredom exhausted her; she felt continually tired, irritable, the smallest sounds annoyed her. She snapped at the servants, chiding Francis for his cough and then hastening to apologise, until the bewildered man took to running for the kitchen each time a cough threatened in his throat.

The long days hung hot and vacant. She tried to think of the child. The arrival of a cot from the Coast prompted her to rearrange the guest room which was to become a nursery. She borrowed old magazines from the Club and dreamed of soft carpet, of delicately flowered wallpaper and almond-pink paintwork.

'You can't have wallpaper, dear,' Clare Bowen told her. 'We don't use it out here, the humidity makes it come unstuck.'

'And doo-doos get into the cracks,' added Vera.

She wrote to Harry, could he send her a litre of almond-pink paint? It arrived within a fortnight, unloaded from the Beechcraft and brought straight to the house by Kangeni.

'Patrick says you must have this straight away.'

Full of excitement Julia tore open the carton. Pinned inside was a brief note from Harry. 'I couldn't get the shade you wanted. I hope this will do.'

The paint was cream-coloured, the same off-white that covered every window-frame and door-frame in the house.

Julia's eyes filled with tears.

'Mrs Whitman.' Kangeni put out his hand. 'You mustn't weep over a little thing like this.'

'Why not?' Julia left him standing on the lawn. The torn carton containing the paint tin stood at his feet.

Julia wrote to thank Harry for his trouble. 'You have no idea how much the colour mattered. It is these small details that rule our lives in Ledorot.'

Bartholomew came less often, his visits were shorter. She had the feeling, more than ever, that the house on the hill had become her prison. Her keepers were many-faced; the heat that exhausted her, the sack-shaped cotton smocks that constrained her unfamiliar body; time that dripped as slowly as her sweat in the airless nights; Patrick's heavy hand on her belly, his stained smile as the foetus kicked; Bartholomew, who came less often, whose manner had changed, from a deft-handed friend to that of gaoler, watching, smiling as a scientist might smile at his experiment.

'Can you help my friend once more?' He was back in the canvas chair, sipping his drink, his fourth finger delicately poised above the glass. 'His mother's funeral was so expensive.' She had heard of their funerals, feasting and drinking that lasted a whole day and night and sometimes even another whole day and night. She-beens. Half the pickers turning up too drunk to see the leaves.

'Isn't it a waste? To spend so much on a funeral?' she asked.

Bartholomew smiled, an unkind, ironic smile. 'Does motherhood make you mean, Julia?'

He leaned towards her and very deliberately patted her stomach. 'How much will you expect this little one to pay for your funeral?'

Julia pushed his hand away. 'No more than he can afford.'

'Well then!' cried Bartholomew. 'My friend can afford

nothing. So it is up to you. How much will you give him?'

His dark eyes were close to her face. 'How much did you pay for your mother's funeral?'

Julia did not answer. She remembered the undertaker's bill, four hundred and seventy-five pounds plus VAT, with ten per cent discount for payment within a month.

He lit a cigarette while she fetched her wallet. She noticed the carton on the table, Dunhill International, and a new throw-away lighter that had replaced the boxes of matches.

She gave him twenty pounds, laying the notes out flat on the cool glass top of the table. He gathered them absently, folding them away without a glance, as if the amount was of no consequence, only the acquisition.

The weather worsened. Each day was hotter than the last. Even the breeze from the tea was warm, waterlogged. Clouds glowered blackly from the hilltops, billowing like a peasant's skirts until the rain fell, a bladder bursting over the land, so hard that the water bounced off the earth and fell again like an encore with thunderous, clapping applause.

Rain brought no respite from the heat. Warmed by the baked earth, it rose, even in the darkness, to gather again as clouds, trapping the moisture-laden air against the land. She hated the rain as much as the heat, blamed it for her bloated, constipated body. Each day she thought, would be the last. She could grow no bigger, she would burst.

Nightmares ravelled her sleep. The growth in her womb was a monster, a tumour masquerading as Patrick's child. Patel wouldn't know. How could he tell, with only black women – half-cows to practise on?

In her waking hours these night thoughts horrified

171

her. How could she think such things? But the images remained, Vera Ellis's mincing voice, 'If it were my baby, Donald would insist on a white doctor.'

Night after night she dreamed of Bartholomew, of his hands on her body, waking up awash, her narrow bed sodden with sweat, as drenching as the rain, until, at last, four weeks before its time, her own cloud burst, belching water on to the sheets.

It was almost dawn. Her watch was in the bathroom, too far to fetch, she must count the time on her fingers, two hundred and ten, two hundred and eleven, two hundred and . . . Patrick!

He leapt at her, clumsy with sleep, backed in dismay from the stained sheets.

'I'm going to get Vera.' Still in his pyjamas. Gravel hit the window as he spun the car.

Vera wore a white apron. 'There's no rush, my dear. You're nowhere near. You've given Patrick a dreadful fright.'

It took all day. Heat and the knotted mosquito net. The flap of servants' feet hushed in the passage. Patel had gone to his weekly clinic in Kibwezi. 'We can do without him,' said Vera, 'I've brought enough *mtotos* into the world to know a thing or two.'

Clare came soon after breakfast, bathed her face, whispered to Vera in the hall. She had brought the girl.

'Can you hear me, Julia?' Clare's voice was low, straining to be gentle. 'This is the girl Patrick has chosen for you.'

Julia opened her eyes. They had waited for an interval, a pause when Julia had fallen back onto the pillow, tears of sweat on her cheeks.

'I don't need an *ayah*.'

'She even knows a few words of English.' Clare Bowen beamed over the bed.

The girl stood behind Vera. A green pinafore pinned across a tight yellow blouse.

'I don't need an *ayah*.'

'Of course you do. You can't manage a baby up here all by yourself.' Clare pulled the sheet from where it lay crumpled at Julia's feet. 'Patrick thought you'd be pleased to have one of the girls you know.'

Once more Julia opened her eyes. Hope Njori. The one in the corner who did not understand; who had bought a bra and been sick.

'Her father is a foreman. He's very reliable.'

'I don't want an *ayah*.' She tried to sit up. 'I want to look after my baby myself.'

'But you will, dear. It's just sensible to have someone to help. Hope can deal with the nappies, give him his daily bath and so forth.'

'I don't want her.'

'Nonsense dear, Patrick has chosen her specially.'

Vera leaned forward, cupping her hands round her mouth, 'Patrick chose this one because she doesn't smell,' she whispered loudly.

The time was up. Clare bustled the girl away from Julia as the pain began again, roaring up. 'I don't want her!'

The clock on the dressing table said eleven. A tray of coffee on the bedside locker. Vera brought it. She had sent Francis to his quarters, coughing, the corners of his apron stuffed into his mouth.

In the afternoon he boiled all the linen in the house; Julia heard the clang of the tin tub over the stove, the thump of the scrubbing brush on the side of the sink; and then, through a gap in the curtains, a pantomime in the garden, Vera running out to gather in the towels and sheets from the bushes. 'You must *dhobi* again',' she cried, 'there are doo–doos in the bushes.' And Francis walking after her, heaping the linen over his shoulder, shaking his head.

It was out again within the hour, blinding white in the sun, and Julia, lying in the spare room with the pains almost constant, singled out the flap, flap of colour-drained linen, crackling like canvas sails on the line outside the window.

Tea time. Her body was a bruised bag. Whispering in the hall. Patel was still in Kibwezi, rain had made the road impassable.

'Push dear, push now.' Clare and Vera with blood on their arms.

The flannel grew warm-moist on her forehead. Smoke on Clare's breath.

Repeating the words over and over, 'Push dear, push now!' As if their rhythm would assist her. And the room going dark. And Julia crying and pushing, trying until she would explode, her body fragmenting into a thousand particles of pain and frustration and hopelessness. And then the bulb going on; the single sharp stab of light. And then, as if the light had tricked it, the last shuddering heave and the over-spread, spraddled space filled, and emptied, and filled again. Wetness on her thighs. Vera's cry, louder than her own. And the room going dark again. And silence.

They were a long time gone. When she opened her eyes it was just the bedside light. Like an ordinary evening. With the hum of visitors in the living room and now Vera too, smelling of whisky.

'Did you sleep, dear?'

And the question coming, voiding from her lips.

'Don't you remember, Julia? You knew before you went to sleep. We explained it all to you.'

And it was gin on Clare's breath, and the lighted cigarette.

And the rigour of her jaw which she had not felt, suddenly going, and the wash of tears falling over her face and her neck and even into her ears as she rolled against the pillow.

'That's right now, a few tears will do you good.'

And weeping and blubbering. 'I want to see him.' And the shaking of heads, even when she screamed, howled as the child that was not would have howled for the great swollen teats that leaked, even now, on to the bedclothes. Not all her screaming and wailing would stop their shaking heads. 'It's gone, dear, it's gone. The men have taken it away.'

Out of sight. Frozen in her mind. A shrivelled rat foetus she found in the sixth-form dissection class. His face a wide messy-tongued cave shaped to make a howl to match her own.

Patrick came later. Beer on his breath. A different man, pale, cold-skinned, sitting beside the bed.

'It was too hot. We should have sent you back to England.' Taking her hand and holding it against his face. The gentlest gesture she had known of him. 'We should have sent you home.'

And, extraordinary, after all the pain of the day, tears on his cheeks. Wet eyes. Softly she stroked his face, feeling the stubble under her fingertips. He pushed her hand aside and bent down, frowning through the tears. 'I'm so disappointed in you, Julia.'

In the middle of the night was the *ayah*. A dark shape at the end of the bed. Stirring on the ladderback chair that had been brought in for Vera the midwife, Vera of the not birth, running after the sheets when she was most needed. When it was still there, a something, pushing her legs wide, still there, something to show for the bleating and panting, a use for the *ayah* that she had not wanted and did not need.

The girl was awake. The bedlight caught the flutter of bored hands, a flash of tongue when she yawned.

Hope Njori. The one who had not understood; who had later learned to lay a table, fingered mother's china, 'Hello! Hello!' into the dead receiver. Like a prayer.

Had they pulled straws for the job of Whitman's *ayah*? Had it been a joy to see the short straw in her hand? A pleasure, gladdening to know that she would nurse a white baby, mix feeds, change nappies, have the run of the white man's house instead of picking tea?

175

A straw too short; the infant child no more than a disappointment, dead on arrival, taken by the not-midwife, tossed away, buried, a white man's refuse.

Where?

Could there be a place for such things?

She sat up, fighting the nausea to grab the girl's hand. 'Where did they take my baby?'

'It is buried.' The hand squirmed from her own. 'You should sleep now.' Standing up, making a move to plump the pillows.

She shook her head, sweat-raddled hair sticking to her face. 'I want to see him.'

'The doctor says you must rest.'

'He wasn't here.'

'Yes. He came this evening. To write the certificate.'

'I didn't see him.'

'You were asleep. He gave you the needle. See the mark on your arm here?'

'Not the doctor. The baby.'

'You must rest.'

She sank back. 'We'll keep the *ayah*,' Patrick had said. 'We'll keep the *ayah* for you.'

'What for?'

'To make sure you rest.' Vera clucking, 'You've had a bad experience, Julia. You must rest well, and eat plenty of fruit, and who knows? In a few months you might start another baby.'

21

Bartholomew waited two weeks. Physically she was almost healed. Able to walk about, slack-bellied, squeezing back into the high-heeled shoes she had abandoned when she could no longer see her feet. It was better to be tall, to cast aside the shapeless sack-dresses they had heaped upon her, to leave them for Francis to *dhobi* and wear her own things; tee shirts she had worn in London, eighteen months ago, a lifetime.

'Well, Julia, are you strong again now?'

She looked down at her clothes, the skimpy tee shirt and cotton skirt. 'I have recovered.'

'We must do it better next time.'

Her head shot up. 'We?'

'Of course, we. Wasn't that the trouble with this one? *Café au lait?*'

'What?'

'Don't you know the expression? The French have a delicate ear for these things.'

'What are you talking about?'

'The child. Was it coffee with milk, or plain black?'

Julia jumped out of her chair.

'Is that what you think?'

'Isn't it obvious?'

'No!' The word came out like a cry of pain. 'You're quite wrong.'

'How do you know? Did you see it?'

She shook her head. Vertigo. Blackness spinning

before her eyes. A coffee-coloured rat foetus. She groped for the chair and sat down again.

He waited until she opened her eyes. 'We'll do it properly next time.'

The shake of her head became a shuddering, unstoppable spasm. He was shouting at her. 'What is it? Is the idea too awful to contemplate?'

'No!'

'Good then.'

He had slapped her. Stopped her mouth.

'I will come again, Julia, when you are well. I am a patient man, I will wait until you are healed.' A hand between her thighs, gentle. Just a touch.

She stayed in the chair. Long after he had gone, Francis came out to clear away the empty glasses.

'No, leave them.' She took the glasses from his hands. 'Let the bwana find them.'

As she put them back on the table the old man shook his head. 'Eh . . .'

The glasses were there when Patrick came home, one still with its half-inch of melted ice.

Julia waited, breathless for him to notice them. Unable to speak herself, she longed for him to talk, to ask 'Who was here?' To have it out, to tell him she was afraid of the friend she had made; the boy on the veranda. She would even confess. 'It was me, I, who led him on. I misunderstood, as he did.'

But Patrick made no reference to the glasses, simply pushed them aside, as one would in a cafeteria, pushing away the evidence of the previous occupant.

Bartholomew resumed his visits, coming every day, every afternoon, just as he had done before. She made herself sit on the veranda to wait for him, trying to recall how she had felt before; the joy of seeing his confident stride across the lawn.

There was no joy, only dread, of his eyes, of the persistent question, 'Are you ready yet, Julia?'

One afternoon she tried to hide from him. Abandoning the pretence of her welcome, she stayed inside the house, hoping the closed door would send him away. He strode across the veranda and burst through the french doors. 'Julia! There you are! Were you fetching our drinks already?'

Like a miscreant child, she scuttled across the room. He remained on the threshold, legs thrust apart, his hand on the door. He had never been inside the house; not since the first day, when he had told of the shooting at the Office, had he come into the living room. She saw him look around, keen eyes on the changes she had made, the ornaments and pictures, cushions and lampshades that had come by sea from England.

He saw that she was watching him. 'But it isn't Bartlett Road, is it?' he said softly.

'What do you mean?'

'All the little touches – these, and these.' His hands wandered over the porcelain ornaments. 'These would have looked better at Bartlett Road.'

He was right. She looked again at the ornaments, seeing them with fresh eyes. They were out of place. The house on the hill was better plain, as Patrick had it, or, even better, decorated only with photographs, as Vera Ellis had her living room, littered with fading snaps and portraits, memories of Ceylon, relics, just as Ledorot was a relic, of times long gone.

'Come, Julia, shall we sit outside where it is cool?'

She followed him out, wondering what excuse she could give today. For once he did not settle into Patrick's chair but remained standing, lounging against a pillar. His fingers traced the courses of the brick, idly following the lines of mortar.

'I feel I am no longer welcome, Julia.'

She said nothing, but watched the slow-moving finger.

'I am beginning to change my mind about you.' He turned and pointed his finger towards her. 'I thought you were not the kind that likes a black boy for a pet.'

Feeling light-headed, Julia moved across the veranda and lowered herself into a chair.

'Well? Have you nothing to say?'

'You were never a pet,' she whispered.

'But not quite a friend either, is that it? And now that you have grown tired I can be discarded, dismissed, without the awkwardness that accompanies such circumstances between white people?'

Julia could think of nothing to say. The truth was too complicated.

'Well?' he demanded.

She ran her hands over her face. 'What is it that you want, Bartholomew?'

He answered quickly, as if she had given him a cue. 'I want five hundred and eighty shillings.'

She looked up in astonishment. 'Whatever for?'

'You owe it to me.'

He came forward and put his hand on her knee. She pushed his hand away but he put it back and began to move slowly up her thighs, his fingers slipped under her skirt.

'Bartholomew!'

'What is the trouble? You liked it enough before.'

'Bartholomew, stop!' She pushed him away, trying to raise herself from the chair.

His hand was back before she could stand. 'Five hundred and eighty shillings and I will ask for nothing else.' He squeezed the skin at the top of her thighs. She squirmed away from him. 'Please! I can't bear it.' Tears sprang into her eyes.

'It is I who am saying please, Julia.' His voice was low, his breath warm on her face.

'Let me go. I'll get you the money.'

Five hundred and eighty shillings was the price of a second-hand motorbike that had stood outside the general store for a month. She had seen the For Sale notice that dangled from the handlebars. The motorbike had belonged to a man in Kibwezi, one of the African assistants who had managed to save up for a car. For a five per cent commission the storekeeper had let him park it outside the store, to be sprayed with dust and doused with rain until someone found five hundred and eighty shillings to pay for it.

Bartholomew rode up to the house, a fearsome figure in a black helmet and mirrored glasses, roaring up the drive. He stayed on the lawn, straddling the machine, stroking the chrome.

There was no threat, no reference to the ugliness of the previous day. He told her he would be driving the motorbike down to the Coast.

She tried to hide her relief.

'Will you stay down there long?'

'Just for a short visit. I have business to see to.' He smiled, his cheeks fat against the sides of the helmet. 'Perhaps there is something I could bring you?'

Julia paused.

His face was impassive, eyes hidden by the sunglasses. She pretended to think.

'No. I don't think there is anything just now. Thank you.'

He shrugged. 'I will have to leave soon.'

'Yes,' said Julia.

'You will be ready when I return.'

She looked away, out over the Rift to the plains, wallowing, silver-gold in the afternoon light.

'Let me bring you something.' He stroked the chrome. 'Perfume? Cosmetics?'

'I don't want anything, Bartholomew. I would prefer it if . . .'

He interrupted. 'What would make you happy, Julia?'

I should ask him to bring something, she thought. Face powder, writing paper. Anything. It would draw a line, crystallise the new distance between us to send

181

him on an errand; to give him the correct number of shillings and some small change for a cold drink.

He shrugged again, faceless behind the glasses. The machine burst into life. He smiled as she jumped back. Then he was gone, bouncing down towards the track. Without a wave.

22

She grew strong again. The blackness that came down
each morning when she got out of bed, or stood up
too quickly from her chair, took less time to disperse.
Unlike the blackness in their lives; unforgiveness, the
disappointment in Patrick's eyes, mirrored in her own.

His dreams were as dark as hers had been before the
birth. He would wake up shouting, clutching out for
her as she crossed the space between the beds. He was
back on the farm, the encampment in the furthest field;
confused in a dark nightmare with the baby born dead
and the black boy on the veranda. She let him press his
head against her breasts until it hurt and nursed him
back to sleep, waiting until his snore was steady before
creeping back to her own bed.

Patrick had no recollection of these nightmares. He
would complain of tiredness, of the 'damned heat' keeping him awake, even of her being restless, disturbing
him 'crashing round in the dark' when she went to the
bathroom. Julia watched his face to see if he knew the
truth but there was no sign of it, only his accusing,
disappointed eyes.

He took to leaving her alone at night, going out
with Jack Bowen and Dickie Dickinson, drinking at
the Club and then cruising the estate looking out for
'trouble'.

'We'll keep the peace on these estates if it's the last
thing we do,' the men would boast, full of beer and
bravado, leaving their women alone in the bungalows.

Julia no longer cared. She was glad to be alone, to go to bed early and listen to the rain on the roof.

The sound of Patrick's car disturbed her sleep, the slam of doors and the watchman's mumbled greeting. She burrowed deeper under the bedclothes and closed her eyes.

It was impossible to pretend. He came into the bedroom and switched on the overhead light. She felt him pull up the mosquito net, heard the creak of his bed as he sat down. She opened her eyes and found him staring at her. Blood was flowing down his chin.

She sat up. 'Whatever's the matter?'

'I fixed him,' said Patrick thickly. 'Fixed your lover boy.'

'But he's at the Coast.'

The words were out, spoken before she drew breath.

Patrick shook his head. 'No he's not. He's lying in a storm drain feeling very sorry for himself.'

She got out of bed and brought cotton wool and a bowl of warm water from the bathroom. The weight of the bowl tugged the newly-healed muscles of her stomach.

His breath was foul with beer. She turned her face away to take a gulp of air but he grabbed her hand and squeezed until water ran from the cotton wool crushed in her palm. 'I told him to stay away from my wife,' he said fiercely. 'Fucking nigger, I told him I'd kill him if he came here again.'

When he let go she began to dab gently at his lip with the cotton wool. 'Are you hurt anywhere else?'

He shook his head. 'But that woggy boy has more than a cut lip. The way he was howling I should think he's missing a few teeth.' He pushed her hand away. 'I found him on the track. The others thought he was just a picker but I knew who he was. I told him to get lost but after I dropped Dickie at home he was still there, not a hundred yards from this house. Just standing down there, looking up at the lights.'

She emptied the water into the toilet and washed her hands. When she returned he was asleep, snoring, muddy boots on the bedclothes. She pulled off the boots and brushed the soil from the blankets before getting into her own bed and turning off the light.

Bartholomew in a storm drain, unconscious perhaps, mud and insects close to his face. She wondered what he had done. Had he begun the fight, raised his hands to the drunken white man? Or was it his expression, the bland ironic smile that had provoked Patrick's fist?

In the morning Francis was late with the tea. When he arrived Patrick shouted for an explanation but there was no answer. The old man wheezed loudly and sighed as he tied up the net. Patrick shouted again and Francis stood still, looking sadly at the floor.

'Eh?' said Patrick.

'Ehhhhh . . .' said the old man at last, raising his head and looking, not at Patrick, but at Julia.

'He wants to apologise,' said Patrick. 'He is sorry for the trouble his son has caused.'

Julia looked away. She wondered how the old man saw her. Had he been proud of his son, sitting with the memsahib on the veranda? Or had he seen the way it would go, the mutual seduction, his son flattered by her white skin and she by Bartholomew's easy charm, all the mysteries of Africa in his round brown face. He had mended her house and she had given him friendship; he had stroked her legs and she had given him money. They were a microcosm of a continent, the clash of reflections, civilisations as thin as veneer, as bright and misleading as a dancer's mask, a rhythm too subtle for white men's feet. 'Eh . . .' said the old man and Patrick called it an apology. 'Eh . . .' echoed Julia. She stared up, trying to catch the old man's eyes, but he was looking down again, watching his own feet as he shuffled through the bedroom door.

Harry stared at his desk. The fan creaked above his head, clucking and squeaking as it stirred the sluggish air, causing a continuous flutter of paper.

Earlier that morning his fountain pen had leaked into his pocket, a bright blue dribble on his handkerchief.

'You' lucky it does not come on to your clothes, Mr Thomas.' Mrs Holu had twittered around him, whisking the handkerchief from his hand. 'That no good to you now, Mr Thomas.'

No good to me, thought Harry ruefully, but someone will find a use for it. He fully expected to see the handkerchief, folded so that the stain would not show, peeping from the liftboy's pocket. And who could blame them?

The liftboy was also a night porter. Muthaga had given him permission to stay on the premises at night. There was no pay for any extra duty he might perform; answering the telephone, listening for intruders – only the chance to sleep on the dry floor space behind the reception desk.

Harry had learned of the arrangement by chance, coming in early for a meeting and finding the liftboy asleep, like a small animal, curled on a grey blanket behind the desk.

'This must be stopped!' he cried to Muthaga. 'This is outright exploitation.'

Muthaga shrugged. 'Would you rather he slept on the street?'

'Surely he has somewhere to go?'

Muthaga's voice conveyed more than his usual bitterness.

'Apparently not.'

'Don't you have a home?' Harry inquired of the liftboy, who had rapidly woken up and stood to attention, jamming his battered janitor's cap over his ears.

'Right here, Mistah Thomas,' the boy said loudly. 'I am keeping an eye while the big men go to bed.'

'But how do you sleep?' He looked at the thin blanket on the floor. 'Don't you get cold?'

'Not cold. Very warm. More better than outside.'

Muthaga smiled. 'You see, Harry, Chaachi looks after its workers.'

Harry shook his head. 'I shall write to Head Office.'

Muthaga gripped his arm. 'Why must you interfere? The boy has a place to sleep, Chaachi has a night porter.' He waved his free hand. 'Surely everyone is satisfied.'

'Hardly satisfied,' said Harry. 'Hardly satisfied.'

Muthaga's eyes bulged. 'Can't you see, white man? The Company doesn't need a liftboy. Does anyone in England employ liftboys these days? If you interfere they will look at their payroll and say he is redundant.'

The liftboy interrupted, straightening his cap once more and raising his hand in salute.

'Liftboy reporting for duty, sah!' He grinned. 'Night porter has gone to bed!'

Harry smiled at him.

'English more better every day,' said the boy, still grinning.

Harry nodded, noticing that Muthaga had turned, his expression full of distaste, as though an unpleasant smell had entered the room.

Harry sighed and looked once more at the gently fluttering papers on his desk. He had interfered. He had arranged for an old mattress to be laid behind the reception desk, and brought a blanket of his own from home. Within days the mattress had gone and though Harry's blanket remained, the original grey one no longer appeared. In their place came a transistor radio, a pink plastic case that was rarely far from the boy's ear.

Muthaga put his head round the door.

'There is a lady in Reception, asking for you.'

'Who is it?'

Muthaga shrugged. 'An English lady. They all look the same to me.'

A white woman? Someone from Ledorot? Julia?

Muthaga watched from the doorway as Harry ran a

comb through his hair and put on his jacket. 'I hope you are not disappointed.'

Harry pushed past him and ran down the corridor, through the double doors, past the reception desk. A woman sat in the armchair by the lift. A wide-brimmed hat. She was rising, smiling, holding out her hand. 'Clare Bowen,' she boomed. 'We met once or twice at the Club.'

Harry gaped. 'Of course, I remember you well.'

'I'm here for a bit of shopping,' she said brightly. 'Jack's gone to see some tiresome man about fishing tackle, so I thought you and I could have lunch together. I gather you don't get much of a social life down here.'

He took her to the café across the road. They sat at a table on the pavement under a coloured umbrella. Mrs Bowen settled herself into a chair and called the waiter to the table.

'I'm going to have a gin,' she announced, 'what about you?'

Harry glanced at his watch. It was just after eleven. 'I'll have a beer.'

The waiter brought the drinks and Mrs Bowen sent him back twice, the first time for ice and the second for a bottle of bitters that she shook over her glass until the gin was marbled with red, like a bloodshot eye.

'Cheers.' She raised her glass.

Harry raised his in return. 'Cheers, Mrs Bowen.'

'Call me Clare.' She stared around at the other tables, turning her face away as if what she was about to say was of no consequence. 'Have you heard about Julia's boy?' Her eyes swivelled back in time to catch Harry's expression. 'Disgraceful business.'

She emptied her glass and signalled the waiter for another. 'Why don't you have something a little stronger? How about a whisky chaser?'

It was ordered before he could reply. 'Disgraceful business,' she repeated.

'I don't . . .' Harry began.

'Of course, you wouldn't. It was only a day or two ago.'

'What happened?'

'Well, he got what was coming to him of course. The wonder is that Patrick waited so long – '

'Who?'

She stopped in surprise. 'But you know about Julia's boy, surely?'

'I don't, I haven't been up there for a long time.'

She looked at him over her glass. 'But you used to come up regularly.'

'Yes I did, when Patrick was on his own. Once Julia was there it seemed an intrusion.'

Clare Bowen smiled and patted his hand. 'I quite understand, Harry. She is a difficult girl to be friendly with.'

Harry shook his head. 'I didn't mean that. It's just that with them being newly-weds, and then Julia being pregnant, it didn't seem right to go barging up there as often as I used to.'

A waiter interrupted to offer Harry his change, a shower of coins on a tray. In the centre of the tray was an advertisement for beer. Harry noticed that most of the coins had been spread over the centre picture, where they were hard to see. He picked out the silver coins and left the waiter a string of coppers.

Clare Bowen's eyes were sharp. 'You've left him an awful lot, Harry.'

'I know,' said Harry quietly.

Clare Bowen opened her mouth to comment but then leaned forward, as if remembering a more interesting topic.

'You know she lost the baby?'

He nodded. 'Patrick told me over the phone. He sounded quite cut up.'

'Nasty business.' Clare took a swallow of gin. 'I'm not a religious woman, but it's hard not to feel that there's some divine retribution in what happened.'

'Retribution for what?'

'She made friends with a boy from the township,' said Clare. She fumbled in her handbag for a packet of cigarettes. 'A young kaffir. God only knows what they found to talk about. It's been going on for months. She invites him up every afternoon while Patrick's at work. Everyone knows about it of course. Best piece of gossip for years. Improved in the telling too – there are women at the Club who refuse to speak to her. Not that she notices. She hardly ever goes there.'

Clare struck a match and lit a cigarette, screwing her face against the first wash of smoke.

'When she got pregnant we thought she'd settle down. People were willing to give her another chance. But she kept on seeing this boy, she even had the cook baking biscuits for him. And now, since she lost the baby, she's been giving him money.'

She paused to gulp her gin and puff at the cigarette. Her lipstick had left an imprint on the glass, a pink, creased kiss mark under the rim.

'It's not that I don't understand,' she went on, 'Patrick is limited enough, poor boy. They always are, these local chaps. My Jack is the same.' She smiled at Harry. 'You know what I mean, Harry, not quite like us. But this, this Bartholomew.' She spoke as if it were the name of an unpleasant species. 'I don't know how she could stoop to it!'

Harry tried to interrupt, 'Stoop to what?'

The woman ignored his question. Harry had the feeling that she had told the story over and over, repeating it until she could recite without hesitation. 'Jack didn't want me to know about this latest business; I got it from my houseboy. I can always tell when there's something on his mind and that day he was being more woolly-headed than usual. I had it out of him in no time.' She shifted in her chair, Harry caught a glimpse of white, dimpled thigh.

'What happened?'

190

She took out another cigarette and lit it from the end of the first.

Two more cigarettes were smoked through before he knew the story, embellished with details and commentary, sharp asides and pauses between the puffs of smoke and gulps of the dark, blood-brown gin.

Mrs Bowen took his arm as they walked back to the Office. 'I'm quite fond of the girl really but she's been so silly, she just will not take any advice. The business with the baby was a dreadful tragedy, but you know, there was potential there. She could have been the making of Patrick Whitman.'

'Well,' said Harry, 'perhaps they will make a go of it now, after losing the baby and everything. Perhaps it will bring them closer.'

Clare shook her head. 'No. It's too late. She's made a fool of him. He won't forgive her for that.'

She planted a moist kiss on Harry's cheek. As he stepped into the lift he wondered which it was that Patrick would not forgive, the lost child or the township boy?

Returning to his office, he found a message from Patrick on his desk. He had dictated to Mrs Holu over the telephone. 'Charter coming up on Saturday. Room for another passenger. Can you squeeze in?'

No word of the fight with the township boy. No word of Julia. But an appeal nevertheless.

23

Harry shared the Beechcraft with the Bowens, strapped beside a huge cylinder for a drying machine, cartons of groceries, a box of video films for the Club. Clare Bowen squeezed into the seat in front of him, with Jack Bowen beside her.

Harry tried to make conversation but it was difficult to hear above the roar of the engines. Clare shared out coffee from a thermos, splashing packets of sugar in the carton at Harry's feet. Jack Bowen spent the journey sorting out a box of fishing flies. Harry watched him examine the bright, delicate morsels against the light. Almost concealed by intricate patterns of fur and feather, the fine steel hooks glinted in the sun.

Patrick was waiting at the airstrip.

'My good friend, Harry. It is great to see you.' He pumped Harry's hand and made no reference to the split in his lip and the purple bruise that stretched from his eye to his ear.

Waiting for them on the lawn, Julia was paler than ever, china-white skin against a pale blue dress, and hair scraped back in a ponytail that exposed the veined skin of her neck.

She greeted Harry quietly, brushing his cheek with a kiss and offering her own, eyes down, so that in the brief second of the exchange he mistakenly kissed her eyes, soft lashes against his lips.

'I never saw the baby,' she said, as they went into the house.

Harry caught his breath. She looked up at him, blank-faced.

'It's all right, we can speak of it. No-one in this house thinks of anything else.'

The old guest room had been turned into a nursery. A mobile of birds, cut from silver foil, hung in the window. Julia showed him the cot in the corner. 'It's empty, as you can see.'

Harry put down his bag and held out his hand. 'I am so sorry about what happened, Julia. It was a terrible tragedy.'

Her voice was suddenly harsh. 'It was born dead. Not black or milky coffee, just dead!'

Harry took a step backwards, as if she had slapped him.

'I'm sorry.' Her voice was normal again. 'I asked Patrick to invite you up here. I thought that at least you would say it was a tragedy, not divine retribution – which is what the women think – or carelessness, as Patrick seems to think.'

She walked to the door. 'He has kept the *ayah*, you know. You'll see her wandering about. Patrick says I must find an occupation for her.'

Harry walked across and took her hand. 'Perhaps I shouldn't have come, Julia, it's too soon.'

'No. I'm glad you've come. It might help us all to see how crazy we are.' Suddenly she gestured grandly round the room. 'I hope you'll be comfortable.'

There were flowers beside the bed. Harry smiled.

'Thank you for the flowers, they're very welcoming.'

She smiled for the first time. 'Patrick doesn't like flowers. He thinks they bring insects into the house. He'll probably tell you I killed the baby with birds of paradise.'

Harry shook his head. 'Julia, that's crazy talk.'

As she left the room, Harry noticed the tendons of her neck, standing out like stretched rubber bands.

He sat on the bed. It was all worse, much worse than

194

he had imagined. Outside, the sun glared down on the garden. He could hear the call of the hornbills, starlings chattering in the acacia, but he felt no enchantment; only the weight of the heat, the still air trapped in the house, oppressive and sour.

24

Patrick's line swished back and forth. His raised arms revealed fresh sweat stains in the folds of his shirt. 'Have you seen him?'

'No,' said Harry. 'I heard about him from Mrs Bowen.'

'Ach, she's got a big mouth.' Patrick flicked his wrist and lifted the fly off the water.

'She told me about the fight you had. That you whipped the boy and left him in a storm drain.'

'He had it coming to him.'

The fly dropped silently on to the water, causing barely a ripple.

'Is it true?'

'Is what true?' Patrick raised the rod and the line swished upwards.

'That this Bartholomew visits Julia?'

'Maybe.' The fly hit the water with a plosh, loud in the silence.

Minutes passed before he spoke again

'Harry, I tell you, I don't know what to think any more. I know Ledorot must have seemed a bit quiet after London. I thought she would get used to it, I thought she'd make friends with the other women and settle down. Instead she makes friends with this bushhead.'

The boat rocked gently on the flat water.

'So I got her a job, teaching in the pickers' school. I thought it would make her forget about the kaff, keep her occupied until we could get some children.'

'I gather she made quite a go of the teaching.'

'Yah, but it didn't get rid of the kaffir. When she became pregnant we all breathed a sigh of relief. I was sure it would be all right then, with the baby and all to think of.'

He sat down abruptly, his voice suddenly whining, peevish. 'I was so excited about that kid, Harry. A son of my own. Little Patrick, Mark II.

'I couldn't believe it. After all those months, all the friendship she was given, the women making her dresses, giving her good advice, even Kangeni asking me every day "How is she?" After all that, she couldn't do it right. A simple little thing like that. Kaffir women do it every year, squatting in a field, back at work the next day. But not Julia.'

A pied kingfisher hovered near the boat, shuddering its wings like a huge insect buzzing against the sky.

'Perhaps she should have gone to a hospital?'

'Why? She had everything right here. If the kaffirs can do it here why can't she? We even had an *ayah* lined up for her. One of the girls she'd been teaching. But no, Julia didn't want an *ayah*.' Patrick slapped his legs and took hold of the rod again. 'She'd have run a mile if she'd had to scrape shit off his nappies. But Julia didn't want an *ayah*.

'She is so stubborn. All this business with the kaffir boy. What was I supposed to do? For months I ignored it, thinking she'd see that it was wrong. She used to taunt me, Harry, as if I was some sort of dummy. I'd find his leavings, his old fag ends, his empty glasses. The son of my servant! How could she do that to me?'

The kingfisher plunged suddenly, as if jerked by an invisible wire, down into the water and out again, a wriggling fish in its beak.

At the same time Patrick's line pulled taut and for a minute all conversation ceased as he hauled in a plump, glistening trout.

'I'll bet you ten bob that's a kilo!' cried Patrick.

Harry laughed. 'I wouldn't waste my money.'

Patrick gutted the fish swiftly over the side and packed his catch away in the cool box.

'She's been giving him money. Did Clare tell you that?'

Harry nodded.

'What am I supposed to make of that?'

The kingfisher came near again, hovering and dipping above the golden afternoon water.

'Was it her money to give?'

Patrick nodded. 'She got it from her mother.'

'Her mother died just before you came out, is that right?' Harry asked.

Again Patrick nodded. 'These days I wonder if that was the only reason she came – because she had nothing to stay for.'

Harry watched him casting out once more, feeling the gentle rock as the boat moved in rhythm with his arm. 'Perhaps things would be different if she wasn't left alone so much?'

'But I have to go to work,' Patrick retorted too quickly, as if he had rehearsed the answer.

'Yes, but today, for instance, it's Sunday and yet we've left her alone in the house with nothing to do but brood.'

'She was glad to see the back of us.'

Harry looked away. The sun was slowly subsiding across the sky. On the horizon the clouds were gathering, low slung puffs stringing out into a line.

Patrick laid down his rod. 'I wouldn't say it to anyone else, Harry, but I am fond of her. Even after all this. I just want her to be a wife to me. Not to have all these strange ideas. Just to look after my house and give me healthy sons. Is it so much to ask?'

'You must give her time to heal,' said Harry. 'I think the *ayah* upsets her, she's a constant reminder of the baby.'

'I want her to remember!' Patrick cried. 'I want her to get it right next time.'

Harry plucked at the rim of his sunhat. How to

persuade him? How to make him send the *ayah* away to restore the house to some sort of peace? 'Surely it's a waste of money,' he said finally. 'To keep the *ayah* when there is no work for her.'

Patrick shook his head. 'It's not a waste of money. As long as that *ayah* is there, Julia will remember what she has to do. Don't you worry about the money. That *ayah* is worth every cent.'

They rowed back to the shore just as it was getting dark. The fishermen were waiting for them on the bank. They waded in to pull up the boat and Patrick was left to tie it down while they helped Harry carry the tackle back to the car. When it was done they stood near him, waiting in silence.

'Did you get your ten bob's worth then?' asked Patrick.

Harry dug into his pockets and found a handful of change. Not quite ten shillings. The men did not blink as he counted every coin he had into their waiting palms.

25

The first time she heard it, she went outside to wait on the lawn, anxiously watching the rise where he would come up, head first, from the long grass.

He did not come. She went back inside and watched the garden through the window.

Twice, three times, she heard it, like a menacing insect, back and forth below the ridge, filling the air with its high staccato whine; baiting her, leading her out to look, to stand at the edge and look down where she could see nothing for the long grass that had grown back thicker and more impenetrable since the cutting.

It was almost mid-day when it stopped. Not fading as it had done before, dying off into the tea, but ceased as if a key had been turned, shutting off the engine. She went out to the lawn, scattering the starlings that had come for the pineapple, the hard core that Francis put out automatically now, breakfast for the memsahib, fruit for the birds – part of his routine.

'Hello Julia.'

He had come from the back of the house, white plimsolls silent on the path.

'Did I frighten you?' He stood too close, casting his shadow over her. 'My apologies.'

His face was covered with bruises, purple discolouration showing through the pigment of his skin. He walked to his chair with a limp; his left plimsoll was unlaced to make room for a layer of bandage.

'I won't stay long.' After sitting and staring at her for a moment.

'Actually . . .' She gathered her courage. 'It's rather awkward for you to visit just now.'

'Rather awkward?' he repeated. There was a gap in the row of straight white teeth. He saw her look and rolled back his lip so that she would see the wound in the gum.

'I mean, it's lunchtime. I'm expecting my husband,' Julia lied.

'Of course.' Throwing up his hands. 'I must not be here when the bwana comes. Silly of me to come at the wrong time.'

'I'm sorry he hurt you,' said Julia.

'You are sorry?' he repeated in a high sing-song voice, mocking her. 'Everybody is sorry. Even my father is sorry. Do you know he will not speak to me? My father is ashamed.' He pointed to the gap in his teeth. 'You see this? I have lost one of my teeth. And this?' pointing to his bandaged foot. 'Today is the first day I am able to walk. And all for you.'

'I'm sorry. I didn't know he would go after you. I thought you were down at the Coast.'

'My visit was postponed.' He got up and stood beside her. 'But I hear you have a visitor.'

He bent down, she could see tiny droplets of sweat on his upper lip. 'Is he better than Patrick?' he whispered.

Julia turned away.

'Is he?'

'I don't know what you mean.'

Bartholomew bent closer still. His breath was a warm breeze on her face. 'It is just too late to be prim with me, Julia.'

She wanted to push him away, to reach up and dig her nails into the dark, beguiling eyes.

He straightened his back to look down on her, the stretched fibres of his jeans were close to her eyes, minutely visible, the threat palpable in the rise and bulge of his body inside them.

'How much do you want, Bartholomew?'

The answer was quick and sure. 'Eight hundred shillings.'

'But I don't have that much ! I've given you practically everything.'

'You have it in your wallet.'

It was true, she had exactly eight hundred shillings, all that was left of the bundle of coloured notes she had changed for her sterling.

'It's got to stop, Bartholomew, I can't give you any more. People will talk.'

'Ha!' It was a shout. 'So that's it. You don't like people to talk.' His face closed, shut like a trap. He held out his hand, clicked his fingers at her. 'Eight hundred shillings.'

She shook her head, turning towards him, ready to hit out, slap, punch, push him away but his hand was in her lap, a swift sharp movement thrusting his fist into her groin.

'Wise up white lady.'

She cried out. The fist twisted up against her, sending pain deep into her body.

Then he was gone; straight through the house, plimsolls squeaking unevenly on the polished floor.

She waited, panting, for the pain to subside, for her thundering heart to still, and then, moving slowly, she picked up her chair and carried it out on to the grass. She placed it in the shade of the acacia, where she could look down over the ridge and see the bike pass along the track.

She sat for a long time. The hill was silent, nothing but birdsong and the click and hum of insects in the grass. Sunlight dappled her arms and legs, like a disease of the skin. Below the ridge the grass whispered dryly. She waited for an hour, listening for the bike, the quick kick and roar as he rode away.

More than an hour; the sun no longer overhead but tilting through the leaves, a change in the light signalling the passing of noon. There'd been no sound, no kick and roar, nothing but the drone and buzz of flies and Mshoki singing to himself in the kitchen.

He was still there!

She was up before the thought had fully formed, tossing aside the chair, charging across the veranda, through the living room, surprising Francis with his broom in the passage. The suitcase was on the bed, the dolls' house gone as she had known it would be. Grabbing her shoes, stuffing her wallet into her handbag, she ran out through the back. Along the path by the vegetable garden, past the quarters, an unknown *bibi* staring from the step, and on, down through the long grass at the back and into the tea. He was waiting for her on the first terrace, truncated by the bushes, a half body hurrying away as she approached. The heavy track of the bike, even the twisted print of his sprained foot was visible in the dust.

He started the engine, sat astride, rode a few yards and paused to look back. The flat pieces of the house were bundled under his arm. She ran along the track. He let the space between them grow smaller, rode a few yards and waited, then rode for a few yards more, filling the air with the roar and pause of the engine, his progress marked by a broken ribbon of dust above the path.

Stones in her shoes, a blister weeping, her breath whimpering out of her, she hurried on, hemmed in by the tea that crowded up against her arms as she passed. The path wound round and round, the tyre marks showing a clear zigzag print on the murram, eddies where he had paused, prints where he had put down his feet, favouring the right leg.

At last she reached the bottom, limping herself now, against the stinging blister, He had led her into the township. She slowed a little, shocked by the strangeness of the place.

The township was quiet, square huts set in the dirt, row after row; curious faces appeared in doorways. She followed the tyre tracks and found the bike propped against a wall. Bartholomew was smiling behind a door that swung open to greet her. He was sitting on the floor, drinking from a plastic beaker; the pieces of the dolls' house were propped beside him, out of reach unless she leaned across. She let herself sit down. Her legs were red with dust. He refilled the beaker from a carton that stood in a shallow trough of water in the corner. It was milk, lukewarm. She guzzled, letting it wash the dust from her mouth and throat.

He unlaced his right plimsoll, revealing a threadbare sock, the heel pushing through like a smooth brown skull. The bandage was streaked with dust. He took time to take off his shirt, spreading his arms to show her the tight muscles of his chest. The large-buckled belt clattered to the floor.

She made a dive for the parcel. Missed. He caught her from behind, pinned her arms. She started to scream, slapping, scratching whatever she could reach. He dragged her across the floor; a glimpse of the street through the open door. A crowd was gathering, round heads echoing the round 'ooh' of mouths opened in surprise and laughter. He kicked it shut but it bounced open again.

'Now you are ready.'

The buttons of her dress sprung easily; she heard the shriek of material ripping. Strong hands forced her down, forced her legs to open, pushing her down, as it had been on the rock and not so, more and less and worse as she tried to struggle and thumped useless elbows against the floor; worse and better with the pain of the not-birth and raw, unhealed skin. She tried to kick but he was there already, thrusting fast, like a dog. His face almost against hers, eyes crossed, a strange mixture of surprise and helplessness and, only seconds after it began, it was done. He rolled away across the floor.

She raised her head. The door hung wide open to the street but there was no-one outside: as if the crowd had withdrawn, guided by a collective shame that overcame their interest in the spectacle.

'Where is it?' He was pulling up his trousers, standing gingerly on the bandaged foot.

'What?' Her voice seemed to come from a distance.

'The money.'

'In my bag.'

He took out the wallet and dropped the bag on the floor. Then he went outside, tucking his shirt as he went. The door banged. Her face was wet, she felt cold, the hard cement floor seemed to drag the warmth from her body.

He was back.

'How is it with you?' A plimsolled foot under her chin.

She pulled closer to the wall but he squatted beside her, put his index finger directly on to her nipple.

The finger pressed, her eyes filled with tears at the pain.

'What do you want?'

'Want? Nothing! I have it all, the whole eight hundred shillings. And you have something in return. Not only what you so much enjoyed, but a lesson well learned.'

The finger was like a knife. He beamed at her, the gap in his teeth like an open gate into the dark cave of his mouth. Then his hand was between her thighs again, the horror starting over, a searing dry pain as he thrust in, thumping her head against the concrete. A nigger, a servant boy laying his seed in her. Vomit spilled from her mouth, a patch of spewed milk such as an infant would leave.

Once more he stood to zip his trousers, grinning.

'Please let me go.' She could barely focus her eyes.

'Of course! Nobody will stop you. Nobody wants you here.'

'And the dolls' house?'

'Take it, take it! What would I want with a model house, when I have all this?' Gesturing to the hut. 'Take your model, Julia, and remember this place.'

He laughed as he went, loud African 'Ha ha' along the street.

26

'For God's sake, why haven't they closed the curtains?'

A quarter of a mile ahead, the house shone out like a lighthouse above the tea, lights burning in every window, beaming down across the track.

Patrick stopped the car. There was no moon but the horizon was distinct against the stars. He wound down the window and they listened.

Nothing; the ordinary night sounds, a dog barking somewhere in the valley, the singing of the crickets, the soft hushing of the tea on either side.

'I can't understand it,' said Patrick. 'The place will be teaming with mosquitoes by now.'

'Perhaps she's asleep,' suggested Harry.

'No. It's the boy's job. Every night he goes fussing around, shutting the windows and closing the curtains. Before it's dark. He wouldn't wait for her to give him an order.'

'Could it be a signal?'

Patrick gave him a quick look, his eyes gleamed large in the light from the dash.

'From Julia?'

'Yes, or the boys. They know you will see it from here.'

They sat in silence and stared at the house, searching for a sign, a message in the lighted window squares. Harry suggested that they leave the car and go up quietly on foot.

'Too dangerous,' said Patrick.

'But we have the gun.'

'Nah.. We'd be sitting ducks blundering up there, two white faces like moons sticking out of the dark.'

He turned the ignition and the car moved forward. Insects flurried like snow in the headlamps. At the foot of the drive he revved hard and they jolted upwards, swinging round near the house, parking away from the usual space under the trees.

No sound greeted them. No watchman's salute. Just the dog, yowling now, down in the valley, and the bright electric light spilling out on to the grass.

Patrick knelt on his seat and hefted his gun out of the heap of fishing tackle. Harry heard the click of cartridges and the breech snapping shut.

'Keep your eyes open.'

Harry followed him into the house. His jaws ached from the tension of listening. They walked right through the living room, through the dining room, into the kitchen and back again, switching off the lights in each empty room. Patrick bellowed Julia's name. His voice echoed but no answer came, nothing but the tick, tick of insects against bulbs and the intricate flutter of flying ants that lay dying on the floors.

The bedrooms, too, were empty, mosquito nets still tied high above the beds, the overhead lights alive with insects circling and hurling themselves against the hot bulbs.

The back door stood open to the darkness. They walked along the short path that led to the servants' quarters. No light there at all. The garden was very dark after the brightness of the house. Harry stuck out his hand, feeling his way like a blind man, and almost tripped on the wide step where the servants did their cooking and eating. Patrick banged on the door with his fist. 'Mshoki, you bastard, where are you?'

A single heavy blow burst the Yale housing from the frame and they were inside. Patrick snapped a switch and the room was filled with the dull glow of a low watt bulb. The room was sparsely furnished, a scarred table, a single bed and above it, a picture, torn from a magazine, of the Nativity. Two white serving jackets hung neatly from a hanger on a nail in the wall.

Patrick shouted in Swahili, 'Where have they gone?'

Harry had missed her completely, a young girl crouched in the furthest corner, hugging a baby in her arms.

'Where is the memsahib?'

Patrick stalked across the room, his face full of menace. 'Where is she?'

After the third or fourth try the girl seemed to emerge from her stupor and hear him. She gestured towards the valley, her outflung hand pointing south. Patrick made no answer but turned and strode out of the room, stopping so suddenly that Harry cannoned into him from behind.

'Bring the bloody woman. She can't stay here.'

Harry beckoned the girl to follow but she remained on the floor. Impatiently Patrick took her arm and yanked her to her feet. She clung obstinately to the door, one hand clutching the child and the other the shattered frame. Patrick was swift, prising loose her slender fingers in his great freckled fist and pulling her along the path.

He pushed her into the kitchen and on to a chair. 'You bloody sit there until I tell you to move.'

Patrick slammed home the back door bolts. The girl sat on the chair, bent over her child, while Harry followed Patrick on a second tour of the house, shutting windows and drawing curtains across the gaping darkness.

Most of the insects had gone with the dousing of the lights, flown through the open windows or crawled through the gaps under the skirting board. Patrick left Harry to chase the rest away and close the curtains in the main bedroom. A pile of clean laundry lay at the foot of each bed. Harry stared at the folded clothes, Patrick's pyjamas, a pair of socks, and on the other bed a blouse

211

and a pair of faded jeans. The small domestic detail seemed to mock the deserted room. Beside the pile on Julia's bed lay an open suitcase, empty. Reaching up, Harry undid the mosquito net and tucked it round the two beds, pulling it taut as he had taught his own houseboy, so that air would flow through the mesh.

In the living room Patrick was gulping whisky.

'What are we going to do?'

Patrick shook his head.

'I'll go down there and get her,' he said. 'Tomorrow.'

'Where do you think she is?'

'Down there.' He pointed as the girl had done, south, towards the township. The whisky had begun to slur his speech. He rubbed his eyes, working his fingers into the crevices of his face, like an old man.

Harry sat beside him on the sofa. 'Shouldn't we go down right away?'

Patrick shook his head. 'She's been there all day. If there was any danger it is passed now.'

'But shouldn't we try to get help?'

'From whom?' He took a gulp of whisky, straight from the bottle. 'Who would help me fetch my own wife from a kaffir's bed? Who could I ask?'

He took another gulp from the bottle. Before long he would be insensible.

Harry shook him by the shoulders. 'Patrick! She could be hurt. She could have been kidnapped!'

Patrick waved his arm around the room. 'Is there any sign of a struggle? Does this look like a house where a prisoner was taken?'

'There's an empty suitcase on the bed.'

Patrick snorted. 'It's empty now, is it?' He put his mouth round the neck of the bottle and winced as the whisky poured over his cut lip.

'What did she keep in there?'

'Some bloody dolls' house her father made.'

'A dolls' house?'

'You can picture them going, can't you? Julia riding

212

pillion on the back of his bike?' With fumbling fingers Patrick began to unlace his boots, belching as he leaned down. 'I hope she got what she wanted, silly cow.'

Harry went out to the kitchen. The girl was sitting just as they had left her, bare feet on the floor and the baby resting in the flat of her spread thighs. Harry poured a glass of water from the bottle in the fridge and she took it in silence.

'Does the baby need anything?'

'*Hapana*,' the girl said softly, dipping her finger into the water and pushing it between the baby's lips. It sucked instantly, mouth puckered around the brown finger.

Harry pulled another chair and sat facing her, resting his chin on the high back. He smiled at her and, after one or two tries, she smiled shyly back.

'Are you Mshoki's wife?' asked Harry.

She shook her head.

'Is this Mshoki's *mtoto*?'

Again she shook her head. 'No, this is my child. I am the sister of Mshoki's wife.'

Harry nodded. 'And are you visiting your sister?'

'Yes. I have come this morning. To bring news of my family.'

'What happened here today?'

She shrugged. 'I do not know all.'

'Will you tell me what you know?' Harry smiled at her again and once more she smiled back, pulling her lips down in modesty.

After some prompting she answered. Told him, in a sing-song mixture of English and Swahili, how she had come up in the morning to find Francis and Mshoki asleep in their quarters. The two bwanas (she spoke of Patrick and Harry in the third person, disassociated from the white man who sat before her) had gone out in the so early morning, drinking only coffee and setting out in the still dark. Mshoki had not risen, the bwana had said he need not, only Francis who had put on the

213

coffee pot and gone out (rubbing her arms to denote the cold, dew damp morning) to see the white men away. The memsahib had been up to wave *'kwaheri'* from the veranda but she returned to bed as soon as they were gone. And so too, Francis until seven-thirty when she, Florence, had arrived and roused him to go to work.

During the morning there had been a holiday atmosphere. Mshoki singing in the kitchen, kneading bread on the huge floured board, his song drifting out across the garden to his wife and her sister they sat on the step shelling peas. A joyful day with the white men gone until sundown and the memsahib sleeping still at nine o'clock. Hope had come, the *ayah* who was not wanted, for the baby that did not come, passing along the back path barely greeting the women on the step. Such a grand lady with her sandals and her white woman's dress and, and (mouth stuffed, stopping at the last moment the flow of spite which would describe the brassiere that held Hope's breasts aloft to dazzle the tea picking boys around her father's house). While the memsahib is still sleeping the *ayah* can sneak away. The memsahib will not complain that she has not been for there is no child in the house and it is pain for the memsahib that still the *ayah* is coming.

And the memsahib is sitting under the tree for one hour, not coming in for the meal which is laid out on the table, the meat that goes cold and the fresh milk which the Memsahib Bowen is saying she must drink every day to make another baby. The meat is uneaten and the milk undrunk and then comes Mshoki running out of the kitchen for his wife to go away for there is trouble coming to this house. And she, Florence, sitting on the step with the child she had brought for company and remembering the noise they had been hearing and not hearing all the day, the whine so familiar the ears no longer picked it out, of the motor horse of that young fellow, coming and going along the track at the foot of the house, on the motor horse that someone,

214

everybody knew it, had bought for him and for why? Nobody knows. And him creeping past, pushing the machine, ignoring her wave as she, Florence, all alone, sat shelling peas for the devil makes work for idle hands.

And then the shouting and the running white face on the path, the memsahib, the wife, shouting and calling over and over, knocking the dish of peas from Florence's hands, 'Where did he go?' And her baby crawling and pushing the hard peas into his mouth so that she was all the time trying to take them out and answer the white woman's crying face. Still calling after her running down the slope.

The two men had come to her, Mshoki and Francis, to help gather the peas and wonder at the meaning of all these things and there is much said and each person has their idea of what is to be done and so the afternoon passes with all talk and talk until dusk is on the step. What should they do? They should go to the next house, the Bwana Dickie's house but Francis would not for fear of the shame. They should go and should not go and would go and would not, all afternoon until sundown when the watchman arrived with the idea of the lights and Francis, going against Mshoki for once, sets his signal of lights and open windows to let the white men make their own story from it. And then gone all the men, to the beer stall to have just one drink to help them for the tiredness that overcame them in the empty house.

'Eh . . .' The girl sighed, the tale ceasing as suddenly as it began.

Harry sat on with her, straddling the chair, while she smoothed the head of the child that rested in the crevice of her thighs. A patch of unwiped mucus bubbled under its nose as it snored.

27

Patrick had fallen asleep on the sofa, his deep, regular snore could be heard in the kitchen. The girl settled further into the hardback chair and composed herself for sleep, her bare feet careless of the cold stone floor.

Harry put his elbows on the kitchen table and rested his head on his hands. The electric light cast shadows in the corners of the room, distending the square edges of cupboards in silhouette against the walls. In the corner the old Frigidaire came abruptly to life with a glass-rattling roar that echoed in the silent house like the engine of an ancient ship. He wanted to think of Julia, of where she might be, of the empty suitcase on her bed. A dolls' house, Patrick had said. Harry shook his head. He wanted to feel fear for her, or rage, but it seemed she had gone willingly, not driven or abducted.

His head felt heavy; sleep was like free-falling, feeling his head flopping forward, easing him into a dream, all hands lost to the great black ocean and the captain drunk in the mess. The image flickered as he drifted in and out of sleep, the captain's wife, a soft woman in Edwardian dress, hoisted overboard in a flash of white petticoats, calling his name as the patch-eyed, filthy pirates fondled her breasts.

A loud knock catapulted him awake.

'Who is it?'

'Mshoki.' A voice muffled by the door. The girl was stirring. She opened her mouth to yawn, shifted the baby on to one hip and waddled over to the door. The electric light had faded, diminished by the grey dawn that filtered around the curtains. Still holding the baby, the girl stretched and bent to shoot the bolts. She caught the door handle with her free hand and stood in the threshold so that her body entirely filled the gap.

There was a murmured conversation, a low rumble of words in her own vernacular, interspersed with hums and 'eh . . .', exclamations of wonder or sadness.

'Mshoki,' Harry called. 'Is there anybody with you?'

The girl turned and pushed the door wide open to show the solitary man on the doorstep. He wore his apron, reporting for work, but hanging his head, as if to avoid confrontation, verbal or physical. The girl let him pass and, at a brief word from him, she was gone, waddling down to the quarters with the child still sleeping on her hip.

Harry remained seated while the servant shuffled about, laying trays for early morning tea; beaded fly nets on the milk jugs, and frayed lace tray cloths. He poked the ashes under the stove and went out, leaving the door ajar so that Harry could see him gathering an armful of wood. He threw it into the stove piece by piece, heavy logs thundered against the iron walls. Harry shouted above the din.

'Where is Francis?'

'He will come now.' Mshoki lit a taper and turned his back to light the stove. Harry helped himself to a glass of milk from the Frigidaire and drank it standing, tilting his head so that the liquid flowed down his throat in a thick stream. Mshoki took the empty glass from his hand and rinsed it at the sink.

The garden was cool and damp, filled with the noise of the dawn. Harry walked around the house, peering in at the still-curtained windows. By the veranda doors he paused. Patrick was sprawled on the sofa, his chin sunk upon his chest like an old man, dozing. Harry opened the doors but he barely stirred. The whisky bottle was almost empty. Harry put it back into the cupboard and went to draw a bath.

The water was tepid, yesterday's left over. Francis had not been there to light the fire under the tank. Harry rolled over to lie face down in the stained water, expelling his breath in slow bubbles. Returning from the bathroom, he found a tea tray beside his bed; the curtains were open, the day begun, as if he lay beneath the covers, undisturbed. He poured a cup and added three spoonfuls of sugar. The hot, sweet liquid scalded his throat, warming the milk in his belly. Francis must have been in. Mshoki would have lost enough dignity in laying the trays. Drawing the curtains was no task for a cook.

The door to the main bedroom stood open and there too, a tea tray had been placed on a locker between the beds. Two cups and saucers, extra hot water; as if she were there, a bundle under the bedclothes, instead of the flat bedspread with the suitcase and yesterday's laundry.

In the living room, Patrick had opened his eyes.

'Tea in your room,' Harry said. 'Did you see Francis?'

Patrick nodded.

'Did you ask him where he's been?'

'No.'

Patrick stretched himself, pressing his elbows into the upholstery and rolling back his mouth to reveal his brown stained teeth. 'I've told them to cook up eggs and bacon,' he said. 'It's the only cure for how I'm feeling, eggs and bacon. Stuff your gut so that it can't dwell on what it had the night before.'

Was Patrick pretending too? Would the whole house conspire to forget the absence of its mistress?

Harry went out to the back and found the houseboy sitting by the door. Pairs of freshly polished shoes were laid out on the lower step: three pairs of Patrick's and one of Harry's. A pair of woman's sandals lay askew in the dust, as if they had been kicked there by tired feet.

Harry sat down and felt the servant edge away from the contact.

'Where did you go last night, Francis?'

Silence. The sound of brush against leather, long dark fingers gripping the inside of a shoe, pressing in the fist to get a good hold.

'It must be told, Francis.'

No pause in the brushing, only the feeling of ears pricked all around; Mshoki listening in the kitchen behind him and the girl in the quarters, waiting behind the broken door.

'Too many beers, bwana. I am drinking too many beers.'

He started to cough; tight dry spasms that grew in volume as the seizure took hold. Spreading his arms to give space to his shuddering lungs, he knocked the clean shoes off the step into the dust. Harry picked them up and set them back on the step. 'Do you have any *dawa*?'

Francis gestured, speechless between coughs, to the quarters.

Harry hurried down the path. The girl was on the servants' step, and another woman, Mshoki's wife. They looked at one another, a quick, African-sly glance and then the older woman came forward proffering a bottle of red syrup.

It became a ceremony. Francis got up, still staggering with the force of the coughs. He paused to spit a gobbet of phlegm into the dust before preceding Harry into the kitchen. Mshoki guarded the cutlery drawer as Harry tried to reach for a spoon. Francis palmed water into his mouth and the coughing subsided a little.

'This one,' he said eventually, extracting a white plastic spoon from the pocket of his apron. 'Memsahib says this spoon.'

It was the kind issued free with prescriptions in England.

Mshoki filled the spoon from the bottle and handed it, quivering, to Francis. He took it full in his mouth like a child and licked it clean. The process was repeated and then Francis polished the spoon vigorously on his apron.

He coughed once more, less loudly, as if to show that the medicine had worked.

Harry went to join Patrick in the dining room.

'Julia's always giving them *dawa*,' said Patrick. 'I've told her the stuff just puts them to sleep but she won't listen. That's the third bottle he's on now – probably flogging it round the estate.'

The smell of frying bacon drifted from the kitchen.

'Look,' said Patrick, raising his voice against the clatter of cutlery being laid for the meal. 'I've got to get down to the factory this morning. Will you hold the fort?'

He answered Harry's expression.

'What do you suppose I should do? Send out a posse? I've got to go to the factory, I've got a job to do. We'll go down there when she's had enough time to get whatever she went for and in the meantime you will be a friend to me if you will face it out. Come down to the Club at lunchtime. We'll have a few beers and see who can't look us in the eye.'

He was determined. There was nothing Harry could say to sway him. He tried to paint scenes of danger, murder, rape, but Patrick shook his head.

'I know these people. They won't harm her. It'll be money they want.'

'But she could be hurt, kidnapped, at this very minute lying in some hole and clinging to the belief that you will rescue her.'

'I understand what you're saying, my friend, but you're wrong. Julia is my wife and these are my people. I've been in this country all my life and I know what goes on. Julia has to learn it for herself.'

He left immediately after breakfast, leaving Harry dry mouthed with fear and rage, stranded with the silence of the morning and the faint breeze off the tea.

Harry waited all day. For what he could not tell. The whole morning on the veranda sleeping, on and off, against the sweep, sweep of Francis's broom and

Mshoki's high, insistent plainsong. Much as the girl had described the previous day. Like and not like, no motorcycle whine to break the stillness, no calling and crying and Julia running off to God knows where. No interruptions at all, except coffee arriving, unasked, brought out on a tray with one stale macaroon and the skin of over-warmed milk spooned out to hang like a peel of sun-burned flesh on the lip of the jug.

Was this Julia's world? Harry tried to imagine it. To be so still, to stare into the absolute distance of the Rift and wait for the days to pass.

He woke to find Patrick beside him on the veranda munching the macaroon. He was dressed in shorts and a tee shirt, as if it were a holiday.

'We must go, Patrick. We can't leave her there.'

Patrick shrugged and brushed the crumbs from his lips.

'We'll go later on. I've got too much of a head to go driving down there now.'

'Patrick, we must go now,' Harry pleaded.

Patrick shook his head. 'If she wanted to come home she'd be here by now. She got there on foot, didn't she?'

'How far is it to the township?'

'Only a mile or two down the back path, but quite a long way in the car, you have to go right down to the bottom and then double back.'

'Couldn't we go on foot?'

Patrick snorted. 'No way. It's bad enough as it is – I'm not going walking down there like a kaffir.'

'She could be injured.'

'Francis would have said something.'

'You haven't asked him.'

'If Julia was hurt, Francis would tell me. If she's not hurt, if she's lounging in bed with that fucking kaffir, I'd rather not hear it from my houseboy!'

It was late afternoon when they finally set off; the first drops of rain hit the car roof like the droppings of some huge bird.

28

There was dust in her mouth. Dry, powdery dust that clung to her lips, swollen, sore, huge when she pressed them together.

He had come back twice. Each time more drunk; hurting her, opening the wounds, filling her body with his pink-tinged black enormity.

The last time she fought him, gathered the shreds of her anger and clawed his face. He slammed her against the wall, knocked her head until it rang like a gong. Darkness fell like a veil over her eyes, still there when she came round, a heart-stopping moment of blindness until she saw that it was night, wafers of light from the street spilling through the open door. She lay still on the floor, unyielding granular cement against bruised limbs, slipping in and out of oblivion, dreaming, the smooth round face returning as a nightmare, bulbous, bloated. Patrick and the servant's boy, interchanging, a three-legged dog named Harry pulling at her skirt and behind them all her mother weeping, 'Julia, I can't find your father. He's not here. I've looked and looked and there's no-one with his face.'

Daylight. Sleep like a drug weighting her limbs. He had not come again. Afternoon light. Mottled cloud above the roof of the opposite house. The pool of vomit had been wiped from the floor, someone had dressed her in a cardigan, covering the torn dress. The cardigan was blue, buttoned from the neck, a rim of reddish dirt around the cuffs. She sat up slowly. Her shoes lay in a corner of the room, like drunken feet. She propelled herself towards them, arching her toes under the high ankle straps that had looked so fashionable in London. Leaned against the wall, the whole world reduced to a fiery pain between her temples.

Something moved. Across her eyes-closed awareness of the light a shadow fell. She pulled back into the corner. Not again. Dear God, not again. A man in the doorway. Something familiar in the hang of his hands. He began to cough, a prolonged, breathless hack.

'Francis!' She tried to rise, to hug the familiar skinny frame but she could not stand, her legs buckled back to the concrete.

The room was filled with voices, low grunts and whispers bouncing between the walls. She opened one eye a crack and saw Francis sitting against the opposite wall. His legs were stretched out towards her, the soft pink pads of his feet held up like a greeting. He saw her opened eyes and started to move, coughing again. The other man raised his hand in greeting. It was Mshoki.

They watched while she set her feet flat on the floor and levered herself up, unsteady as a new-born calf. Mshoki put out his arm and she used it to pull herself upright against him.

'I would like to go home.'

There was no response. She repeated herself in Swahili, regretting the translation, her vocabulary supplied only an imperious demand.

Mshoki answered her, a flood of words gesturing to the sky. Meaningless. The pain swelled in her head.

He said it all again, gabbling, jabbing his finger at the sky. The speed was deliberate. Come on, said his eyes, you should understand us by now.

She caught one word she knew, '*mfua*', rain.

They were waiting for the rain. It wouldn't be long. The sky had turned black, the humidity in the little room a tangible presence, welding the nylon cardigan against her skin.

'Better,' said Francis, 'Better we go in the rain.' Safer perhaps? For her not to be seen walking the hills with the servants?

Moments later something hit the roof, like a sharp stone on the bare metal, then another, and another, a sharp metallic clatter that accelerated to a deafening crescendo. The men were all smiles. The rain had come.

She followed them. Her head spun, floor and sky lurching as she staggered to the door. Mshoki pulled his shirt up over his head; it was sodden before he had gone two yards. Julia shuddered as the curtain of water engulfed her. The noise was deafening, the force of it closed her eyes. As if in bright sunlight she shielded her face with her hands and stumbled after them. Mshoki looked back once, a single glance over his shoulder to see that she was following before he set off down the deserted street.

Water pummelled her limbs, driving away her dizziness. She held herself out to it, offering her soiled body to the downpour. Mud oozed over her shoes. In the middle of the road the gutter had burst its banks, spewing a stream into the street.

The house!

They had left the township, reached the place where the path crossed the main road when her brain finally cleared and she remembered it. She shouted to Francis. Like Mshoki he had pulled up his shirt, wrapping his arms, ape-like, above his head. Stumbling up the slope she lunged at his back, slipped as he spun round, landing on her knees in the mud.

Mshoki stopped. The two men scowled down at her through the downpour.

'I must go back,' she shouted. 'I've left something behind.'

Francis shook his head, '*Hapana*.'

'Please!'

Her cry was lost in the din of the water. He pointed up to the road.

'No, we must go back. I have left something important.'

'*Hapana*.'

They smiled as she knelt before them in the mud. Francis's huge yellow teeth bared at her through the rain. He gabbled, waving long, gangly arms up towards the hill.

There was nothing to do except follow them. She forced herself to stand and the mud that had caked on her knees was instantly rinsed away.

Her skirt clung to her legs, weighted with water, hampering her stride as she half ran to keep up with them. They climbed up to the main road and walked at its edge, teetering on the steep banks of mud beside the rushing burnt-red torrent in the storm drains. The tea, only yards away, was almost invisible. They trudged blindly, in single file. Intermittently, through the roar of the water, Julia heard the rack, rack of Francis's cough.

They had travelled about half a mile, reached the second tier of the escarpment, a flat stretch where the tea grew in wide terraces on either side. Julia was numb with exhaustion, the pain in her head had concentrated into a fiery ball behind her eyes, blocking out all vision, all sensation save of wetness and darkness, and the weight of her water-laden skirt pulling her downwards into the mud. She had wandered out into the road, blindly seeking firmer ground, when a car appeared ahead, approaching like a shadow, the sound of the engine drowned in the noise of the drains. Kangeni? The car stopped beside her.

'Julia!'

Not Kangeni. The passenger door was flung open and a white hand took hold of her own.

'Get in, for God's sake. I don't want the car full of water.' Clare Bowen, unmistakably, over everything, her voice.

Julia clambered in, falling across the seat, the remains of her energy draining away with relief.

'Here, put your feet on those.' Clare spread a pair of newspapers under her mud-caked feet. 'Where are your shoes?' Julia couldn't remember.

Nineteen sixty-eight. Her mother's voice. 'Where are your shoes?' She had put daisies in her hair and gone barefoot. The year before her O-levels. 'Your father would be so ashamed.'

She closed her eyes and curled herself against the seat. Clare was wiping her face. The rag smelled of polish. The coarse cloth scraped off a scab of dust and her lip bled afresh.

'Silly, silly girl.' Her mind swirled back. Falling over on Brighton beach, cutting her knee on a shard of green glass. Mother's impatience. 'Silly girl.' Blood from her knee running unheeded, staining the white socks, a warm trickle under her heel. 'Silly girl.'

The servants had gone on, heads bowed against the rain. Clare slowed to minimise the splash from the tyres.

'They came to get me,' said Julia.

Clare glanced at the driving mirror.

'So did I,' she said.

29

The stubble on Patrick's face glowed red in the bright, wet-grey light. They drove in silence, deafened by the roar of the rain on the roof. Water sheeted past the windows, splashing and puddling in the hollows of the road. A thick, musty smell of wet earth filled the car.

Harry had almost dragged his friend into the car, pulled him to his feet and half-dragged, half-pushed him through the rain, ready to hit him as he started to make the rain another excuse to postpone the journey. The windows steamed over the instant they were inside. Harry reached for a wad of tissues stuffed under the dash and dislodged a small brown teddy bear. He leaned down to retrieve it from the floor.

'It was for my son,' said Patrick.

Harry watched him cradle the bear for a moment, a small ball of fluff in the large freckled hands, then it was stuffed back on to the dash, wedged with tissues so that it looked out at them both with its button-eyed stare.

Harry wiped the screen while Patrick put the car into gear. For the next twenty minutes conversation was impossible. The car spun and skittered down the escarpment, veering one way and then the other through the rain, defying the steering-wheel, slipping and plunging within a short breath of the edge and back again, a changing pattern of mud-wall and precipice that caused a rivulet of sweat to run between Harry's shoulder blades and found him, at the bottom of the hill, white-knuckled, clutching the grab-handles, and out of breath.

Patrick was plain faced, breathing shallowly, bland as a man sleeping.

As they reached the lower slopes the rain began to ease. Shafts of pale brown sunlight filled the car as Patrick turned onto the unmarked road that led to the township.

Harry remembered how he had pointed out the township on an earlier journey; a conversation as remote as the moon from the journey they made now. Patrick had called the single-room houses 'bloody palaces', pointed with pride at the straight lines of the streets, the outside taps where the women queued, carrying their huge containers on their heads. Then it had been just after dawn, the first rays of the sun catching the topmost shoots of the surrounding tea as light ripples on green water, throwing long, concealing shadows across the scrapyard gardens. Now, at evening, in the sun's final passage through the brief band of clear sky between storm cloud and horizon, the shadows were in reverse, exposing the twice-thrown refuse; a refrigerator door in the murram, a gleaming white stain among heaps of broken boxes, the upturned legs of an ironing board like a stricken insect on the littered ground.

They parked the car by an outcrop of rocks. There was a vast open space of churned mud in which to park but Patrick went to the rocks, backing the car up between the stands of grass that clustered there. They locked the car doors and Patrick filled his pockets with cartridges from a box in the boot.

There were no street lights. Through unshuttered windows came the white glow of kerosene lamps and the occasional flicker of a candle, throwing moving shadows on the muddy, footprinted ground.

In the centre of each street was a gutter, a small stream of rain water, draining over the unpaved earth, carrying away the scraps and slops that littered the road.

It was the supper hour. People lounged in doorways

or stared through windows; round, cropped heads, ears breaking the oval against the unsteady light. Pots banged, they could hear radios playing, and women's voices raised in anger and mirth. The air was full of smells, cooking fires, roasting maize, occasionally a whiff of charred meat. Children stopped to stare at the intruders, picking a nose or scratching a groin, without censure or comment, simply looking.

They had walked half the length of the street. Harry realised that, just as Victorian explorers had waited for the natives to show themselves, he and Patrick were waiting for one to come forward. None did. A group of youths sloped past, keeping to the high sides of the ground, lowering their heads to stare under hooded eyes. Those in doorways looked away or straight through the white men as they passed.

'Julia!' Patrick's voice boomed out. Harry closed his eyes, striving to hear. For a moment the other noises faltered; a pause in an argument, a broken laugh; but no answer came, nothing but the yap and snarl of a pye-dog standing with its feet in the gutter a few yards ahead.

The twilight had gone, lost in the glare of kerosene and the red glow of charcoal stoves. Harry moved closer to Patrick, bringing his elbow into contact with the cold metal of the shotgun. Mutely they exchanged glances in the dim light.

To the left a door creaked open. Patrick spun round, raising the gun. An elderly *bibi* stepped out. She banged a metal fire tray once against the wall and, without looking at Patrick, went back inside and closed the door.

'Julia!'

They were listening now. The intruders' ears, made sensitive by fear, caught the change. Radios going off one by one, voices reduced to a murmur. After another full minute they called a third time and the name fell upon silence.

A movement in the shadows to the right. Together

they wheeled round, the gun barrel swinging between them like an outstretched arm.

'She was over there.'

They could hardly see him. A small man in shorts, barefoot, his face in shadow.

'In the next road. House number six.' The voice expressed neither interest nor involvement. 'I can show you the way.'

He led them along a narrow path, passing between bare concrete walls. Small, litter-strewn yards backed on to another row of houses.

The second street was identical to the first, tin roofs crouched against the sky and pools of flickering light in the windows. A beer stall glowed at the far end, electric light spilling luxuriously on to the guttered earth. A sign had been painted on the wall, 'The Sweetheart Hotel'. For an instant the silence was broken, pierced by the wail of an electric guitar, cut off as soon as it began, like a baying hound shot down in the chase.

Their guide stopped, pointing to a doorway. Patrick lit a match and a white painted number sprang into view, a figure six crudely brushed above the door frame. It was the only house without light, the door a dark space in the unplastered wall.

Patrick had taken another deep breath, about to call her name again, when a figure appeared in the doorway, just visible in the lurid borrowed light from the bar.

'Where is my wife?' Patrick's voice was hoarse.

A shrug. The figure moved forward, pulling the door closed behind him. It was a young man.

'You should not have come here,' he said. 'This is not your place.'

Patrick climbed the shallow rise of earth to the wall of the house. The door gave easily against his foot. He lit another match and went inside.

Harry waited in the street. The youth offered his hand.

'How do you do. My name is Bartholomew Wagirii.'

With a feeling of unreality, Harry shook the out-stretched hand, conscious of strength in the fingers.

'She has left, the white lady. She was here and now she has gone.'

A lamp was lit inside the house. Harry could see Patrick's shadow, huge against the wall. After a moment he emerged, clutching something in his right hand. It looked like a piece of cloth.

'You fucking black bastard. What have you done to her?'

The movement was so sudden that Harry missed the sequence. Bartholomew let go of his hand, he saw Patrick move and then he was on the ground with the gun across his throat and Bartholomew's knee buried deep between his thighs, shoving hard against the groin. Harry moved towards them but his path was blocked. A group of men had encircled him. One took hold of his left arm; the grip tightened when he tried to shake it free. Other hands took his right arm and he was turned around, marched towards the next house and made to sit in the doorway. The crowd grew. A lamp was brought out and placed by the wall; dark eye-bright faces jumped in the light. Patrick was still on the ground, with Bartholomew kneeling above him, but the youth was in difficulties. Both his hands were occupied keeping Patrick's head pinned down with the gun-barrel, leaving Patrick's free to push and scrabble at his face. The youth was wasting his breath, too, talking, yelling, 'I show you, white man. You think you can call me a bastard! You think you can spoil my face and break my teeth!'

The hands that restrained Harry were not violent. Their faces were turned to watch the fight, but when he tried to pull away, they tightened their grip once more and a deep African voice spoke from the darkness of the house behind him, 'Keep away, well away. This is not your fight.'

'But I must help him.'

'No. One week ago this man attacked that boy at night. His foot was hurt, a tooth broken away. Now the boy must have his revenge.'

Harry peered between the legs of the crowd as the struggle slowly turned in Patrick's favour. He was half sitting, his fingers stuffed into Bartholomew's mouth, stretching back his lips, pulling so hard that his arms were streaked with Bartholomew's blood. Suddenly Bartholomew relaxed his grip and Patrick was up, wrapping his leg around him and tumbling him to the ground. He kicked him as he fell and continued to kick, hard enough for Harry to hear the thud of his boot against the slack, rolling body of the youth. Patrick was shouting at the crowd, 'You lot can just go and fuck off. Bugger off, all of you, this isn't a bloody circus.' He brandished the gun like a stick, as if to beat them away. Those immediately in front stepped back but the sides closed in, keeping just beyond arm's length. One reached forward and pulled Patrick's shirt from behind, like a child playing tease. Patrick spun round. Failing to see his assailant, he aimed another kick at Bartholomew. The youth groaned and the ring of men drew closer. Patrick whirled about, the gleam of the gun metal making a fiery circle as he jabbed at random into the space around him. His face was wild, hair spiked with sweat, teeth bared.

Once more Harry tried to rise but his captors pushed him back, turning him away so that he could no longer see the fight. He was pushed through the doorway, almost into the hut. He smelled sweat and burned meat from the charcoal stove that glowed dimly in the corner. Outside the crowd began to murmur, the sound rising and falling as if in rhythm with the unseen struggle. There was a loud crash and the men around Harry were suddenly very still. Bartholomew's voice came through the darkness.

'Your wife won't want you now, white man. She's had nigger cock now!'

The crowd started to back off. Harry could sense the movement all around him, a change of mood, fear in the voices that muttered in the darkness. He was trying to turn, trying to look out when the gun went off; a single shot that vibrated back and forth among the houses.

The crowd broke up, shadows scattering into the darkness. The hands that had restrained him were suddenly gone, leaving him sitting against the wall in the mud. They had left the lamp. Harry picked it up and walked out into the street. A hand touched his shoulder. He wheeled round, clutched with fear. A youth stood behind him.

'What do you want?'

'I am showing you the house.' The outstretched palm was pink in the lamplight.

'Oh, of course.' Fumbling, Harry dug into his pocket and dropped a couple of coins into the waiting hand. The boy bowed. 'The bwana is inside the house.'

'Thank you,' Harry said, unnecessarily. The boy had gone.

Holding the lamp in front of him he went into the house. Patrick was on the floor, facing the wall, slumped over as though he had fallen asleep. There was blood on the wall, a wet streak slipping down to the concrete. Harry walked round and bent down to look Patrick in the face. He had none. A mess of tissue and bone and blood dripping on to the floor.

He turned back to the faces in the doorway. Five pairs of eyes, flickering, silent, mouths hanging open and mouths clamped closed, all hushed in the still-ringing echo of the gun. Into the smallest hand he poured every coin from his pockets. 'Go quickly. Fetch the police. Tell them there has been an accident.'

30

The car door closed with a thump. Harry felt in his
pockets.

'I'm sorry, I have nothing left to give you,' he said.

The leader of the men shook his head, leaning forward
to check if the car door was properly closed. Satisfied,
he started to move away. The others followed. In the
dim light Harry saw that their clothes were stained with
blood from Patrick's body. He looked down; his own
shirt also had a stain, a wide, dark circle where he had
cradled the head in his arms.

Patel's certificate was in his back pocket. The doctor
had arrived soon after the policeman, rattling down in
an ancient station wagon and hurrying into the hut to
be brought up short by the sight of Patrick's body lying
near the wall.

'What happened here?'

'It was an accident,' said Harry.

The policeman shuffled his boots on the concrete floor.

'This is Mr Whitman?'

Harry nodded.

'Terrible,' muttered Patel, 'terrible.' He looked up at
Harry and pushed his heavy rimmed spectacles further
up his nose. 'I treated his wife recently, you know. Her
baby was four weeks premature.' He gestured with the
pen. 'I was over on Kibwezi, a mudslide after the rain.'
The heavy spectacles slid once more down his nose.
'And now this.'

Harry held the lamp while the doctor wrote out the certificate.

'I must go and see Mrs Whitman,' he said as he handed the certificate to Harry. 'Has she been told?'

'Not yet.'

The pad of blank certificates went back into Patel's bag. 'You can bring the body to the clinic, but I have no storage facilities. We do not have much time in this heat. It must be buried within forty-eight hours or flown down to the Coast.' The clasp of the doctor's bag snapped shut. 'Shall I call on Mrs Whitman?'

Harry shook his head. 'Later, perhaps.'

'She will be in shock, she may need a sedative.' The doctor gestured to the row of faces watching in the doorway.

'These men will help you with the body. I shall go ahead to prepare the clinic.'

The policeman stepped forward, the shotgun held loosely under his arm. 'You will drive me to the station.'

The doctor stopped. 'You are on foot?'

'The patrol car is broken.'

Patel looked for a moment as if he would argue. Then he shrugged, turning back to Harry. 'I shall have to make a detour.'

Harry nodded. 'I'll see you at the clinic.'

Three men came forward from the crowd as the doctor's car rattled away. Strong dark arms encircled Patrick's body. Harry took the head and they staggered unevenly along the streets to the outcrop of rock where Patrick had left the car.

A shadow moved on the veranda as Harry drove the car up on to the lawn. He swung the wheel and caught the watchman jumping to his feet like a startled animal. Beside him a jam jar lay on its side, a trickle of liquid dripping down the veranda step.

There were lights on in the house, leaking out around closed curtains. The hands on his wristwatch showed just after two. He tried the veranda door and found it open.

Clare Bowen was asleep on the sofa, mouth open, a blanket over her legs.

She stirred as he closed the door.

'Why aren't you wearing your shirt?'

Harry stopped, startled by the question. 'I left it at the clinic.'

Clare sat up, her eyes still heavy with sleep. 'Why? Where's Patrick?'

Harry sat down. He shook his head. 'Is Julia here?'

'Yes, she's asleep. But where is Patrick?'

Again Harry shook his head. 'He is at the clinic. Doctor Patel has him.'

Clare frowned. 'What happened?'

In the briefest words, leaving out any explanation or comment, Harry related the events of the evening: the drive through the rain to the township; the house with the painted number; the cloth in Patrick's hand; the fight with Bartholomew; how he himself had been restrained, had not seen the end of it, only heard the shot, the single report that had shattered the night.

'What am I going to say to Julia?' Harry asked.

The woman spoke as if she had not heard him. 'We could have prevented this,' she whispered. 'We all saw it coming. We warned her. We warned Patrick. You cannot mix with these people.' She shrugged. 'I don't know, maybe in the future, with the intelligent ones it will be possible. But not with these people. That boy was the son of her servant. It was wrong to let him come here.'

She stood up and folded the blanket into a square.

'What shall I do?' Harry asked, suddenly wanting to be told, wanting the large, comfortable woman to tell him what to do.

'Go and see Kangeni. He'll know what to do.'

'What about Julia?'

'I'll tell her.'

239

'But I ought to see her.'

The woman looked at him. Her face was still soft with sleep, grey tendrils of hair hung down over her forehead. She pushed them aside. 'Time enough for that.'

She followed him to the door. 'Would you like me to get one of Patrick's shirts? I'm sure I could find one.'

Harry shook his head. 'I'm not cold.'

Her hand touched his back. 'You'll be no use to anyone if you catch a chill.'

Harry shrugged. 'I'll borrow one from Kangeni.'

Clare Bowen frowned. For a moment Harry expected her to voice the thought in her mind, objecting to the loan of an African's shirt. She simply patted his shoulder. 'Go on, then, I must speak to Julia.'

Harry waited on the veranda. Clare's voice came through the bedroom window, sound without words, and then Julia's harsh cry.

Kangeni's house was in darkness. A chained mongrel barked at the car. Lights came on and the front door opened a crack. At the sight of the car Kangeni hurried outside.

'I thought it was Patrick.'

Harry got out of the car. 'There's been an accident.' Harry told the story as Kangeni ushered him into the house.

'This is a bad business.' The African clicked his tongue. 'That boy should be punished.'

'Which boy?'

'Wagirii. He had no right to go there. It was a bad business from the start.'

No fault of Patrick, or Julia, thought Harry. Even this African blames Bartholomew.

Kangeni's wife appeared, sleepy-eyed.

'Bring Mr Thomas a shirt to wear,' said Kangeni.

Harry had forgotten his bare chest. The shirt was too big but it felt crisp and clean against his chilled skin.

Kangeni's wife brought him a cup of tea. The strong, factory brew, heavily sweetened, restored him, calmed his nerves. He looked around the room, feeling a strange sense of displacement. The house was like his own, like Patrick's; slightly smaller but furnished with the same standard Chaachi furniture. Like and yet utterly unlike; a batik print on the wall, unframed; finger marks around the light switch, a smell of goat-meat and dust.

They drove to Patrick's office. It was just before dawn. A stream of pickers filled the road, pouring from the township with vast empty baskets strapped to their backs and heavy plastic aprons flapping against their legs. Harry had seen similar scenes at the Coast, the dawn army moving along roads and pathways, huddled under shawls and blankets.

These tea pickers moved silently, as if word had already travelled across the estate, every picker knew what every house servant knew, what the white householders would learn with their breakfast.

Kangeni was calm and efficient, Harry watched him telephone the Chaachi Head Office, speaking to Muthaga in the rapid bursts and sudden pauses of English spoken among Africans. Kangeni's black arms rested comfortably on Patrick's desk. Harry pictured Muthaga at the other end of the line, smiling, smug at the news of the white man's tragedy.

At the end of the conversation, Kangeni put down the phone with a sigh. 'These Coast people have no manners.'

Harry smiled.

'Excuse me,' said Kangeni. 'Is Mr Muthaga a friend of yours?'

Harry shook his head. 'Just a colleague.'

Kangeni spread his hands. 'Men like that give Africa a bad name.'

Forgetting, for an instant, the circumstances, Harry laughed aloud.

'I'm serious, Harry.' Kangeni prodded the desk in

front of him. 'These Coast people think they must be rude to everyone, that if they are not rude they will give something away.'

'You sound like Patrick.'

Kangeni stood up, rubbing his face. 'No more,' he said hoarsely, black fists covering his eyes. Harry looked out of the window. In the distance he could see a row of pickers bent over the tea. He looked back at Kangeni. 'There is nothing more we can do here. Would you like some breakfast?'

Kangeni shook his head.

'Some coffee then?'

Kangeni took his car keys out of his pocket. 'We ought to go and see how Patel is getting on at the clinic. He will have some coffee for us.'

The doctor was outside the clinic, seated on the long wooden bench where the patients queued. Beside him was Julia. Both held mugs of steaming black coffee.

Kangeni held out his hands to Julia. 'Mrs Whitman . . .'

Julia looked up, shaking her head a little. Her face was bruised, a swelling on her temple and blue-dark shadows around her eyes. Harry looked for signs of grief but found none, only the shadowed eyes and a chilly calm as she inclined her head to Kangeni.

'Is Clare Bowen here with you?' Harry asked.

'No,' said Julia, in a voice as calm and clear as her eyes. 'I told her not to wait.'

Dr Patel straightened the collar of his white coat. 'We are just waiting for the coffin.'

Kangeni turned to Julia. 'It will be only a makeshift affair, Mrs Whitman, the best we can provide at such short notice. There will be a proper coffin ready when you reach the Coast.'

Julia made no response, but stared vacantly into the distance. Harry turned to Patel.

'We were wondering if you would have any coffee for us, Doctor Patel.'

'Of course, of course . . .' The doctor bustled away, calling for his clinic assistant. Kangeni followed him.

Harry sat on the bench beside Julia and cleared his throat.

Julia looked at him. After a moment she said, 'He wouldn't let me queue here, you know.'

'Pardon?'

She touched the wooden seat of the bench. 'There was a long queue of people waiting but Patrick pushed me to the front.'

Harry watched her hands, smoothing the grain of the wood. 'It's what they would expect,' he said.

Slowly she nodded, staring out at the clinic garden, her eyes wide, unfocused, not seeing the trim grass and the small frangipani that spilled its sweet fragrance over the musty smell of rain-soaked earth.

'I had such expectations when I came,' she whispered. 'Patrick promised me a house on a hill, a place where a woman would be content. I imagined a kind of paradise.'

She looked up at Harry and the shadowed eyes smiled at him. 'He believed it, Harry. He never tried to deceive me. I deceived myself.'

Her hands clutched the wooden seat. 'Bartholomew didn't deceive me either. He was always what he appeared to be. It was I who misunderstood.'

From a distance came the noise of an engine grinding slowly up the road to the clinic. A loaded vehicle trundled into view, one of the estate pick-ups with three Africans in the back and a long wooden box resting at an angle beside them. Julia stood up and kept close to the workmen as they unloaded the box and carried it into the clinic. Stencilled along its edge was the Chaachi store code, a series of numbers and LEDOROT printed in black. The box was laid beside Patrick's body and immediately it was obvious that the box would be too short.

Kangeni slapped his hands in frustration. He shouted at the workmen, 'This at least you could have done

243

properly! You were given the measurements, why could you not make it the right size?'

The workmen looked at their feet.

Julia smiled, turning steady, dry eyes on Kangeni. In a calm voice she said, 'Of course they couldn't get it right. They didn't have Patrick there to guide them.'

Kangeni's eyes rolled. 'I'm sorry, Mrs Whitman. I'm so sorry.'

Julia watched, unblinking, as they began to force the stiffened corpse into the undersized box. Twice the face cloth that Patel had used to cover the wound slipped, exposing shattered bone and flesh. After the second time, Patel secured the cloth to the sides of the box with sticking plaster.

Harry took Julia's arm. She squeezed his hand tight against her but kept her eyes on the box, on the efforts of Patel and the assistant to make the body more comfortable.

'Why don't you have the funeral up here, Julia?' Harry whispered.

'No,' she answered aloud, 'I shall take him home.'

'But surely his home is here in Ledorot?'

She shook her head; a stiff, unyielding movement as she continued to watch Patel. 'He doesn't belong here any more, Harry. There is no place for his kind. He can be buried in England, beside my mother.' She glanced up. 'Though they never met, my mother and Patrick did have certain things in common.' She smiled. 'Mother was afraid of the brown skins who worked in the bakery. She gave up tea cakes, for fear of infection.'

A workman stepped forward, holding aloft the lid of the coffin. One held down the edge while another banged in the first nail.

Harry steered Julia outside. For a minute he thought she would weep. She slumped on the bench, holding her head, hands covering her ears against the noise of the hammer. He touched the back of her neck.

'What will you do?'

244

The hammer paused and her answer was loud and clear in the silence. 'I'm coming back.'

'To Ledorot?'

'No. To the real Africa. There is a place for me out there somewhere.'

'But not a place for Patrick?'

She lifted her head to look at him. 'There is nowhere left for people like Patrick. Africa needs people who have something to offer for the future. Patrick had nothing to offer, he was simply left behind.' She stood up. 'I shall get a proper teaching qualification in England and then I shall come back. I have mother's money, I needn't be a drain on the country.' The hammer began again, echoing from the concrete building of the clinic. She stepped out on to the grass. The ground was soft. On the clinic drive pools of rainwater had begun to shrink in the rising heat of the sun.

'There will be a pension from Chaachi,' said Harry.

Julia touched his hand. 'I want you to arrange something for me, Harry. I want the pension to be paid to Father Dominic, for his school.'

'But Julia — '

'I insist. However much it is, you must pay it to Father Dominic.'

'There may be a lump sum as well,' said Harry. 'You must take that at least.'

The hammering had ceased. She turned back towards the clinic. 'I'll write to you about that, Harry. I shall want you to give some of it to the boys. They'll be out of work, but Francis should be retiring anyway. He's only working to keep his youngest son at school. Tell him the schooling will be paid for, he must go back to his village.'

'And Mshoki?'

'Mshoki too, they must both return to their *shambas*.'

'Is that a condition of having the money?'

She nodded. 'Why not?'

Harry smiled. 'You mean you'll only pay them if they do what you think is best?'

She paused, at her feet a pool of water threw back her image, a white fool made huge, hovering over a blue reflected sky.

'No,' she said. 'You are right. They can have the money, and make their own decisions.'

Patel came out of the clinic. He had taken off his coat.

'Everything is ready, Mrs Whitman, and the boy has brought another flask of coffee.'

Julia turned to Harry, as if she had not heard the doctor speak. 'And you must give something to Doctor Patel here, for the clinic.'

Julia held Harry's arm as the coffin was loaded into the Beechcraft. The others had followed them across the strip. They stood in a group around the plane, watching as Kangeni made the coffin secure, pulling the straps tight with strong, capable hands.

Vera Ellis clutched a small bunch of flowers, pale yellow roses and a spray of fern.

'They're a bit overblown,' she said. 'But the others were only buds.'

Julia stood at the foot of the steps. Beside her, holding her suitcase, was the *ayah*. She took Vera's flowers with a smile. Dickie Dickinson stepped forward and patted her arm.

'Patrick was a good chap.'

Julia nodded, two spots of bright colour had appeared on her cheeks. She gestured to the men who had helped Kangeni load the coffin.

'Will these men be paid overtime?'

Donald Ellis cleared his throat. 'It wasn't overtime, they were due to start work in any case.'

'But they're not paid to make coffins,' said Julia, 'and I don't suppose they volunteered, not for Patrick.' She pulled a bundle of notes out of her purse. 'Here, this is his money, give them five bob each.'

She turned to Hope and thrust a second clutch of

notes into her free hand. 'This will buy you another pretty dress.'

The girl looked at the notes in her hand and smiled shyly at the floor.

Kangeni gave the straps a final tug and stepped down beside Julia. 'Everything is in order, Mrs Whitman. You will be met by Mr Muthaga at the airport. He will look after you.'

She smiled at him briefly, and turned to walk up into the plane.

Vera Ellis called after her, 'Goodbye, Julia!'

The rest called with her, as if anxious, at the sight of her departing, to make their peace. Julia paused and raised her hand. Vera's yellow roses waved slowly at their upturned faces.

Harry watched as the doors were pulled closed and Julia could be seen taking her seat beside the makeshift coffin. He looked round for Clare Bowen and found her standing at the edge of the group. Her face looked grey and exhausted. He took her arm and led her to where the cars were parked haphazardly on the grass.

'Things have changed, you know,' she said, as the plane taxied in a semicircle and lined up for take off. 'I thought that whatever happened elsewhere, Ledorot would remain as it was – a happy place, with everyone looked after and knowing where they belong.'

'Things will certainly change now,' said Donald Ellis, who had handed the five-shilling notes to the workmen with a sour expression and then followed Harry over to the cars.

The plane began to accelerate.

Clare Bowen looked at Donald Ellis as if to say, 'That isn't what I meant,' but something else came over her face.

'Oh damn!'

'What is it?'

The plane lifted off the ground. Through the distant

porthole Harry saw Julia's face, white and remote, looking out at them all.

'I had something to give her,' said Clare. 'One of Patrick's boys brought it to me this morning. He was awfully keen that she should have it.'

The plane turned east over the hills. They watched in silence until it was out of sight.

'What was it?' Harry asked.

Clare unlocked the boot of her car and extracted a large parcel. It looked like a flat-pack of furniture, a bundle of boards tied together with string.

'I can't think what it is,' said Clare.

Harry took the parcel from her hands. 'I'll keep it for her,' he said. 'She told me she'll be coming back.'

FAY WELDON

LEADER OF THE BAND

Starlady Sandra, astronomer, wife, strumpet, TV personality and discoverer of the planet Athena, forsakes fame and fortune to run off one night to the South of France with Mad Jack the trumpet player. But at her heels come the ghosts of her past, and of a whole generation . . . Now read on –

'Creative energy is here . . . the book fizzes and zings'
Carole Angier

'Monstrously, intoxicatingly partial'
Anita Brookner, The Spectator

'A sparkling river of wit'
The Mail on Sunday

'Intellectual froth, teasing, exhilarating and challenging – as black and glittering as a jet necklace – vintage Weldon, in fact'
Evening Standard

'Immensely well-nuanced enthusiasm'
The Guardian

Post·A·Book

A Royal Mail service in association with the Book Marketing Council & The Booksellers Association.
Post-A-Book is a Post Office trademark.

MORE TITLES AVAILABLE FROM
HODDER AND STOUGHTON PAPERBACKS

FAY WELDON

☐	59183 3	Leader of the Band	£2.99
☐	36379 7	The Life and Loves of a She-Devil	£2.95
☐	23827 5	Little Sisters	£2.50
☐	33965 9	The President's Child	£2.50

MAVIS CHEEK

☐	49747 5	Pause Between Acts	£2.99

SYLVIA MURPHY

☐	49486 7	The Life and Times of Barly Beach	£2.50

JOANNA TROLLOPE

☐	50066 2	The Choir	£3.50

MAEVE BINCHY

☐	42802 3	Firefly Summer	£4.50

ANABEL DONALD

☐	50609 1	Smile Honey	£2.99

All these books are available at your local bookshop or newsagent, or can be ordered direct from the publisher. Just tick the titles you want and fill in the form below.

Prices and availability subject to change without notice.

Hodder & Stoughton Paperbacks, P.O. Box 11, Falmouth, Cornwall.

Please send cheque or postal order, and allow the following for postage and packing:

U.K. — 55p for one book, plus 22p for the second book, and 14p for each additional book ordered up to a £1.75 maximum.

B.F.P.O. and EIRE — 55p for the first book, plus 22p for the second book, and 14p per copy for the next 7 books, 8p per book thereafter.

OTHER OVERSEAS CUSTOMERS — £1.00 for the first book, plus 25p per copy for each additional book.

Name ....

Address ....

....